Ana had j——
clinic when she saw a man ————
tery light of the ghost moon; he looked half
ghost himself, too pale, and in his arms—

Oh, God. She flung open the door, grabbed
the child from his arms and carried her to the
nearest treatment bed.

"Ambulance is on the way," the man gasped
in English. There was bright red blood smeared
on his hands, on the crumpled white of his collar. He was wearing a bulletproof vest.

And then she recognized his face, as if a camera had suddenly pulled him into focus. No
time to feel anything. She dismissed the problem of Pete and focused on the child she was
holding. There was too much blood. She
worked in silence, putting pressure on the
wound from the front and tossing aside the
girl's blood-smeared backpack.

Pete reached down for it. "It's heroin," he
said. "They were using her for a mule."

"I guess you taught her a lesson she'll never
forget," Ana said grimly. In the distance, sirens
screamed. "If she lives."

BRIDGE
OF
SHADOWS

Roxanne Conrad

AN ONYX BOOK

ONYX
Published by the Penguin Group
Penguin Putnam Inc., 375 Hudson Street,
New York, New York 10014, U.S.A.
Penguin Books Ltd, 27 Wrights Lane,
London W8 5TZ, England
Penguin Books Australia Ltd, Ringwood,
Victoria, Australia
Penguin Books Canada Ltd, 10 Alcorn Avenue,
Toronto, Ontario, Canada M4V 3B2
Penguin Books (N.Z.) Ltd, 182–190 Wairau Road,
Auckland 10, New Zealand

Penguin Books Ltd, Registered Offices:
Harmondsworth, Middlesex, England

First published by Onyx, an imprint of Dutton NAL,
a member of Penguin Putnam Inc.

First Printing, November, 1998
10 9 8 7 6 5 4 3 2 1

 REGISTERED TRADEMARK—MARCA REGISTRADA

Printed in the United States of America

PUBLISHER'S NOTE
This is a work of fiction. Names, characters, places, and incidents either are
the product of the author's imagination or are used fictitiously, and any resem-
blance to actual persons, living or dead, events, or locales is entirely
coincidental.

To my husband—Cat Conrad,
who puts up with me.
That deserves more than a dedication.
Maybe a medal.

And to the Weirdos, as always,
for pointing out to me (too late, alas)
why Peter was such a dangerous
name to give a character.

Chapter 1

July 7, 1992
Esmeralda Elena Sanchez and Peter Alan Ross

Esmeralda Sanchez would never have paid money to the *coyotes* to take her over the border if she hadn't already been caught and deported by *la migra*—the U.S. Border Patrol—seven times. She was desperate to get across and stay across—not only for her own sake, but for Jaime's. He was six, and small for his age, and she was afraid of what would happen to him if they stayed in the grinding poverty of the Ciudad Juárez barrio, within sight of the nice American homes and cars.

And the *coyotes* hadn't seemed so very bad. They'd shown her the car—a nice car, American, with air conditioning.

And after she'd paid them the money, they'd shown her the trunk and, under the spare tire, the tiny, cramped metal compartment just big enough for her and Jaime. She hadn't liked the way they'd looked at her. She shouldn't have gotten in the compartment. She knew now, knew it for certain, that if they let her and Jaime live at all, it would be after a terrible ordeal of pain. It had all gone wrong, and it was her own fault.

"Mama? It's too hot," Jaime whispered through dry, cracked lips. He remembered to speak English— she'd told him to practice it, practice it all the time. "Mama, make it cold. *Frío*, Mama."

She couldn't remember the sky. A clear blue sky, she thought, with the sun a brutal white shimmer rising toward noon. How many hours ago? The heat of his small body against hers was almost unbearable, but she cradled him as best she could, muffling his cry as the car shuddered and their heads banged painfully into the false metal wall above. A coffin, it was a metal coffin, he was dying in the dark, her *pobrecito*, and there was nothing she could do.

"*Chito*," she whispered, and kissed his sweat-soaked hair. His skin felt clammy. "Shhh, no, it will be over soon, I promise."

"*¿Verdad?*" He sounded so pitifully weak.

"*Te lo promesar.*" He was dying. Better *la migra* catch them. Better deportation, better starvation, better *anything* than the sound of Jaime's breath in her ear.

He was only six years old. *Dios mío, ayuda me*, she prayed. *Don't let him die. Not because I wanted something better.*

It would be over soon. The driver would stop, he'd open the trunk and let them out, and she and Jaime would laugh and drink cold water and—

Jaime whispered, "*Tengo frío, Mamá.*" *I feel cold.*

Esmeralda screamed, screamed as loud as her dry mouth could stand, battered her blistered hands on the metal plating, kicked with all the strength in her cramped muscles. She screamed until the heat made her dizzy and sick, and without meaning to she vomited, managing to turn her head away from Jaime only at the last second, and then she felt his hand on her face, startlingly cool. He said, "Mama? It's all right, Mama. *Está bien.* I'll take care of you."

She would have wept, but her eyes were dry and parched, her throat scraped raw. The heat filled her lungs like sand, and it was so much effort to breathe. The stink of her sickness came muffled and distant, like the smells of hot tar and metal and sweat. The constant vibration of the road was a soothing hand on her back.

She slid away into the dark for a while, jerked back when she felt the car lurch. They were stopping. *They were stopping.*

"Jaime," she croaked. Her lips felt wet; when she licked them with her thick, dry tongue, they tasted of blood. "Jaime, *mijo*, wake up."

They had survived hell.

Rámon Cruz loved the desert. He had grown up in the small town of Tortilla Flats, near long stretches of white salt deposits that men had fought and killed for a hundred years ago; the desert had taught him many things, not the least of which was that whatever lies men told, the land stayed truthful.

The hot-brass sun, the velvet dunes, the harsh beauty of cactus and mesquite and desert sage. *The land of our fathers.* No sense of time passing here—only wind whispers, and the subtle movements of snake, lizard, bird.

He was more than two hours outside El Paso,

Texas, but he could have been at the edge of the earth. The evidence of human occupation—old bottles, rusted, dirt-scoured cans, faint shreds of plastic—these would fade with time. The shack creaking in the wind behind him would dry up and blow away. The cars, including the ancient green pickup that had brought him here, would rust away to nothing. Only the land was forever.

He closed his eyes and breathed in eternity. *Aztlan.* This was the empire his ancestors had raised and where, with the will of the old ones, he would raise it again. That was his pure and certain destiny in this life. That, and revenge, in the old ways, on the betrayers of the people.

A shadow fell across him, and he looked up at the sweating leathery face of his *padrino,* Miguel Sanchez. Miguel swiped a hand across his forehead, knocking back his battered straw hat, and took a seat next to Rámon on the sand. He smelled of fresh, metallic blood.

"It's done," he said, and wiped his hands on his faded pants. "*Ay,* it's hot out here."

"Heat is good for you," Rámon answered. "Burns the stains out of the soul. Here, *cerveza.*"

He passed over a sweating bottle of Dos Equis; Miguel twisted the cap and drank thirstily. His fingers were blunt and hard, cracked at the tips. Blood around his fingernails. Rámon looked past him at the distant purple mountains shimmering in the heat. A fly buzzed close, then veered away toward the shack behind them.

"To the cause," Miguel said, and held up his half-empty bottle. Rámon focused on him again, lifted his own beer, and clinked glass.

"To the cause," he echoed. "Our time is coming. Eh, *amigo*, I'm grateful, you know? I couldn't have done this without you."

Miguel nodded, swallowed, shrugged. It was all work to him, digging irrigation trenches or digging shallow graves. Rámon glanced over his shoulder at the others sitting quietly in the shack's meager shade. Two of them were asleep, snoring gently; the third was watching him with narrow, dark eyes.

"What do you think about the Maldonados?" he asked Miguel. "Good men?"

"Good enough. Nestor's reliable, he's with us."

"You're sure we can trust them?"

Miguel eyed him sideways, tipped his bottle, and drained foam. "Why shouldn't we? They're our brothers, Rámon. Nestor came up from La Raza."

Rámon nodded slowly. Loyalty was one thing, but they were about to steal more than a million dollars of heroin; that was money Aztlan couldn't afford to lose. Unlike the *cabrones* they would take the drugs from, Rámon did not intend to sell the heroin in the *barrio*; he intended to market it where it would achieve the most good—in the predominantly Anglo neighborhoods of West El Paso. More profit, more money for the cause.

The Maldonado brothers were too quiet, too watchful. He would not turn his back on them.

"Rámon." Miguel elbowed him and jerked his chin toward the shimmering black highway in the distance. A car was turning off—a big car, expensive. An Anglo car.

"*Ya veo.*" Rámon stood up, feeling the heat suddenly like a close-clinging vampire. Dark spots swam before his eyes, swarmed like ants. He dropped his half-finished beer to the sand and pulled a gun from his waistband. "On to Aztlan," he said.

"God willing," Miguel murmured. He had a shotgun. Behind him the Maldonado brothers mutely got to their feet.

"Let's kill these *cabrones* and get the hell out of here."

The tires crunched off the pavement onto loose gravel. Rocks pinged, and the smells changed to burning oil and sour, smoky exhaust. The engine shut off, and the rumbling vibration Esmeralda had grown so used to stopped. Without it she felt her muscles trembling, close to collapse, and the fear she'd pushed back threatened to smother her like the bad air.

The car shifted. The driver's side door opened and closed.

"Jaime," she whispered again. "Jaime—"

Men's voices outside the car. She caught pieces of the rapid Spanish: . . . *the heroin? I don't do business with you. Where's Luis?*

Men laughed. *He's out of business. You do business with us now.*

All right, one of the *coyotes* said after a short, comprehending pause. *Glad to see you, amigo. More money for your cause, eh? Power to the people.*

The *coyote* who'd talked her into this horror said, with a smile in his oily voice, *That's right, Rámon.*

We're with you all the way, man. Soldiers for the new land.

"I'm glad to hear it," a man said in English. "You can die like soldiers, then. Kill them all."

The soft desert wind whipped away the sharp sting of gunpowder, and in the silence Rámon thought for an instant he heard the crying of a child, but his ears were ringing from the noise of the gunfire. Three more dead men, staring sightlessly up at the cloudless sky. He looked across the bodies at Miguel, whose serene expression had not changed even as he shot a seventeen-year-old *vato* in the face.

"Put the bodies in the shack," he said. "Get the drugs and let's get out of here."

"What about the car?" Miguel said. He gestured toward the big, shiny Lincoln the *coyotes* had arrived in, now pocked here and there with bullet holes. Nestor Maldonado reached into the car and popped open the trunk. He lifted out an old, oil-stained cardboard box and carried it to the truck. As he opened it to check the contents, Rámon stared at the empty trunk. He walked over and clicked it shut.

"Leave it." The Lincoln had two flats now, and Rámon was in no mood to change tires. The car disgusted him. It was the symbol of everything he hated—money, power, pointless luxury. Even the cash he'd get for it wouldn't make that taste leave his mouth. "Let the buzzards shit on it."

Like good soldiers, they methodically picked up the ejected brass cartridges from their guns, and Miguel started the truck. Rámon rode in the back, one arm across the loosely taped box of heroin, staring at Nestor Maldonado's dark, narrow eyes and knowing that one of them would die before this day was finished, because there was greed in those eyes, not dreams of a homeland for the people. If the man couldn't see the future, he would die in the past.

For no reason, as the rattletrap truck lurched onto the smooth blacktop of Carlsbad Highway, Rámon turned and looked back at the shack where they had left sacrifices on the altar of Aztlan. The Lincoln Town Car gleamed like a dark diamond in the sun.

He did not know why he was so uneasy.

It was dark, so dark; it felt as if the dark had shape and weight and stuffed Esmeralda's mouth with its rancid heat. The only sound in the world was Jaime's breathing and the pounding of her own heart.

The bullets had missed them, but it was so very hot.

Jaime stirred against her and in a voice old with pain croaked, "Water, Mama."

She had no water, no tears. Even her sweat was gone. Out of terror she had let the sound of the other car die into silence; now she heard nothing outside. No one.

"*Está bien*, Jaime," she said, and as best she could, in the dark and in the heat, in a space the size of a child's coffin, she rocked him to sleep. "*Está bien*."

Christ, he thought, *it all looks the same*. Peter Ross squinted through the Mercedes' tinted windshield, trying to pick out the meandering tracks of dirt roads leading from the highway. In the west, smoke blue Franklin Mountains sawed the sun bloody, and clouds soaked up the spill—red edges, brilliant orange centers fading into a delicate pink. The stars were already out to the east in thick diamond clusters.

"Damn desert," Larry said from the passenger side, and pointed up ahead at some barely noticeable gravel turnoff. It was Larry's car, Larry's booze in the backseat, Larry's girlfriend's picture dangling from the rearview mirror. "Gets on my nerves. Everything's got edges, you know? Cactus, rocks, everything."

"Why'd you move out here, then?" Pete asked, and turned the wheel. The Mercedes responded, smooth as butter, and even the bump of leaving the highway felt like a gentle tap.

"Watch the fuckin' mesquite, man." Larry eyed the spiky, thorny bushes warily, like they might reach out and key the car for the hell of it. He slumped down in the passenger seat and gnawed a much chewed thumbnail. Pete slowed the car to a leisurely crawl. Headlights lit up red sand, rough mesquite, the occasional pod-crowned spike of a sotol cactus. All the same, the desert, and all so deceptively different.

"I thought we were going to El Paso," he said to Larry, not quite a question, more a way to make Larry stop chewing his cuticle.

"No, man, I didn't say that. I said we were going *kinda* that way. Get too close to the city, you get cops, Border Patrol, DEA, Customs—they're just aching to bust our asses. No, we always meet out here."

"Well, where is here exactly?"

"Red Sands." Larry, who was the size of a defensive lineman, combed his long, dark hair over his shoulders. He had two earrings in his left ear, both gold rings, and he was wearing all black. His drug dealer look, Pete thought, and with a fair amount of self-disgust, *Like I have room to talk? What the hell am I doing here?* Not his car, not his girlfriend, not his money—"It's like White Sands—"

"Only it's red, yeah, I get it. Why here?"

"Dunno. Ask Luis, man, I just work here. Hey, what're you going to do after this? You catching a plane back to Dallas, or you want to hang around?"

He didn't know. The fight with Ana had nearly destroyed him this time. He was afraid for her and he was furious with her. She was the kind of woman who always had a cause, and the causes were always dangerous; this one, the one that had earned her death threats, was because she was consulting physician for a Dallas abortion clinic. It was a subject they could not discuss, so the anger came out in other ways—little cutting comments about money or jealousy or the color of sheets on the bed. He and Ana were over. They just hadn't admitted it yet.

A tumbleweed the size of a Christmas tree rolled across the gravel road, its branches tinseled with yellowed paper, candy wrappers, a limp, pale condom. It hesitated in front of the Mercedes, and Pete stepped on the brakes to let it roll ponderously past. Wouldn't want that stuck under the grille. He already had itchy, bloodless punctures in his fingers from pulling out the last one.

Larry was very particular about his ride.

The headlights caught a flare of red from another car's reflectors. Pete stepped on the brakes again, this time with a surge of fear. Cops? He didn't know he'd said it aloud until Larry said, "No, man, it's okay. That's Luis' car, they're just early."

Pete put the Mercedes in park. In the cool white beams of the headlights, dust swirled red and gold. The air conditioning breathed its last, and the fading heat of the summer day closed around him like a steel wool blanket.

Larry got out, stretched like a cat, and tossed his hair with another one of those girlish gestures. The gun at the small of his back—black like the rest of his outfit—was hard to see unless you were looking for it. Pete gripped the steering wheel hard, feeling the cool leather give like skin, and took a deep breath before stepping out of the car.

Even with the evening breathing hot on his face, there wasn't much smell to the desert—a faint bite of mesquite wood and the weirdly dead smell of ultradry air. The tick of the engine as it cooled sounded loud as a cartoon bomb.

Nobody moved at the other car. Larry ambled over to peer in the Town Car's windows, and Pete stayed where he was, door open, ready to dive at the first sign of trouble. He was *not* a drug dealer. He didn't much care about pot, could take it or leave it. It was Larry's show, Larry's money, but that wouldn't matter a damn; he was driving the car. He was guilty, too, and he couldn't even figure out why he was taking the risk.

Yes, he could. Because apart from going back to another useless fight with his wife, there was absolutely nothing else to do.

The mountains had finished off the sun, but the

sunset's ghost remained. By its glow he saw that the
car parked next to the windowless shack had Mexican license plates. He'd seen a lot of those since coming into West Texas—they all said FRONT CHIH.
Frontera Chihuhua, Larry had explained, playing
tour guide. The plates were good in the U.S. only for
about three hundred miles from the border.

"Luis!" Larry called. No answer. In the profound
silence the little whisper of tumbleweeds made Pete
paranoid. He wished he had a gun. No, he didn't.
He wished he were somewhere else, anywhere but
out here with a lunatic long-haired freak buying a
kilo of grass. Larry, the rebel without a fix.

It was also a little late to be having second
thoughts.

"Fuck me," Larry muttered, and went up to the
shack. There was a doorway but no door. He poked
his head in. "Luis? Hey, man, quit screwing around,
let's do it."

"Anybody in there?" Pete asked. Larry looked
back at him and shrugged.

"Can't see a goddamn thing. Get me a flashlight."

Pete popped the Mercedes' trunk and rooted
around, found a slim little MagLite and switched it
on, rotated the lens to its widest halogen beam. Larry
pointed it inside the doorway.

"Hey, guys, if you're in there, just remember, black
widows love places like this. I'd be careful if I—"

He yelped and jumped back two feet. Pete's first
thought was, *Great, snakebite,* and then he saw Larry's face.

"Fuck," Larry said softly. "Oh, fuck, man, this isn't
happening. Get in the car."

He scooped up the fallen flashlight, switched it off, and headed for the Mercedes. Pete hesitated, frowning, looking at the shack.

"Get in!" Larry ordered.

"What's in there?"

"You don't want to know."

"The hell I don't!"

Larry shook his head. "Some dead guys, okay? Luis and some other guys. Jesus, get *in*, will you—"

He broke off and looked sharply past Pete at the Town Car.

"You hear something?" he asked. Pete shook his head. Larry took a step closer to the other car, listened, took another.

This time Pete did hear it—a muffled thump, like something hitting metal.

"Shit!" Larry jumped back. "Oh, man, that's *it*. Come on, Pete, we've got to go. *Now*."

"Wait—it sounds like—it's coming from the trunk." Pete bent over the trunk and listened, listened hard. "Yeah, somebody's in the trunk. Open the car and pop the latch."

"No way. You put *your* goddamn prints all over a murder scene, not me."

Pete shot him an exasperated look and opened the door with a fold of his shirt over his hand, popped the trunk release the same way. The inside of the car was clean and very hot. It smelled, faintly, of vomit. There were no keys.

"Nothing," Larry reported from the back. Pete walked around to stand beside him, both of them staring like idiots at the empty carpet, the spare tire. The smell of vomit was stronger.

They both jumped at the sound of another thump. This one rattled the spare.

"Underneath," Pete said, and dragged the carpet out of the way. The metal plate below was bolted at the corners. "Hell. Got any tools?"

"No, I don't have any tools. What do I look like, a mechanic? Oh, man, I can't believe this is happening. Where's my shit? Somebody ripped Luis off and they took my shit. What the hell am I going to do? I got obligations, you know."

Pete found a crowbar wedged in one corner of the trunk, jammed the forked end under the plate, and heaved up. Metal bowed and popped.

"You're fucking crazy." Larry backed up a step or two, watching as Pete snapped the first bolt off and started on the second. "You don't know who the hell's in there. Could be a cop for all you know."

"Yeah, that would make sense. Drug dealers always stick cops in smuggling compartments."

Larry made the obvious connection—smuggling compartment, missing drugs. He grabbed his own crowbar out of the Mercedes and worked on the other side of the plate, and within five minutes all four bolts were sheared off.

The plate was still hot to the touch, like coins left in the sun. Pete hissed in pain and held it up with the palm of his hand, squinting under it as Larry helpfully turned on the flashlight.

"Jesus God," Larry said, and backed off.

A woman lay at a torturous angle in the tiny compartment. Her swollen, blistered face was smeared with dried vomit, her lips cracked and bloody, and in her arms she held a little boy with skin the color of delicate ivory, his open eyes gone opaque and dry.

Her lips parted, the cracks splitting open to stitch threads of blood down her chin.

"*Ayude mi hijo*," she croaked. "*Ayude Jaime.*"

Larry backed off, all the way back to the Mercedes, breath rasping hard in his throat. Pete stood frozen, looking down at her, and after a long few seconds he reached down and took the boy out. The small body felt so heavy, limp as a sack of sand. There was no muscle in him at all.

The reality of it hit Pete in a hot wave, like pepper in his throat and eyes. His lungs felt hot and compressed, and he had to put the kid down, quick, before he dropped him.

No matter how limp he was, he didn't look like a sleeping kid ought to look. Pete worked at the buttons on his own shirt, fingers clumsy, got it off and draped it over the little boy's pale, sad, somehow knowing face.

"Help me," he said. He wasn't sure who he was saying it to for a second; a breeze, startlingly cool, blew up goose bumps on his bare back. Oh, yeah, Larry—Larry was standing there, staring at him like a stranger. "Come on, Larry, help me get her out."

"Out?" Larry repeated. "And put her where exactly?"

He was too tired for this shit. Pete got up, moving maybe too fast, and Larry made a nervous move for his car. Pete held out his empty hands, palms up.

"In the backseat. Come on, Larry, don't bullshit me. We've got to do this. She'll die out here. The kid's already—" For some reason he didn't want to say it. Larry shook his head and avoided looking down at the blue and white shirt fluttering in the evening breeze.

In order to avoid that, he ended up staring in the direction of the highway. Pete saw the red and blue lights flashing in the distance at the same time Larry did.

"Oh, shit!" Larry yelped. "See? See what I told you? No fucking way, Peter. If I go down, it's for the third time. Why're we even talking about this? You saw her, no way she's going to last until morning. I'm not getting my ass busted for a goddamn dead wetback!"

"Shut up and help me, Larry!" Pete screamed, and it was the wrong thing to do because now Larry had the gun out, a flash of black in his hand, and he had one hand on the driver's-side door of the Mercedes. "Larry, you can't do this, man. You can't leave her here. You're better than that."

"The cops are coming. They'll pick her up. Get in the goddamn car, Peter, or I swear I'll leave you here. We got history, man, but I'll leave your ass."

For a second it was very tempting. Get in the car, relieved of responsibility because of Larry and his gun. *I had no choice.*

"I can't," he said. Simple truth.

"I'm not saying it again." Larry got in the car. He started the engine, closed the door, rolled down the window. "Don't get yourself busted over her, buddy. She's dead by morning no matter what you do. Okay? Okay. I'm leaving. Bye-bye."

He put the car in reverse with a smooth click of gears, the backup lights shooting white flares over the sand. He turned on the radio very loud, the heavy beat of AC/DC thudding like hooves. Stalling. Waiting for Pete to change his mind.

Pete walked to the passenger-side door, opened it, reached in the back, and took out the quart of bottled water Larry kept for roadside emergencies, like mixing with his scotch. Larry grabbed his arm.

"Pete," he said, and let go of him when their eyes locked. "This is a bad fucking scene, man. You don't have to do this."

"Sure, I do," Pete said, and shut the door.

The boom of the stereo continued to stomp long after the Mercedes was out of sight. On the highway, the police car zoomed by without stopping, pursuing somebody else, maybe even Larry. Pete might have stood stupefied for hours, staring into the gradual dark, except he heard the woman whisper, *"Señor?"*

Oh, Christ. He fumbled for the water, reached into the trunk, and held it to her mouth as he supported her shoulders. Her skin was sticky with exploded blisters and body fluids. She stank like—he swallowed hard. She wouldn't last out here; she was already shaking like an epileptic. He had to get her to El Paso, to a hospital, to the cops, *something*. The Lincoln had two flat tires, but it was better than nothing. Keys—

No keys in the ignition. He scrabbled in the lush upholstery, the suffocatingly hot carpet. No keys *anywhere*. He'd skipped hot wiring in shop class, had no idea how to begin, and from the back he could hear the woman making faint gasping noises. There wasn't time to experiment; he had to *find the keys*.

Larry had talked about dead bodies in the shack.

Pete took a deep breath and headed for the shadow-streaked wood, the sunset a bloody eye watching him.

The woman grasped weakly at him as he passed the trunk.

"*Señor?*" she croaked. He gently took her hand. "*Mi hijo?*"

He knew that much Spanish, at least. No way to break it to her gently. "He didn't make it, *Señora.* I'm sorry."

Her eyes blinked slowly. He felt her muscles tremble violently. No tears. She probably didn't have enough moisture left for tears.

"I'm going to get the keys," he said, and tried to let go of her hand. She held on with surprising strength.

She said something, with great effort. He didn't understand it. "Take it easy. Easy. I'm not going to leave you."

She said, her voice just a thread, "Esmeralda." He leaned forward and gently stroked her hair back from her ravaged face.

"My name's Pete," he said. "Peter Ross. You hang on, Esme. I'll be back."

He searched five bodies in the dark, brushing away mounds of glistening ants to get at bloody jackets and pants. At the bottom of the pile, a pair of car keys with a silver cross for a key chain. He stood there in the dark, with the stinking, crawling bodies, and for the first time he was afraid.

Up to him. All up to him now. *Live or die, Pete. Time to do something right.*

He jolted the Lincoln along fast enough to spin

rubber off the flat tires, while Esmeralda lay on the backseat with her dead son in her arms. A highway patrolman stopped him thirty minutes down the road. The CareFlight helicopter arrived fifteen minutes after that, and Pete became curiously redundant, just another onlooker as paramedics intubated and IV'ed and medicated. When he tried to go to her, the cop taking her statement restrained him and shook his head.

"I'm responsible for her," Pete said. The cop looked attentive. "I'm paying for her treatment."

"Yeah?" The patrolman sucked on the side of his cheek, regarding him with cool blue eyes. "Why?"

The question stunned him. He said, "What?"

"You know her?"

"I've never seen her before."

The cop gave him a pitying look. "Not from around here, are you? Buddy, if you let one of them start riding your gravy train, they'll suck you dry—"

He pushed free and climbed into the helicopter with her, held her hand as they soared into the empty sky, and it seemed to him that somehow he was leaving everything behind him, even his name. His head felt empty and very, very quiet.

She opened her eyes as the chopper landed. She didn't try to speak, and he couldn't have heard her over the roar of the engine even if she'd tried, but the message in her eyes was clear. *I'm afraid. Don't leave me.*

He didn't. He stayed through two weeks of hospital rehabilitation, and through Jaime's funeral, accompanying Esmeralda through the long Catholic mass under the eyes of two burly police officers. He stayed for the police questioning. He left out any mention of Larry or the incomplete drug deal.

After that he was free to go. His wife wouldn't return his phone calls.

Two days after Jaime's funeral, Esmeralda was deported back to Mexico. There was nothing in the world he could do to stop it, not even marry her. He was still married to Ana.

A month later, Peter Alan Ross enrolled as an agent of the United States Border Patrol.

Chapter 2

Four Years Later—October 26, 1996
Dr. Ana Maria Ross Gutierrez

I hate this.

Dr. Ana Gutierrez leaned her forehead on clasped hands, closed her eyes, and tried to reach for calm. Detachment. It was a part of her job, but she had never grown used to it, not during residency, not during private practice.

The death of a child was never easy for her.

The girl's name had been Lupe Navarro, and she had been a bright seven-year-old born into a family of eight other children, an overworked father, an exhausted mother. No one had paid much attention to Lupe's fever until it had lasted for two days. Until she'd begun convulsing.

They'd brought the girl here to *La Clínica Libre*, the Free Clinic, instead of sending her to the hospital— because they had no money, they were illegals, and they were afraid of American doctors and police. Ana had done the best she could. One look had told her the girl was breathing her last; she'd grabbed the child, thrown her into her nurse Rafael's arms, told him to *drive, damn it*, to the closest emergency room. It was faster than calling for an ambulance in this part of town, at this hour of the night.

He had done his best, Rafael.

She had done her best. And it hadn't mattered a damn.

Lupe Navarro had died a terrible, agonizing death.

In the privacy of her office, unseen by anyone except the silently recording surveillance camera, Ana Gutierrez cried. Not a lot of tears, just enough to take the edge from the dull knife of grief in her stomach. When she'd been a resident in Parkland Hospital in Dallas, her mentor Dr. Johnston had always said, *Don't be afraid to cry, it lets out the steam.* He'd also told her, with grim sincerity, *Just don't do it where anybody can see you. A weak doctor is a useless doctor.*

Ana never allowed herself weakness, except in private.

The tears ended, leaving no sign of their departure except a soggy tissue and some faint smudges of mascara under her eyes that would be taken for simple exhaustion. She blew her nose, finished writing the cold, clinical details of Lupe Navarro's death in the clinic chart, and disposed of the tissue in the waste bin beneath her desk. No more weakness for the rest of the night. No more *anything*, she hoped; it was late, and she was utterly drained.

Wishful thinking. It was Saturday night—early Sunday morning, but in the *barrio* it was Saturday night until morning mass—and she would be seeing the usual parade of knife wounds, gunshot wounds, beatings, and rapes. Not all of them came here, of course—only those illegals who could still talk when they were found. And many of them she sent on to the hospitals, where they would take their chances with police and *la migra*, who knew all about Saturday nights. Immigration officers hung around like crows picking at road kills.

She killed the anger when it tried to rise in her. Anger was like tears. She couldn't afford it.

Out the window—reinforced with thick wrought iron, for her protection—she had a view of a street only weakly lit by a single streetlight, the buildings gray and brooding, the street decorated with swirling trash, beyond it the sluggish gray Rio Grande river. It looked harsh in full El Paso daylight; it looked ghostly and dead at night. Peaceful. *What a lie*, she thought. If she listened hard enough, she'd hear the arguments, the screams, the shots. El Paso passions ran like blood, just under the city's skin.

Her battered chair squeaked as she rolled it up to the desk—a Salvation Army reject, gunmetal gray and military green. Her in-box held a thick wad of mail. She made two piles: an envelope from Health and Human Services went in the handle-it-later pile; mail from MEChA, the Chicano student organization that sometimes volunteered in the clinic, joined it. She paused over a letter from her lawyer, tapped it against a short fingernail. Probably another bill. She hesitated, then pitched it in the growing do-it-tomorrow pile.

The next letter had no return address. She frowned at the block printing. It couldn't be from an Anglo, not addressed to *Dr. Ana Maria Estrella Ross Gutierrez*. The formality of it was wholeheartedly Hispanic. The postmark was from Juárez, Mexico. She reached out

for the letter opener and ripped open the envelope—
a better grade of paper than she'd have expected.

Single sheet of paper. She unfolded it and felt her
cheeks flush with shame at being tricked. *Peter.* After
the embarrassment came the anger she'd thought
she'd shut away; she could imagine her ex-husband
painstakingly lettering the envelope, knowing what
she'd think. Another way of showing his superior-
ity—*See? I can make you read my letters even if you
don't want to.*

And she did read it. *Ana,* it said. At least he'd
stopped calling her *Dear. Please give me a chance. It's
important that we talk—important to both of us. If you
won't accept my call, please call me on the pager and I'll
find a phone.*

I really need to talk to you. No fooling.

She crumpled it up and threw it at the trash can.
It bounced out again, just like Peter, who wouldn't
stay in the trash where their marriage had ended up.
She didn't know how many times she'd told him to
leave her alone, but he didn't seem to get the point.
Persistent. He'd always been persistent. It was the
way he'd gotten her to date him in the first place,
that and his infectiously beautiful smile, the slow,
dry humor—

Stop thinking about his good qualities. Pete had plenty
of negatives. One, he was an Anglo, which she'd
overlooked for far too long—and even if she did, *he*
never forgot. Two, he'd become the enemy. She could
never be friends with a man who was a *la migra,* the
face of the oppressor. He knew that.

Being kind and considerate didn't make up for that
kind of betrayal.

After a moment of thought she picked up the letter, smoothed it out, and stuffed it back into the envelope. She sealed the tear at the top with tape, slashed in red across her name and address and wrote, *Return to Sender.*

She tossed it in the out basket and wondered why she didn't feel any better, all things considered.

He'd be hurt when he got the letter back.

"I'm glad," she said aloud. It wasn't how she felt. "I am."

A cough startled her; it echoed like a gunshot through the quiet office. She turned in her chair fast enough to feel a tense muscle twitch in protest; the chair provided the appropriate squeal of protest. Just a boy standing in the open doorway, nothing to be afraid of. He couldn't be more than fourteen—except there were no such things as children in the *barrio,* not at his age; he'd seen death, drugs, despair, suffered beatings, delivered some himself. He had the look. She forced a smile to her lips.

"Dr. Ana?" The boy had deep brown eyes, long, soft lashes. They were startling in a face tense enough for a man twice his age. A thin scar ran down one cheek, ending in a dark blue homemade tattoo of a tear. "*Vamanos.*"

The hell I will. She dropped automatically into Spanish. "I don't leave the clinic." Ana was too canny and too experienced to let herself be lured away from the relative safety of *La Clínica,* though she was asked, begged, and ordered many times a day. The police, much as she hated them, checked on her at irregular intervals here. "I can call an ambulance if you need one."

The boy jerked his head toward the door. It wasn't manly for a gang member to take orders from a woman.

"What's your name?" she asked him. His soft brown eyes took on a hard plastic shine. Dangerous territory. They didn't like it when she pried.

"Gato," he said. It meant *cat*. "Move, Doctor."

It occurred to her that he might be here to rob the medicine cabinet. It was part of why she stocked only the very basic supplies; there was no real profit in stealing aspirin and antibiotics. She kept the syringes locked up separately, the real narcotics in a concealed cabinet in the storage room.

"I'm not going, Gato," she said. A calculated risk. She still had a knife scar from the one time it hadn't quite paid off, but the odds were good if she held her ground, very poor if she didn't. Gato—all the Gatos of the *barrio*—respected strength.

He moved away from the door frame. In his right hand, which had been hidden, he held a gun. Her blood slowed in her veins; her heart ticked like a tired clock. How long until the police came by? What did it matter? If Gato wanted to shoot her, he would. Nothing could stop him.

It took a huge effort of will to stay where she was, to keep her face politely blank. Gato gestured with the gun, impatient and baffled now. He was used to unquestioning obedience at the sight of the weapon.

"You shoot me, I won't be any good to you. What do you want?" She met his eyes, looking past the terrible magnetic attraction of the muzzle's stare. "Where do you want to take me?"

"You don't need to know!" He sounded unnerved.

She remembered to breathe, didn't know when she'd stopped. The rush of fresh air in her lungs tasted like metal and made her heart beat too fast. She couldn't afford to be weak now. *Never let them see your fear.*

"Get up, bitch!"

"I don't think so, Gato. You tell me the problem, then I decide what to do, *comprende*? It won't work this way."

A confused child. Fourteen years was not enough time to make these kinds of decisions. Gato blinked his doe eyes and shifted his weight, nervously looking into the shadows, out the window to the street.

"He got cut," he finally said. "On his leg. There's a lot of blood. You come to help him."

Worst case, a severed femoral artery, she thought, even as she reached for her bag and began to fill it with the necessary supplies. If it was a severed artery, she'd just wasted precious time. She was peripherally aware of Gato putting the gun away, point made. She hoped she'd established enough respect with him to hold her through this little adventure—no way to tell.

Her knife scar ached, like a ghost's touch, just below her right breast.

She threw in several pairs of sterile gloves and snapped the bag closed, rose to her feet. She was exhausted. Gravity pulled at her like an insistent child.

"Gabe," she said aloud, in English, and looked at the southwest corner of the office, where the hard glint of the security camera's eye watched her. "I'm going out. If I'm not back in thirty minutes, call the police."

Gato looked around, eyes wide, hand diving back for the gun. She pointed up at the camera.

"Gabe is in another room; he records everything that happens in *La Clínica*. He's just here for my protection, okay? So I don't get hurt."

Gato understood protection. He stared at the camera for a few seconds, expressionless, then nodded once. His eyes came back to her face.

"Down the street," he said. "At El Tony's."

El Tony's would have been a bar if it had owned a liquor license; it was a couple of rooms, some surly patrons who brought their own liquor, some prostitutes who'd been known to rob and stab when they didn't pass social diseases. The clinic got a lot of business from El Tony's.

"I'll need someone with me," she said. "For my back."

Gato smiled charmingly and spread his hands. *That's me.* She returned his smile.

"Let me tell my assistant."

Gato shrugged. Ana came toward him, and he backed out of her way, graceful as a cat. She called Rafael's name as she came down the hallway.

"Yo," he called from a curtained treatment area. She stuck her head around to find him stitching up a superficial laceration in a teenage girl's hand. "Trouble?"

"Knife wound at El Tony's. I'm going with Gato here."

"You think that's a good idea?" Rafael paused, the girl's hand in his gloved one, and he seemed completely unaware of the brilliant worship on his patient's face. It was hard for girls not to swoon for

Rafael; he was a big, handsome boy, maybe thirty, with a lithe, strong body and angelic eyes. She had a vague impression he'd been a football hero, but she was dead certain he was a gifted nurse. "Shouldn't you call the cops first?"

"No," Gato said. He sounded sure about it. "There's no time to debate. If I need them, I'll call them."

Rafael touched the girl on the shoulder, signaling her to wait where she was, and came out to Ana's side of the curtain. She wasn't short—five seven—but he topped her by nearly a head.

"I don't like it."

"Look, I'll be careful." She cocked her head slightly toward Gato, who waited impatiently behind her. "I have a guide."

There was something coplike in the way Rafael's eyes took the boy in, as if he were memorizing him for a lineup. Ana shook off the feeling and gestured for the boy to go ahead.

"Doctor." Rafael reached out but did not quite touch her. "Be careful, eh? I don't have time to do your job, too."

Gato pushed past her, teenage arrogance back in place. The gun made an unsettling bulge in the back of his pants. He was wearing the traditional *vato* uniform of baggy chino pants, flannel shirt buttoned at the top button and open the rest of the way. Beneath it, his T-shirt had seen better days. Ana had seen a thousand like him in the years at *La Clínica*.

She tried to imagine being afraid of him, and smiled at the thought. Gato paused to stare at her, his face intense, his eyes blank and challenging.

"What you grinning at?"

She shook her head, still smiling, and followed him out into the dark.

Wrong, she thought the moment she stepped into El Tony's, into a reek of stale beer and body odor. She froze in the doorway, unreasonably panicked by the darkness, the half-seen men she knew were watching her. There was no crisis here, or if there was, it was her own.

I walked right into it. All her clever talk was useless. Gabe and Rafael would abide by her instructions; they'd wait at least a half hour to send police, and by that time she could be anywhere, raped, mutilated, dead, her body dropped in a—

Get hold of yourself, Ana. She took a deep breath and said, steadily as she could, "Somebody need a doctor?"

Something cold probed her back. Gato's gun. She obeyed it, stepping inside even though her knees were trembling and she wasn't sure she could feel her feet. Darkness closed around her.

"Dr. Ana," a man said. A match flared, lighting a weatherbeaten middle-aged face as he puffed a cigarette into life. Her eyes began to adjust to the low light, and she saw that he was no *vato.* He was a working-class man, dressed in a well-worn shirt and faded blue jeans, his work boots battered and dusty. "Dr. Ana Ross."

"Gutierrez," she corrected, too sharply.

"You were married to Peter Ross," he said. He spoke excellent English, she noticed. Unusual in the *barrio*, where you could go your whole life without hearing it if you tried. "Married to *la migra*."

That got her temper going, like a match to a pilot light. "We're divorced, if it's any of your business." Gato jabbed her in the back again, and her temper snapped. "Look, you tell him to put the gun away, or I leave right now and you bury your friend."

The man studied her. After a few seconds he inclined his head toward Gato. The pressure at her back retreated. She controlled the urge to check where he'd gone and kept watching the man who sat so casually on a bar stool, so obviously in charge.

"Miguel," he said by way of introduction. "You've been running *La Clínica* a long time, Doctor. People trust you. They know you were married to an Anglo, but they say it was a mistake, that you're true to *la raza* now. Are you?"

"I'm a doctor and I work in the *barrio* for my people. What do you think?" She waited for a response, didn't get one. Miguel inhaled slowly on the cigarette, and his face flushed bright red in the glow. "My marriage—he didn't become *la migra* until after. I never would have married him if he'd been one of them."

"They're all *them*, Dr. Ana. I'm just trying to find out if you're one of *them*, too."

She cursed him, fluently and comprehensively, in gutter Spanish, the language of the *barrio*. When she was done, the men were smiling. *Look at the little girl.* Miguel shrugged indulgently, poured himself a shot of tequila, and invited her to share. She didn't.

"Gato tells me they like you around here. MEChA tells me you are okay. I am going to trust you, Dr.

Ana, but if you betray me, Gato will put a bullet in your head."

"I understand." She had no doubt Miguel would order her killed, and did not doubt Gato would do it. She would be a robbery victim left in an alley. She'd have a lovely Catholic funeral.

"Come." He finished the tequila and stood up, walked through the silent men and through a tattered, dirty curtain into the other room. She followed.

On the other side of the curtain, the smell of blood was strong; she blinked as Miguel turned on a low overhead light, and by the glow she saw legs sticking out of the shadows. The left leg of the dirty blue jeans was slit to the crotch, folded back, and her whole attention focused on the wound.

Someone had gotten a rough tourniquet on him, but the laceration continued to seep steadily—judging by the pool of blood on the dirty concrete, had been seeping for far too long. Miguel froze, staring at the blood, his face suddenly anything but impassive.

"He wasn't—" he started to protest.

"Out of the way." She pushed by and knelt down to take a look at the wound. Deep laceration, with excised tissue in a triangular shape near the top of its seven-inch run. Blistering around the wound, and crusted black burns at the top. "How long ago?"

"Twenty minutes, maybe." Miguel's authoritative manner was gone; he'd clearly not realized how bad the situation was. "He's going to be okay, *así?*"

"*Idiota*, you should have taken him directly to the hospital, not to me—I'm not a vascular surgeon. Call an ambulance, *now.*"

"Fix him," Miguel said. She looked up, incredulous. "You want to leave the same way you came, you *fix* him."

He wasn't kidding, and he was the kind of man who wouldn't understand honest failure. No choice but to try, anyway; she'd have done that even without the promise of a gun behind her. She snapped on latex gloves, sponged blood away from the wound to look at the deeper damage. The muscles were sliced, and there was a long tear in the thick, rubbery covering of the femoral artery. She was vaguely shocked that the man had lasted this long, even though they'd obviously worked quickly to get the tourniquet on him. No time to worry about her limited knowledge; there was no time to wait for anyone, even if she could convince Miguel to play along. The victim was losing too much blood.

"What are you doing?" Miguel asked. He leaned forward, and the wound disappeared into shadow.

"Trying to save his life! Look, get me light, I can't work in the dark. Go."

After a second's hesitation, he disappeared. She didn't follow his progress. Her overused attention was riveted on threading her smallest needle and beginning the delicate, aching work of stitching. *Deep breaths*. She was an eternity away from her vascular training, and it was impossible work on an unanesthetized patient. The stitches would have to be perfect, or the wound wouldn't close properly.

"Ana?" The shock of her patient speaking her name made her look, for the first time, at his shadowy face, and she found that she recognized him. She had known Rámon Cruz since—well, since high school. Since those wild and strange days in the

Lower Valley of El Paso. Rámon had been a fighter, she remembered, always ready to take on Anglo boys in their cowboy boots and blue corduroy Future Farmers of America jackets. He had been a *vato* before there had been a name for what he was. She had found him dangerous and beautiful and wild, like a jungle animal. She hadn't been surprised when he'd joined the Chicano movement. She hadn't been surprised when she'd heard he was wanted, either. Rámon had always been destined to be art on a post office wall.

She *was* surprised at how fond she was of him after all these years. They'd always been rebels together in spirit.

"I asked them to get you especially," he said. "*Como está*, Ana?"

"I've had better days. So, obviously, have you. Rámon, you've got to go to the hospital." So much to say, no time to say it. "This will kill you, understand? I'm not qualified to do this, and even if I was, you need a transfusion."

"My men will give blood for me." His face, which she remembered as dark, was pale as old ivory, his lips delicate yellow. "They'd die for me."

"This is different. I can't transfuse you here. You've got to call an ambulance!"

"Ana." Fondness in his raspy voice. "I'm a wanted man. I can't go to the hospital."

Footsteps behind her. She turned and saw Miguel with four men behind him.

"Call an ambulance!" she demanded, to Miguel, to Rámon, to anyone who would listen. Miguel ignored her. His eyes were on Rámon Cruz's face. "Damn it, do you want to watch him die?"

A moment of silence. Rámon's decision, she realized, not hers. Not even Miguel's, for all he seemed to be in charge.

"Call the fucking ambulance," Rámon said with a faint sigh. "Dr. Ana says I got to go to the fucking hospital."

Miguel nodded and left, the curtain shivering in his passing. The four men stepped forward.

Ana flinched under a sudden assault of brightness. Four halogen flashlights aimed down at the wound. She blinked back afterimages and turned her attention back to the surgery before her.

"Don't you wonder?" Rámon asked her dreamily. She kept stitching, fine, even stitches like her mother had taught her. Only this time her sewing wasn't saving an old shirt; it would save a friend's life. The man standing behind her coughed and murmured an apology, and she thought, *So much for the illusion of a sterile field.* She pushed away thoughts of infection and gangrene.

"Don't I wonder what?"

"How it happened?"

"For the love of God, Rámon, I'm not blind." She touched the edges of the wound, crusted black. "You were standing too close to something when it blew up. This is a shrapnel wound, flying metal or glass, with signs of contact burns. You'll be lucky if you don't lose your leg. What was it, an exploding gun?"

"You wound me, Ana."

"Doesn't look like I'm the first."

He snorted at the joke, but his amusement was cut

short as she brushed against raw, bleeding tissue. His
eyes rolled back in his head, and he almost went
limp; she felt him hang on to consciousness with a
grip of iron. Strong. He'd always been strong.

This was a mess. She irrigated the wound, stared
hard at the artery, the thin, delicate stitches. No seep-
age. She loosened the tourniquet just a bit, ignoring
his sharp breath of pain, and watched as blood
pumped through the tube.

The stitches held.

"I want you to join us," Rámon said. She kept
watching the wound, sponging away seeping blood
from the tissue trauma. "Ana, listen, we need you.
Where we're going, we'll need someone like you."

"Where do you think you're going?" She packed
the wound with sterile gauze. The conversation was
a meaningless distraction, something to keep his
mind off the pain. He wouldn't even remember what
he'd said in the morning.

"We're going to war," he said. She stopped working and met his eyes.

"You're not serious." He held the gaze. "War. Who
the hell do you think you're going to fight? The government? With what? You've got to be kidding."

"You are a patriot, Ana. The kind of patriot we
need to win back this land for our own." His breath
was coming short, and he had to rest between senten-
ces. She checked his pulse. Thin and weak. "People
are rising to follow us. We'll need doctors in Aztlan
just as we do here. You could be the first."

"Aztlan," she said slowly. "You're talking about
revolution."

"El Paso is a crossroads. It has close ties to Mexico.

It has the—the largest population of Spanish-speaking people of any American city." His voice was getting weaker. His eyelids shivered with the strain of keeping him conscious. "Aztlan—is the homeland of *la raza*. El Paso should be ours, Ana. We can defend it."

"It's part of the United States."

"It was illegally taken." A long pause now. Rámon rested his head against the wall. Sweat glistened on his face, and his skin color was ghostly. "We'll get it back, Ana. I swear we will."

"Rest." She put her hand on his forehead. His skin felt clammy and cold.

In the distance she heard a siren. Around her the men holding the halogens shifted; she looked up as one by one they switched the beams off. The sudden darkness felt oppressive and terrifying.

Rámon's cool hand gripped her hard.

"Why'd you marry the Anglo?" he asked.

So many things to say, so many excuses to offer. Ana settled for the truth.

"I loved him."

Red and blue lights strobed the curtain; something official had pulled up to El Tony's. If it was an ambulance, she was saved. If it was the police—

Gato slipped like a wraith around the curtain. He was carrying a flashlight in one hand and aimed it directly at her face. She could barely make out the gun in his other hand.

"Gato," Rámon said. He sounded very far away. "Take my good friend Dr. Ana home. Keep her safe."

Gato immediately holstered his gun and held out his hand to help her up. She closed her bag and looked down at Rámon, her friend, the dreamer. The criminal.

"I have to say no," she said. "I'm sorry. But I'll pray for you."

"Pray for all of us. Get out of here. Don't let them see you."

As she heard the rumble of a gurney's wheels approaching the door, she followed Gato's insistent pull on her hand to take her home.

Chapter 3

October 26, 1996
Dr. Ana Maria Ross Gutierrez

Gato left her somewhere between El Tony's and *La Clínica*, where she didn't know; he was with her and then gone. She walked the rest of the way alone, with the ambulance's strobing lights marking her path for her, and through the bright windows of the clinic saw Rafael pacing. He looked like he'd had lots of practice.

"Ana!" He frowned when he saw her enter, blanched when he saw the blood soaking her pants. She held out a hand to stop him from rushing at her, dropped into a convenient soft chair that creaked only a little, and closed her eyes.

"It's not mine," she assured him. "I'm tired. What time is it?"

"Three a.m. Listen, Ana, we should close. You need rest."

No question he was right. She was a habitually bad sleeper; the last three or four nights had been impossible. She might have squeezed in ten hours for four days if she was lucky, but she figured the total for far less. Rafael's suggestion made her think of scented candles and warm bubble baths, of deep and dreamless sleep.

"I have to go to the hospital," she said aloud. "Check on Rá—my patient. Thanks for holding down the fort. Any problems?"

"Two cops came looking for you. I told them you were out delivering a baby. They liked that one." Rafael had the smile of a mischievous kid. "I think they were looking for your testimony on some drug-related thing."

"Which one?"

"Yeah, that's what I said. Go on, I'll restock and finish here."

"I—yes. Okay. I need to change."

Rafael nodded and started working. She felt a rush of affection for the boy, thought, *Maybe I should marry him,* and hauled herself wearily out of the chair and through the clinic to a door marked NO PASEN. She unlocked the door and stepped into a gloomy, narrow vestibule with green walls and peeling beige linoleum. There were fifteen steps to the second floor, though her legs insisted it was more like fifty; she flicked the switch at the top of the stairs and turned to the right.

She was home.

It might not have been a condo, but it was cheap; she stayed close to the clinic, was never late for work, and had few transportation expenses. The arrangement had become available as she'd moved out of Pete's house in Dallas; it was supposed to have been temporary, but she liked it, liked the solitude and the security. The sparseness of the rooms suited her, too. She'd left the old-fashioned hardwood floor bare and gleaming, softening the stark emptiness with thick, colorful Mexican rugs next to the couch. Comfortable, unthreatening furniture.

As she passed the plump-pillowed couch, she picked up the remote control and clicked on the television, set perpetually to Univision. She liked to hear voices, especially late; many times she left it on all night while she slept.

From the next room her brother yelled her name. *Not now,* she groaned inside; she wanted to lie down, prop up her aching legs, sink into the cushions as if they were a lover's arms.

But she never ignored Gabe when he called her. She supposed that was unhealthy.

"*Aquí,*" she said, and went toward his door.

Her brother Gabriel sat at his usual post, in front of a bank of cheap black-and-white monitors. He was a small man, but his wheelchair made up in presence what he lacked in bulk; it was a low racing model, with angled wheels, the canvas back and seat a bright tie-dyed yellow and orange.

"So you didn't die," he said bluntly, and looked over his shoulder at her. He must have been able to tell how much blood there was on her clothes from the monitors, because he didn't even blink at the sight of it. "This time. Don't do that again."

"What, save a life?"

"Leave the clinic. You know the rules, Ana. Let them come to you. One of these days you'll get hurt pulling that shit."

He was rocking his chair back and forth, an unconscious motion like other people tapped their feet.

"Papa Gabe," she said with a sigh. "I'm going to get cleaned up and go to the hospital. I'd like to find out what happens to him."

"He who?" Gabe asked, and spun his chair to face her. It was still a shock for her to see the whole of him, the strong, muscular body and the legs that ended in round stumps at mid-thigh. It had been only three years since she'd gotten the call—*Your brother's been in an accident, it's bad.* Only three years to get used to seeing the shadow in his eyes, the anger that flared unexpectedly from that gentle smile.

"Nobody you know," she lied. Gabriel was only two years younger than she, and they'd fought their way through the same high school; he'd remember Rámon Cruz, and not favorably. Gabe was that rarest of birds, a Chicano born of ghetto poverty who'd become completely conservative. He didn't blame the Anglos for his problems, not even the drunk Anglo who'd crossed the median on the freeway to smash head-on into Gabriel's car. It was, Gabe always said, God's way of telling him to get off his ass.

But that was proving more difficult than it seemed. There wasn't a lot of market for disabled football players, or even disabled football coaches. He'd been working for Ana at the clinic for nearly a year now, watching the monitors, waiting for trouble to summon the police. Boring work, but steady.

She wondered sometimes if he hated her for it.

"You're bullshitting me," Gabe said. "Oh, by the way, Mama called today. She wanted to make sure you were coming for lunch tomorrow. I told her yes."

"*Yes*? Gabe, no—"

"Yes. Tomorrow, mass and then lunch. You can do this, Ana. Mama expects it. Oh, and *Tía* Yvonne, too. She's coming, too."

"Great. Who else?" Ana could already picture the chaos that it would turn into—her aunt Yvonne would bring her three uncontrollable children, she'd be expected to coo over them, and Mom would lecture her again about finding some nice Chicano boy and having babies.

"Just Sister Teresa." Gabe grinned at her expression. "Oh, come on, she's not as bad as all that."

"She's a nun," she said. "I can't stand nuns."

As she left the room, she heard Gabe say, just loud enough to hear, "Why? You practically are one."

In the bathroom, she stripped off her bloody clothes and put them in a cold-water soak, threw herself into a brisk hot shower, and let her muscles go peacefully limp for ten minutes before she forced herself to move on. As she was toweling her short dark hair, she wondered if Rámon had really been serious about Aztlan. She'd heard others talk about it, of course, some starry-eyed MEChA students and some ineffectual dreamers, but nobody who'd actually be likely to *do* anything about it. Take over Texas, New Mexico, Colorado, Arizona, California? Turn them into models of a long-vanished Aztec homeland? It sounded like science fiction to her, but there was no denying the sincerity in Rámon's eyes. Or in a lot of other people's when they spoke of it to her. Fanatical dreamers were the most terrifying people in the world.

There was something to be said for throwing the Anglos out, though. No more politicians promising help to immigrants with one hand and shooting them down like dogs with the other. No more *la migra* to protect Anglo fortunes. No more of one percent of the El Paso population—the wealthy *white* one percent—dictating the culture of the city.

And no more Pete Ross.

As if she'd conjured him up, she remembered his body, his skin a rich pale cream, and the taste of him came back with shocking suddenness. She didn't still love the man. She *couldn't*. It was just that her brother was right; two years without sex wasn't good for anyone.

It was shameful. It was *wrong*. She knew Rafael liked her, knew even Rámon wouldn't turn her away, but there was really only one man she wanted.

And she wouldn't let herself have him.

Scrubbed, fresh, clear-eyed, she said good night to Gabriel and took the freight elevator down to street level, where her car was parked. It was a rattletrap of a Pinto plagued with oil leaks and balding tires, but it was her own, and she didn't really need anything more. Her money, what little she made, went back into the operation of *La Clínica*. She unlocked the car door and got in, started it up with a roar and a puff of white smoke that rose majestically into the clear desert air like a loose balloon. Rafael was still inside the building, and she waved to him as she drove past the front door.

One of these days she'd ask him upstairs. Maybe. She wanted to do it tonight, just to forget her ex-husband, but she couldn't ask him to stay and she had to go see Rámon. Some other night, she promised herself. *Oh, sure.*

Fate being what it was, she knew it would never happen.

Nothing that good ever happened to her.

The emergency room at Columbia East was having a normal Saturday night, too; Ana stepped out of the way of a speeding gurney propelled by white-coated interns and nurses, a resident shouting orders alongside. A drunk bumped into her from behind and mumbled a confused apology as he sank down the wall and went to sleep. In the far corner of the utilitarian room someone vomited; a harassed nurse grabbed a mop and shoved it at an intern.

She remembered being that intern, mopping up vomit and far less lovely substances late at night. She remembered gunshot wounds, the shredding effects of head-on-collisions, bad back-street abortions. Not so many of those these days, in more liberal times, but there were still a few old women with their potions and hooked knives. Good Catholic girls didn't show their faces at abortion clinics; at least one of the church groups took photos of everyone who went in or out of the doors. Some of them still considered it safer to trust a wrinkled old *bruja* with a coat hanger than their own families.

That brought back memories, too many of them. She swallowed and put her mind on something else. As she turned toward the crowd at the nurses station, she caught sight of the man she knew as Miguel standing against the far wall, his hat tipped down low over his eyes, his hands hanging limply at his sides.

After a second he pushed away and came toward her.

"Walk with me, Doctor," he said. "Just a friendly walk."

"I'm fine here." She didn't like the look in his eyes. "How's he doing?"

"They tell us nothing. You can find out for us."

"I—" Whatever excuse she'd been about to make vanished as he took hold of her arm; his fingers were brutally strong, and she knew she'd never be able to break that grip if it ever locked around her neck. "Of course."

Miguel nodded, satisfied. The cruel pressure on her arm eased.

"His name is Luis Villarreal."

They'd have given a false name for him; everyone recognized the name of Rámon Cruz, especially the police. Before she could ask anything else, Miguel turned and went back to his post against the wall. Scattered around the room she spotted other men she thought might have been at El Tony's. She got the cold feeling that they had arranged themselves that way, with the milling patients and families in the cross fire, for a reason.

If it came to that, would any of them shoot?

We're going to war, Rámon had said. He'd meant it.

She swallowed hard again and went in search of someone on staff willing to do her a favor.

She found that favor in the frantically energetic person of her best friend from high school, Maria Flores. One or two quick words, and Maria understood the situation—Ana did not have privileges at

Columbia East, at least not currently, due to some bad blood with the chief administrator, and to be caught poking around patients was strictly forbidden.

But not for Maria, who was always eager to break the rules.

"He was half a dead man," Maria said, hiding her mouth behind a cup of hot coffee. Her eyes darted around, searching for listeners; she made Ana nervous just standing next to her. "They say his name is Luis, but I remember the face."

"But they don't know who he is?"

"God forbid!" Maria took a sip of coffee, made a face, and drank again. "I used to hate coffee, you know, but you got to drink something around here. I remember him from high school, you know. I did him, remember? I think I told you about it later. We were in his car, that cherry red Chevy with the hydraulics—"

Maria had been one of the school's wild kids, like Ana herself—they'd both dressed in traditional *cholla* style, oversized men's suits and slicked-back hair, watch chains hanging to their knees. Nobody messed with them, because they were crazy.

Maria had been the first one in school Ana knew to attempt suicide with pills. Hard to believe she was a registered nurse these days, straightened out and married with three children. But old habits died hard. Like not ratting on your brothers. Like Rámon Cruz, who seemed to stir up old loyalties just with a glance.

"You won't say anything?" Ana ventured.

"No." Maria eyed her narrowly. "You neither, *chica*."

"You know it. I don't forget the rules." The conversation could have been twenty years old, straight out of the high school locker room. "He's my brother, I don't screw him over."

"Once a *cholla*, always a *cholla*. Stay here. I'll find out the news." Maria dumped her coffee out in the water fountain next to them, handed Ana the empty cup, and walked down the wide green-walled corridor. Ana turned the styrofoam in her fingers, staring at the pale brown drops that chased inside, and wondered how long it would take to get home and get some rest. Hours probably.

She felt the heat of someone's stare and looked up, startled.

At first she didn't see anyone she recognized, and then he snapped into focus: Pete Ross. He was thinner than she remembered. He stood next to the elevators, frozen in the act of adjusting his dark blue jacket—tall, lean, just a trace of gray frosting the light brown hair. He'd been too long without a haircut, as usual, and his white shirt looked rumpled and as tired as his face.

Just visible under his jacket, the leather of a shoulder holster. She looked from that to his warm brown eyes, and turned away from his smile.

He didn't have the sense to leave her alone, of course. She stared fixedly at the doors where Maria had disappeared, willing her to come back. Too late.

"Ana?" Just her name, spoken very softly. She didn't look at him.

"Peter."

It took him a second to overcome the coldness of her reply. "Good to see you, too."

"Why?" She allowed herself to look at him, now that she was certain she would present the right impression. "You think I *want* to see you?"

She meant all of the levels of meaning, and he got every one. Not a slow man, Pete Ross. Not at all weak, either. It took a great deal of courage to continue to ask for this kind of rejection. *For God's sake, Pete, go away. Don't make me keep hurting you.*

"Visiting a friend?" he asked mildly. She turned her face away.

"Checking on a patient. I suppose you'd better get out there and drag a pregnant woman back across the border by her hair."

She had several seconds of silence to think about the cruelty of what she'd said. That hesitation was very much Pete's style; it was impossible to have a good argument with the man when he considered everything you said. It gave him the appearance of— she hated to admit it—depth.

Not just the appearance, Ana. She stomped the traitorous little voice down, hard.

"Look, let me start over." He moved so that he was back in her sight line again. Wrinkles at the corners of his eyes that she didn't remember being there. Had it been that long? Was four years time enough for everything to change, or was it just that her memory was faulty? "I've needed to talk to you—"

"I got your messages," she interrupted. "We have nothing to talk about, don't you understand that? Now please go."

"Ana—"

She focused on him and shouted, "Leave me alone! Do you understand that, *chingalo*?"

That had always been her secret weapon; Pete, like most Anglos, hated to cause a scene. Her raised voice attracted the attention of everyone in the hallway—patients, doctors, nurses, even a passing uniformed cop. She saw what she wanted to see—shock in Pete's eyes, then an electric snap of anger, quickly banked. He stepped back. Inclined his head stiffly to give her the point.

"Cheap shot, Ana," he said. "But that's always been your style. Sorry to have bothered you."

He turned away. She had a wild, weird impulse to grab him and make him come back so she could shout at him again, see the anger in his eyes. *Ay*, she thought, dismayed. *Am I that bad? All I want is somebody to hate me?*

She wanted somebody to care. Hate was a kind of caring, wasn't it?

"*Ay*, is that him?"

She'd forgotten to watch for Maria's return; the other woman stood at her shoulder, staring at Pete's retreating back. Both hands gripped her stethoscope.

"Yes," Ana sighed. "That's him, the pig."

Maria nodded slowly, examining him with care until he turned the corner and vanished from sight. "He's kinda cute," she said, and reclaimed her cup from Ana's tense fingers. "I'll take you to see Rámon."

"No." Ana felt a chill all of a sudden, a warning that made her heart beat faster. "Pete's *la migra*, he wouldn't be here for nothing. I don't want to raise suspicions. You're sure Rámon's going to be all right?"

"So they say."

Ana reached into her purse, tore off a piece of paper from a pad, and wrote her private phone number on it, no name. She handed it to Maria, who tucked it into her coat pocket.

"Give him that. Tell him whatever he needs, call me."

Maria raised one carefully plucked eyebrow. "*Amiga,* that's a dangerous thing to do. You never know with someone like that. You get yourself involved, you could get hurt."

At least that would be something, she thought, and said, "Maybe it's time I got hurt."

Chapter 4

October 27, 1996
Peter Alan Ross

Pete Ross walked, as he always did on Sunday mornings, from El Paso across to Juárez, Mexico, with two bags of groceries. There wasn't as much foot traffic at this time—no day-pass workers, no tourists. Most good Catholics were at mass. Around noon the temperature and the traffic would both pick up, but for now he was glad of solitude and the warm windbreaker he'd remembered to put on. The wind was cold as a thin-bladed knife, drying out his throat and nose. When he swallowed, he tasted blood. Years here, and he still hadn't adapted to the altitude and climate.

The turnstile creaked as he pushed through it under the eyes of a suspicious, bored colleague. This one was the cautionary poster child for sensitivity training, a tall, hungry-looking Anglo with cold gray eyes and the stare of a concentration camp guard. He shifted his gaze from a passing Mexican woman to Pete, no recognition, just curiosity.

"Let's see that stuff," he ordered, coming out of

his chair. Pete stepped to the side and handed over the plastic bags, waited while the patrolman searched through boxes of crackers and bags of potato chips, canned tuna, and toilet paper. He held up a box of feminine napkins, frowning like he'd never seen them before, which considering his charm and general appearance might have been true.

He stuffed everything back in the bags, not too neatly, and handed them back.

"Pass," he said. Pete suppressed a wild urge to tell him *go long* and took his groceries without comment, following the big-hipped sway of the Mexican woman ahead of him. On the other side of the bridge, the Mexican border guard made the same desultory search of his bags, even to eyeing the Kotex.

And then he was in Mexico, where the wind seemed a little colder, the day a little grayer, and the world a little less hopeful. He followed the street down into the tourist district, past closed shops selling quart bottles of vanilla and cheap serapes, velvet paintings, and tequila by the case. One stall was open, a milk stand. One glance in a mug was enough to kill any thirst Pete might have had for that; the skim on the top looked spongy as old carpeting.

He turned at the next corner, onto Calle Gavanza, and then up a dirt path to a small, painfully neat house painted aqua blue with bright green trim. A cardboard Halloween witch, faded with sun and time, cackled on her broom in the front window. A window box of herbs breathed basil and cilantro as he climbed the steps.

In the window, below the cardboard witch, a hand-painted picture of an open palm, the lines painstakingly drawn. And below it: CURANDERA.

He knocked.

Esmeralda Sanchez opened the door, saw his face, and smiled, and some of the gloom of Ciudád Juárez vanished for him. He kissed her cheek and handed her the plastic bags, and her smile deepened, showing dimples. She was still pretty. The American doctors had done a good job with her burns, and the scarring was minimal, only visible if you knew where to look. Pete did. His eyes traveled the map of her face, finding the faint outline of blisters and burns.

"You don't have to bring me things every time you come over," she said in slow and heavily accented English. "I like you to visit."

"And I like making sure you eat," he said in fluent Spanish. He appreciated her gesture, but they were both more comfortable in her native tongue. "You look beautiful today."

She accepted a kiss on the cheek, and they hovered together for a few seconds, drawn by each other's warmth in the morning chill. Esmeralda was the first to step back, cheeks flushed. She took the groceries into the kitchen.

He remembered how she'd acted the first time he'd visited—flustered, afraid, unsure what to do or what he wanted. That had been before she'd become a *curandera*, though. A long time ago.

He wondered if she measured time the way he did. Everything was either pre- or post-desert for him, and the only thing at the center of it was her.

"Business good?" He followed the restless flicker of candles into the sitting room, where a crucifix hung on the wall with a shelf of flowers, candles, and rosary beads below. Her couch had seen better decades. She'd covered the stains with a clean hand-knitted afghan in bright pinks and greens in ornate cross patterns. In the center of the room was a huge oak table with heavy chairs; the wood was polished to a high sheen. In the center of the table, a gold-framed portrait of a small, eagerly smiling boy with Esmeralda's delicate bones and big brown eyes.

Pete took a new votive candle from his jacket pocket, lit it, and put it next to Jaime's picture, then removed a yellow carnation from inside his windbreaker and placed it beside the candle.

"Yellow," Esmeralda said from the doorway. She had two cups of coffee. He accepted his and sat with her on the couch, the attention of both focused on the picture, the candle, the flower. "He will like that, a little brightness on a cold day. Thank you."

The coffee had a chocolate taste to it, subtle and rich. She probably drank thin instant most of the time, except on Sundays. Except with him.

"I saw Ana," he said after two or three silent sips. Esmeralda nodded. "At the hospital."

"She's well, then?"

"She told me to go to hell."

A knowing, dimpled smile. "Ah. She's *very* well, then."

"I don't know why I try, Esme, I really don't."

"You talked to her, though?" Esmeralda asked. "Told her?"

Pete shifted. The couch muttered, grumpy at the movement; springs creaked and stabbed. "I didn't have a chance."

"Did you really want one?"

He let the question pass. She knew the truth. No sense in either of them denying it. He finished his coffee, let her take the cup and put it aside, and then gave her his hand. She turned his palm up, smoothed it with her fingers, traced the lifeline thoughtfully. Her brown eyes were distant and luminous.

"Read my future," he said. She shook her head, a frown forming. "Why not?"

"No jokes, Peter. Please."

She stood up, still holding his hand, and he let himself be led to the massive oak table. She touched her fingers to her lips, to Pete's, then to the picture of Jaime set on the table. Pete, after hesitating, did the same. Her lips felt warm and satin soft under his fingertips, and he was reminded of how she'd looked that terrible afternoon in the desert when she'd come out of that metal cocoon. Blistered, ruined lips.

So little sign of that now, except for the faint, ghostly scars and the picture of Jaime.

"Sit," she said, and he did, settling into the big, heavy chair without releasing her hand. She took a seat near him. "What do you want to ask?"

"I want to know about Ana."

"Ana." A flash of annoyance crossed Esmeralda's face, temper and mischief in her eyes. "Let Ana take care of her own troubles, Peter. You aren't her husband anymore."

"Come on, Esme, I need to know."

Esmeralda sighed and reached over to grasp his hand with hers. Her fingertips stroked his lightly, not quite a caress. "I should never have told you anything," she said, shrugged, and bowed her head. "Pray with me."

He did, putting his mind at rest the way she'd taught him to do, walking in his mind through a peaceful church into stained-glass light, letting the silence wash through him. He was dimly aware of his heartbeat slowing as she prayed, of the subtle pulse of her own life through their joined fingers. That made him think of the pulse at her throat, and how her skin felt on her neck, growing softer as it disappeared beneath the modest neck of her blouse. Seeing Ana had left him feeling—hungry.

"Stop that," Esmeralda murmured. He realized she'd stopped the prayer some minutes ago; the only sound he heard now was the conspiratorial whisper of their heartbeats. "Be a vessel, Pedro. Not a bubbling pot."

He breathed out and let the longing go, let it fall away.

"*Mijo*," she said, and there was such love and peace in her voice that he opened his eyes to look. She was staring at him, past him, into that place he couldn't reach. "Welcome. Mama loves you."

Pete did not believe she really talked to her lost son, Jaime; he couldn't forget the reality of the dead child in his arms, the emptiness of his glazed eyes. But he knew Esmeralda believed, and sometimes that was enough. What he did believe was that for whatever reason, through whatever power, Esmeralda was able to help him where no one else could.

Esmeralda cocked her head to one side, still oblivious to him. A smile lifted the corners of her lips, and Pete felt insignificant against that blinding joy. She reached out with her free hand to touch empty air, as if stroking the face of a child.

"Jaime, *poquito*, you remember your friend Pedro. Pedro is troubled. You remember what you told me about *Señora* Ana? About the black cloud?"

No reply, to Pete's ears, but then, there never was. There was only Esmeralda's half of this strange, disjointed conversation. He waited until she focused on him.

"Jaime says it's starting, as he saw before. There is a sickness inside Ana, not like yours; she is going dark in the spirit. That's what he says."

"Going dark?" Pete repeated, mystified. "How do I keep her from—going dark?"

"Keep her in the light. She wants to follow her heart, and that is bad; that goes into darkness, she will not survive." Esmeralda frowned, her eyes gone far away again. "Not so quickly, Jaime. Tell me slower."

Whatever she heard, it upset her; he saw the shock ripple across her face, felt the sudden tension in her hand. Her eyes blinked rapidly.

Two years ago Esmeralda had looked up from her coffee with an expression like that. She'd told him Jaime said there was something bad in his head. She'd shown him where it was, drawing a circle at the base of his skull. He still remembered the light coolness of her touch.

And a month after that the headaches had started, and the doctor had come back with the bad news. They'd insisted on surgery. And chemotherapy. And radiation.

Jaime—Esmeralda—told him that the surgery

would leave him hooked to machines for the rest of his life, a breathing shell of a man. She had proposed another way. He hadn't believed in Esmeralda's cure, but he'd tried it. Couldn't hurt, he thought, to wait a couple of weeks. Inside of two weeks MRIs had shown the tumor shrink. Since that inexplicable event he'd come every week, sat at this table, and let her massage his head with those cool fingers, seeking the tumor, squeezing it into a tight, tight ball, then a pinpoint—

And now the doctors admitted that it was in remission. There were no more headaches, though he kept the medication in his pocket as a precaution.

Nobody said the word *miracle*. It wasn't scientific.

He listened to her with his whole attention now as she said tensely, "Jaime, *mijo*, you must be sure when you say this. Are you sure?"

He saw the reply make her flinch. She focused on him and blinked.

"There is great trouble coming," she said slowly. "Very bad. Many will die, Peter. And it will be Ana who does this thing, this thing that makes so many die. You must stop her. You must find out what this thing is."

"Jaime doesn't know?"

She shook her head mutely. Her empty right hand curled into a fist in frustration.

"There is more than Ana. There is—a Chicano man—a white man—the hate consumes them in fire. There is a child who sings. There is danger everywhere, Peter, and this was not so before. Something important has happened. Something terrible."

He could tell by the grief on her face that her con-

nection to Jaime was fading; there was always that
terrible loss in her dry eyes. The doctors had repaired
most of the damage, but they hadn't been able to
repair her tear ducts. Her eyes were always dry. Just
now the whites were slowly flushing with distended,
irritated capillaries. Stress made them bloodshot.

"He's gone," she said, and sat back with a sigh.
"Did that make any sense to you?"

"None."

"Me neither. But Jaime doesn't lie. He can't. He
doesn't know how."

She was still frowning, and scrubbed her eyes with
the palms of her hands, an unconscious gesture of
frustration. Pete reached over to a side table and
found her eyedrops; she smiled in gratitude and
dosed her eyes. False tears drew silver paths down
her cheeks.

"Did he say anything more specific? A time, a
place?"

She considered it carefully. "Only—something
about a bridge."

"An international bridge?"

"*El Puente Negro*," she said, and then in English,
to be sure he understood. "The black bridge."

Pete sat back. She resisted his attempt to free his
hand from hers. The feel of her skin was suddenly
distracting.

"What is it?" she asked. He didn't reply, lost in
thought. After a few moments he felt her hand slip
free of his. She stood behind his chair and put her
hands on either side of his head.

"You don't have to—" he began. Her hand slid
forward to cover his mouth, silencing him, then back

to its place on his temple. Her fingers began to slowly move in circles on his scalp.

His skin shivered into gooseflesh. He let himself be soothed by it, like a child, and lost himself in the soft whisper of her singing, in the vision of the quiet church and the sparkling stained glass, the jeweled light.

He sank into a healing sleep, safe.

Chapter 5

October 27, 1996
Dr. Ana Gutierrez

Ana helped her mother down the steps of the Socorro Mission, her mind still on the mass. She couldn't call herself a good Catholic—she didn't go to mass nearly enough for that, and confession was a dim memory—but there was a kind of peace in sitting inside the ancient walls that remembered the Indian wars. The roof beams were black with age. Though the church wasn't large, it had a kind of dignity that a more contemporary building couldn't pretend to have.

Her uncle Julio's name was on the back wall of the church, the one dedicated to the sons of the church fallen in war. She'd forgotten about it until this morning; the sight of his name carved in stone, shrouded in silence and flickers of candlelight, still brought tears to her eyes.

"Demon worship," her mother said.

"I'm sorry, Mama—what?" She dragged herself back to the bright, loud present with an effort. Cars were revving in the unevenly paved parking lot, coughing white smoke and rattling metal. Not a wealthy congregation at the mission—the children of immigrants, or immigrants themselves.

"I said I never let you or your brothers celebrate a devil's holiday. Father Tomás always spoke against it." Her mother, a stoutly built woman, wheezed as she stepped down to parking-lot level. No matter how many times Ana reminded her about heart disease and stroke, she refused to lose weight. *A good Chicano mother is fat,* she'd told her, patting her cheek. *Who trusts a skinny cook?* Ana worried. Behind the humor, her mother's breath sounded wet and fluttery, and she was too unsteady to bear all those extra pounds.

"Father Tomás hasn't been here for ten years, Mama."

"And the world, it changes, I know, I know." Isabel Gutierrez sighed a pale white cloud of disapproval on the cold wind. "And you're *la doctora,* I suppose you know best."

"Mama—" It was an old argument, and Ana abandoned it when she saw *Tía* Yvonne piling her three screaming children into a late-model Ford. Yvonne ran a grocery store near the high school, close enough that she had a steady flow of students buying snacks and sodas. That and her late husband's pension kept her, as Mama liked to say, in tortillas and beans. Mama knew she hated that cliché, and so she delighted in using it at every opportunity.

"And how is my sweet boy?" Mama beamed, and there was Gabe, wheeling himself out from beside Ana's car. As Mama bent over him, her black lace shawl tangled in the arm of his chair, and Ana had to step in to save shawl and her own sanity. Mama gave Gabe two wet kisses, one on the cheek and one on the mouth. Gabe looked long-sufferingly at Ana, but she wasn't sympathetic. After all, he'd "run late" and let her sit through mass alone.

"I'm fine, Mama," he said. "How was mass?"

"Cold. The heat wasn't on." Mama's sharp eyes turned fiery. "And Father Gregory talked about the harmlessness of Halloween. What kind of priest is that, who lets children celebrate the night of the Devil, I ask you? It's not right. Ana, you know it's not right."

"Yes, Mama," Ana murmured. She fixed a frown on Gabe. "How'd you get here?"

"A friend dropped me off. I'm in time for lunch, right?"

"Of course you are." Mama squeezed into the backseat of Ana's car while Gabe maneuvered into the passenger seat. Ana folded up the light graphite wheelchair and opened the hatchback to store it. As she shut it, she caught sight of a late-model brown car cruising too slowly past the mission. Tourists? Most of them had the decency to come after mass, when they wouldn't disturb the services. But there was something about the car, something familiar—

"Ana!" Mama summoned her impatiently. "What are you doing back there? Your brother is cold!"

When she looked up, the brown car was gone around the corner, but the image remained, naggingly unfocused, in her mind.

Pete had a brown car, that was it. She was annoyed at herself when she realized the train of thought—as if what Pete did or said meant anything to her anymore. What had he said at the hospital? *I have to talk to you.* He'd looked so earnest. Was it possible that—

No. It wasn't possible. Not in the least.

Lunch at Mama's house was always an event—small family dinners fed twenty and, Ana thought, could be stretched to feed the downtown homeless, too. She sat with Gabriel in the living room while Mama heated up the feast she'd prepared on Saturday night—tortilla soup, tamales, *menudo*, enchiladas, fresh homemade guacamole. The tortillas were, of course, handmade; Ana remembered as a child learning the art of shaping the bread and baking it just so, not long enough to dry it or burn the edges. She tried not to think too hard about making the tamales and the *menudo*. Not before lunch. There were some secrets of home cooking it was simply best not to know.

"Thank God for *Tía* Yvonne," she sighed, and rested her head against the cushions of Mama's threadbare recliner. It had been Papa's recliner in the old days, but in those days it hadn't been frilled with tatted doilies and smothered with a warm hand-knitted afghan. She turned her face until she smelled the musky lavender of her mother's perfume rising warm from the fabric. Underneath, she could still catch a hint of sharp leathery cologne. *I miss you, Papa.*

"Yeah, otherwise you'd have to be chasing down kids and stirring *menudo*. She lets you sit out here because I might *hurt* myself. Got to keep an eye on the *handicapped*."

Gabe spun his chair around and patrolled the room. She recognized the mood, had seen it often enough at *La Clínica*. Spending time with the family made him remember what he'd lost—looking up to the people he used to be equal to, being cooed over like an infant by the old women. Looked on with pity by cousins and strangers. Oh, she understood. She just didn't feel inclined to deal with it.

"Gabe, grow up or I make you eat *two* bowls of sheep guts. What is it with you, anyway? You set this up for me, and then you don't come to mass?"

"You want to know why I didn't go to mass this morning?"

"Let me guess." Ana picked up a magazine from the end table. A Spanish-language edition of *Reader's Digest*. The jokes weren't much better than in English. "Didn't feel particularly holy today?"

"I was picking up a hooker," he said flatly. He'd stopped wheeling around the room. He faced the big picture window, the one with fading lace curtains, and stared out at the cold morning, the browned grass in the yard. "Had to pay her extra. Because I was, you know, *more work*."

Ana realized her mouth was hanging open, and closed it.

"You didn't."

"Of course I did." He shrugged. "What did you think, I get it every weekend? A girl on every corner? When was the last time I had a date, Ana—two years? Here's a closely guarded secret, if you want to take my confession—it's been two and a half years since I got laid, and that was a mercy fu—"

"Gabe!" Ana broke in desperately. She'd turned to steal a look toward the kitchen, and there, standing in the doorway, was Aunt Teresa. *Sister* Teresa. She stood there in her wimple and severe knee-length black dress. Her order wasn't required to wear traditional garb, but Teresa had always been old-fashioned. "Look who's here. Teresa, how are you!"

She stood up and exchanged hugs with her aunt; Teresa had a well-scrubbed smell, no perfume, nothing artificial. She looked younger than her fifty-two years, her face clear and unlined, her eyes deep as midnight lakes. In the depths of those eyes Ana read laughter, but nothing troubled the serene surface of her face.

"My beautiful Ana," Teresa said, and kissed her cheek. "I see you're doing well, but you look tired. How long since you had a good night's sleep?"

"Two weeks," Ana admitted. "Maybe three."

Teresa touched her cheek gently. "Rhetorical question. Since you were a child, you never rested. And how is my favorite nephew?"

"I'm your *only* nephew," Gabe growled. His cheeks were apple red. Teresa hugged him and kissed his forehead. She pulled up a hassock that put her on a level with Gabriel's eyes and smiled placidly.

"I'm sorry you missed mass," she said, "but I'm sure something came up."

Ana choked and took a deep drink of her orange juice to cover. Gabriel gave her a pitiful *get me out of this* look.

"Aunt Teresa, Mama said you were leaving the school, is that right?" Ana asked. *You owe me one, Gabe.* "I'm surprised. You've been teaching there so long!"

"Since I was thirty," Teresa agreed. "But there's

only so long anyone should have to teach ten-year-olds without training in hand-to-hand combat. I'm eligible for retirement. I thought I'd take it and spend some time doing good works. Maybe I can help you at the clinic, Ana. I had some nursing experience, you know—oh, years ago, but I can fetch and carry, clean up, that kind of thing."

"That would be . . ." *Shocking*, Ana thought. Sister Teresa had always been a figure of terror to her growing up, and she was sure it had been the same for Gabriel. ". . . wonderful. Call me at the clinic when you're ready. I'll put you to work."

"And you." Teresa looked back at Gabriel, who was working hard on a smile. "I'll get to see more of you, young man. It's time we got to talk more."

"I'm sure you'll have plenty to talk about," Ana said, and received a desperate glare from her brother. "It seems we all have a lot in common."

Teresa's smile was so pure she had to have gotten the implication. She came to sit next to Ana and fanned herself with a letter from the table; Ana caught a glimpse of sweat at the edge of the wimple.

"Is it too hot in here for you?" Mama always kept the place warm enough to grow tropical orchids, summer and winter.

Teresa shook her head. "No, dear, I've just been chasing Yvonne's children outside, trying to keep them from playing with black widow spiders and sharp objects. You'd think that a nun's nieces and nephews could show a bit better behavior. I left them trampling your mother's okra in the garden."

"Her okra!" Ana had to laugh. Sister Teresa hated

okra, and it was Mama's favorite thing to can for Christmas gifts. "Well, I'm sure she'll understand."

"God forgive me, no, she won't." Teresa closed her eyes and fanned herself. Gabriel mumbled an excuse and wheeled himself around the corner to the bathroom. Without opening her eyes, Teresa said, "Is he quite all right?"

"Gabe? Of course he's—"

"Don't lie to me, child." A cord of steel under the soft words. "I heard. Did you really think I hadn't?"

Ana folded the magazine she'd been pretending to read. "Well, then you know. There are days when he wishes he was dead. That's really not much of a surprise, is it? But he's getting by."

"Is he really?" Teresa continued to fan herself, the picture of peace. "I wonder. And I suspect you do, too. You're far too smart not to."

They sat in silence until the toilet flushed and Gabriel returned. He took up his post at the window again. Outside, children screamed and laughed, and presently Mama finished laying the table, and they ate a family dinner like any other.

Ana had the sense, even as the meal passed, that they were living a memory, not their real lives.

Somehow, late in the afternoon as she and Teresa sat watching the blazing orange sunset, Ana found herself telling her aunt about Pete.

"Do you want me to give you my opinion about marriage?" Teresa asked, shading her eyes against the glare. The sun's false glory gave her skin a rich golden color. Ana tried to imagine her outside of the habit, but it was useless; the habit was as much a part of Teresa as the quirky humor and the grave, peaceful eyes.

"Not particularly. I've had plenty from Mama about it already."

"Oh, but I don't think we're at all alike, you mama and I. And this may shock you, but I don't let the church tell me everything to believe. What I believe is that divorces are no better and no worse than loveless marriages when no children are involved. If you and Peter were not suited, then I think you did the right thing."

"And if we were?" Ana asked, and couldn't believe she'd done it. "I mean—"

"You mean you're still not sure?" Teresa rocked gently in the old bamboo chair. She and Ana had been excused from kitchen duty—*something to be said for being the doctor and religious in the family*—and from the looks of it Teresa was enjoying the leisure very much. "Well, that's not good. We don't have an eternity to correct mistakes, Ana. God doesn't give us that much time."

Somehow, out here on the porch, it was easier to speak about it. "He's not a bad man, I know that. But what he does for a living, as an Immigration agent—it isn't right, Aunt Teresa. I can't love a man who does things like that."

She had an instant to realize the depth of her mistake, because Teresa let her consider it in the stillness, before her aunt commented quietly "I think he could say the same of you."

Her face burned. "Please, let's not talk about that."

"Why not? You think I'm going to blame you for what you did in Dallas? It's not my place to judge you, Ana. You are a doctor, and what you were doing was in every respect legal before the eyes of the government. You must make the decision about how it appears to God." Teresa somehow made that sound compassionate, but Ana still felt acutely uncomfortable. The last thing she'd wanted to do was discuss her practice in Dallas as physician to the Women's Center.

"It's not the same thing. Look at what *he* does."

"Such as upholding the law?"

"Persecuting our people!"

Teresa shrugged. "It seems to me that there are always different ways to look at things, no matter how much you wish there weren't. I look at these poor people crossing the river, and I think, *It's our Christian duty to shelter them, feed them, and care for them.* But is it? Is it possible to save the whole world, Ana? I think you and Peter have the same idea, but on different scales. Maybe you're trying to save just a few. Maybe Peter's trying to save everyone."

"*Save* them! He throws them in prison! He sends them back to starve!"

"I know the story," Teresa said softly. "About the woman in the desert. And the child. It seems to me that what he felt, looking at that terrible tragedy, was a sense of outrage. A desire, perhaps, to never see such a thing happen again. Maybe joining the Border Patrol wasn't the best way to fight the *coyotes*, Ana, but at least it was an honest one."

In all this time she had never understood that simple truth about her husband. She'd thought—what? That Pete had suddenly come to hate all Chicanos?

That she'd married a bigot who'd managed to hide it all this time?

Teresa was the only one who'd ever tried to look at it from his side.

She swallowed a sudden lump in her throat, stood up, and said, "It's cold out here. I'm going in."

Teresa rocked in her chair, eyes closed. "Your choice, child. Always your choice."

By the time she got back to *La Clínica*, she was exhausted again, so tired that it took all her strength to help Gabe out of the car and up the ramp to the elevator. He went off to his own room, no word to her except a casual *good night*, no mention again of the hooker. Ana kicked off her shoes in the living room, sank into the cushiony embrace of the couch, and flicked on the television. She drifted off into a troubled half-sleep, haunted by voices and screams and the sounds of sirens, woke when she realized that her telephone was ringing. She clawed it off the hook and rolled over on her side, trapped the receiver near her ear.

"Ana?" Rámon's voice, weak but clear. "I wanted to thank you."

"No need to do that, Rá—"

"No names," he said. She sat up, suddenly aware of the chill inside her apartment. The voices on the television sounded annoyingly loud. She muted them and concentrated on his voice. "Listen to me. Thursday evening someone will come. He'll need your help. Do what he asks you to do."

"Wait. I'm not—"

"Ana, we need you. There are people who want

to stop us from taking back this land, and they're willing to do anything. We need people we can count on."

She shouldn't, she knew. Rámon was trouble, from start to finish; she had always been careful to run *La Clínica* strictly legally, always carefully. What he was asking her—

"You already helped me once, *querida*. Help me now."

Querida. How long since she'd heard a man say anything that tender to her? And Rámon was an old friend. That had to count for something.

"Yes," she answered. "But nothing illegal, and you'd better not be lying to me."

"I swear." A smile in his voice now. "*Buenos noches*, Ana. And sweet dreams."

As she hung up, she heard wheels creak in the doorway.

"Is everything okay?" Gabriel asked. She kept one hand on the telephone, staring at it, wondering.

"Yes," she lied. "Of course. Why wouldn't it be?"

Chapter 6

"You got a problem with me?"

Pete decided that if he ever got his hands on the man who'd assigned him to work with Joseph Ryan, he'd ram the bureaucrat's head through a plate-glass window. One reinforced with chicken wire, like the one he was staring through right now. Pete was in a hallway of the El Paso Central Detention Center, a big name for a ridiculously small cinder-block building that served as the jail—correction, "processing center"—for the thousands of illegal immigrants the Border Patrol caught and sent back to Mexico every week.

He would dearly have loved to send Ryan back to his native country, but the plumbing in this building was older than the conquistadors, and he didn't think Ryan's head would flush.

"Hey, did you hear me?" Joe Ryan, taller than Pete by some three inches and broader by at least two, joined him at the window. He had a red face, drinker's nose, and smart cool eyes. Pete didn't like those eyes. They matched what he sensed of Ryan's personality. "I thought you were the kick-ass investigator around here."

"Let me be very clear," Pete said, and turned his head to look Ryan in the eye. "The only ass I'm about to kick is your lily-white one." Ryan had been making a great deal out of skin color.

Ryan's grin grew slicker. "You think I can't do my job?"

"All I know is that you're getting on my nerves."

"Yeah, well, I don't love you either, my man. I got no respect for you INS assholes, just like you got no respect for DEA, so let's just get this out of the way—you're working with me now whether you like it or not."

"Fine," Pete said. "I'm sick of listening to you. If we're going to be working together, let's work. If we're going to be talking, been nice knowing you."

He started walking in the direction of the interview rooms, where Sanchez and Grivaldo waited. If Ryan had been Border Patrol, he would have already been out the door. Ryan's particular kind of attitude wasn't tolerated—but he was, for better or worse, Drug Enforcement Agency, and they had a lot of money and a lot of clout. Pete was stuck with the bastard. It didn't matter if the man told thousands of jokes about Mexicans. It didn't matter that at unguarded moments he called them wetbacks when he thought no Hispanic officers were in earshot.

It *would* matter, gravely, to Pete's career if he took a swing at the guy.

The Border Patrol–DEA cooperative effort was the brainchild of some genius in Washington who thought it would be wonderful if federal agencies could work together like one big, happy family. What they'd failed to consider was that the Border Patrol and the DEA were composed of fundamentally different types of people. Not all the DEA people were as bad as Ryan, of course—but Pete thought that the majority he'd worked with had fit into the cowboy mode. Smart, ruthless, scary. And they looked on the Border Patrol as cannon fodder.

He wasn't about to sacrifice his life for Ryan's headlines.

He was the token liaison between the DEA and two Border Patrol agents, Sanchez and Grivaldo, who'd been working undercover with a group suspected of smuggling heroin across the Lower Valley border—smuggling heroin in, hot cars out. It looked like an efficient enterprise, which meant there was money in it, and that meant guns. People like that protected their investments.

Ryan said, "Hey, somebody told me you're the *culturally sensitive* guy around here. Some kinda poster child or something. A regular All-American guy."

There were days—more and more of them—when Pete suspected he'd made a serious wrong turn post-desert. Esmeralda's peace wasn't really going as far as it used to. Still, he hadn't slammed Ryan's head into the wall. That was something.

Ryan caught up with him, matching him stride for stride. "Seriously, man, is it true you saved some wet—illegal alien out in the desert?"

"I found her," Pete said. "And her son."

"Yeah, the kid died, huh? That's rough." Ryan's

fake sincerity was nauseating. "I heard you asked her to marry you."

He hadn't read *that* in the newspapers. In fact, there were damn few places he could have heard it. Pete said nothing. The door to the interview room at the end of the hall seemed like a mirage, mocking him in the distance. *I'll never make it. I'll be trapped with him forever.*

Oh, hell, just ignore him. You can do that. You ignored your own wife for a year.

"What's a *curandera*?" Ryan asked too innocently.

Pete came to a halt as if he'd slammed face first into a wall. Ryan went on a couple of steps, turned, and grinned at him, palms outstretched.

"Hey, man, just a question. Nothing personal."

He kept walking, whistling as he slammed the interview door open. Pete didn't have any choice but to follow.

Pete had worked with Sanchez before, never with Grivaldo, but he knew the kind of work they were doing took guts and dedication. They'd been boosting cars for two months now, living a life he knew he couldn't imagine, and somehow keeping *them* separate from *us*. It couldn't have been easy, living a lie day and night, doing things against their own codes. He saw the strain in Sanchez's eyes.

Ryan took one look at the two Hispanic men lounging silently around the big table, and grunted, "Great. They've gone native."

Pete grabbed his shoulder. It felt good to dig his fingers in, see Ryan's eyes widen in reaction. "These men are risking their lives for you," he said very softly. "You treat them with respect."

Ryan shrugged him off and sat down at the long Formica table, and that was that. Ryan had his own bosses. None of them would give a damn about the complaints of three Border Patrol investigators. Sanchez caught Pete's eye and gave him a look that clearly said, *Who's this asshole?"* Grivaldo just looked bored. No wonder Grivaldo blended so well; he had a tapestry of tattoos on his arms, flexing and curling as his muscles moved. He also had the dead-eyed look of a true bad boy. Pete wondered just how much of it was an act.

"Yo, Ross, why don't you get us some coffee?" Ryan ordered. He stretched in his chair. "Been a long damn day. That all right with you boys? Coffee?"

Sanchez looked at Pete and said, "Nothing for us. We ain't thirsty."

Pete sat down at the table, next to Ryan and across from Grivaldo. The message was clear. *Get your own coffee.* Ryan might not like it, but he wasn't in a position to kick anybody's ass about it, either.

"Amigo," Sanchez said, and offered Pete a clenched fist to tap. "How's life, man?"

"Shorter every year. How's the family?"

"Wish to hell I knew, I ain't seen them in six weeks. Maybe tomorrow, eh?"

"Yeah, hope so."

Ryan leaned forward. "This is really heartwarming, but let's get to the point, okay? You told us that there was heroin coming over. When?"

Sanchez said, "Word is that it's coming over on the Black Bridge. Tonight."

"Thanks for the goddamn early warning," Ryan muttered.

Pete remembered Esmeralda's words. *El Puente Negro*. The Black Bridge. *Terrible things.* "How?"

"A total of three couriers with backpacks. They're being real careful, but they'll wait until the last one comes over and they'll all get in a car together. You can take them then."

"Welcoming committee?" That from Ryan, who was suddenly all business. Sanchez and Grivaldo exchanged glances.

"Nobody but us," Sanchez said.

"You're shitting me."

Sanchez shrugged. "Hey, that's what they said."

"And you didn't think that was a little bit strange?" Ryan puffed his cheeks, blew out a disgusted breath, and transferred his stare to Pete. "I thought these guys were supposed to be good at this."

"There's some hot cars coming back from Mexico on a hauler, Copia Bridge, early morning tomorrow. Six, seven at the latest. That's where they think you'll be 'cause they're going to give you that one," Grivaldo put in softly. He was staring at Ryan, but Pete knew he wasn't talking to him. "You take that one, the guys you got to watch out for are the ones named Hector Casillas and his little brother Mando. Can't miss them—both got no hair, like to carry two guns, both on the hip. Mando got a knife, too. Keeps it different places. Pat him down good."

"You're telling me that those cars won't be hauling the product?"

Grivaldo gave him an economical little nod.

"Maybe enough to make your weekend happy, man, but it's a sugar bust. You be at the Black Bridge, you get the real deal."

And you guys? You're okay? Pete asked. He handed Sanchez an unopened pack of Camels. Sanchez fished out a smoke and offered one to Grivaldo; they both lit up.

"Yeah." The answer came out foggy and too quiet. "Think so."

"Be sure, man. I don't want you getting your throats cut."

Sanchez exchanged a look with Grivaldo, shrugged his shoulders, and took another deep drag. "We don't go back, they know. This Cruz guy, he's really weird. Don't know what he's thinking most of the time. But if we take off, they're gonna change the plan and it's all shit."

"Yeah," Grivaldo agreed, staring down at the table. A moonscape of cigarette burns mapped the top. "Thanks for the offer."

"Where's this Black Bridge?" Ryan asked wearily.

"Got a map?" Grivaldo grinned as he asked, and Sanchez chuckled.

"Which street?" Ryan tried again. Grivaldo shook his head.

"No street, man. It ain't no international bridge, it's the railroad. Steel and wood slats, right over the river. They'll cross there."

"You really think anybody in their right mind would try that?" Ryan sneered. "They're yanking your puds. This is bullshit. We'll hit the hauler on the Copia Bridge, that's where the stuff will be."

Grivaldo smiled a tiny private smile. Sanchez

looked at the ceiling for guidance. It was Pete who said, "People come over the Black Bridge every night, most of them women and children. Some of them fall and break their necks. Some of them drown. And some of them get run over by the trains in the middle of the night because there's nowhere to go. You're a real expert on the area, aren't you?"

Ryan stared at him, gray eyes hostile. "I don't need to know. I don't work for the goddamn Border Patrol busting women and children."

A silence fell. Sanchez and Grivaldo smoked placidly, watching Ryan with heavy-lidded eyes.

"Heroin'll be here between midnight and four a.m., coming over the railroad bridge. Three couriers wearing backpacks." Sanchez said it slowly, to make sure Ryan understood him. "Is that clear enough, sir?"

"How many guns?"

"Told you already. Us."

Grivaldo was laughing, a soundless trembling of his shoulders. His tattoos pulsed with it. "He don't remember so good. Old-timer's disease. *Ay*, Pete, you watch your ass, okay?"

"Watch yours, man." Pete offered a fist. Grivaldo tapped it. "When you hear us declare, you get the hell out of the way, okay? No mistakes."

"No fucking shit," Grivaldo agreed. Sanchez nodded. "Eh, amigo, you watch him, right? Don't let him get crazy on us." The *him* was, of course, Ryan, who was turning redder than a cherry tomato. Pete turned and met his eyes.

"My word," Pete said. "If Agent Ryan here gets in your way, I'll put him on the ground."

"Good enough for us."

They mutely shook hands all around, except for Ryan, and Sanchez and Grivaldo left, taking the pack of Camels with them. Ryan sat where he was, waiting for Pete to move.

Pete put his feet up on the table.

"Screw this," Ryan said, and pulled out a cellular phone. "I don't believe these assholes for a minute. They've gone native if they weren't there to begin with. We're hitting the Copia Bridge and the car hauler. Nobody's going to put millions of heroin in the hands of a couple of wetbacks coming over a railroad trestle. They're going to want security, and the hauler gives them that. With the right papers it goes right on over."

"You're disregarding inside information?"

"This is a DEA operation. I'll decide what's important." Ryan turned away from him as his connection went through. "Yeah, it's Ryan. We're a go on the car hauler for tomorrow, I want a full team on it."

"They gave you the information," Pete said. "Don't be stupid, Ryan."

"Shut the fuck up, Ross. Call your bosses if you don't like it."

Like it would do any good.

God, he was tired by the time the day had officially ended—the sunset had long since misted away, and the El Paso night was cold, the wind sterile with chill. Pete paused in the act of unlocking his car to stare up at the stars—the best part of living here, he thought. He'd never had any idea how many stars there were, or how clear they could shine, until

Esmeralda had taken him outside and shown him the incredible density of constellations one night like this.

He remembered the feel of her hand in his as they lay on the cool grass, drunk with stars and cold Dos Equis beer. Jesus, he'd wanted her that night, a hard, fierce desire like a fist in his chest. And all he'd done was kiss her lightly as he left.

What the hell's wrong with you, man?

There was a pane of invisible glass between him and Esmeralda. No matter how close they got, they could never—quite—touch.

The glass was Ana, cold as the stars and just as distant. Or it was Jaime? Or both?

"Ross." Irritation crawled up his spine, and he turned to see Ryan opening the door of his own car, a cream-colored Toyota. "Get in."

"Day's over," Pete said. "And nobody told me I had to date you."

"Get the hell in the car and don't give me any shit." Ryan slammed his door for emphasis. Pete stared down at his keys for a few seconds, then walked over and got in the open passenger side of the Toyota.

"Well?" he asked. The car smelled of stale smoke and old grease, but it was cleaner than he'd expected. Maybe Ryan's wife cleaned it out. She'd be a quiet woman, he was almost sure, somebody who could take orders. "What's so urgent?"

"Any asshole with a scanner can pick up our cell-phone line. We're coordinating this on landlines. Five DEA agents are meeting us at the railroad trestle at

ten p.m. What did you think, I was going to hang
your boys out to dry?"

Ryan had started the car and pulled it out of the
fenced, guarded lot before Pete said, "Thanks."

"What for? If they're wrong, they're screwed and
so are you. If they're right, you won't get any of the
credit. What're you thanking me for?"

Good question. Pete settled back in the seat and
watched the stars slide by overhead, cold and distant
as the memory of his wife. He hadn't said anything
to Ryan—no reason to—but Ana's clinic was less
than five blocks from the Black Bridge.

The DEA had some nifty stuff. Border Patrol had
bulletproof vests, of course, but they didn't have the
state-of-the-art body armor, or the suitcases full of
vaguely James Bond-ish equipment. One silver suit-
case opened to reveal a video monitor with a computer keyboard; a canvas bag held a squatty camera
on a tripod that one of the DEA agents took up to a
rooftop vantage point near the railroad tracks. Pete
himself waited with Ryan behind the warehouse, in
a sleek black van with swiveling captain's chairs. It
was way too well appointed for a government-issue
vehicle.

"Yeah, impounded from a smuggler," Ryan said
when Pete brought it up. "Got a wet bar in the back,
too, and a TV-VCR. Okay, we're hot on the camera—
see this screen? Hang on, it's warming up."

The image took a few seconds to solidify, a ghostly
black-and-white picture of the railroad trestle and the
area around the gravel road it intersected. The Rio

Grande was a gray-black ribbon beyond the darkness of the ground.

"Night vision?" Pete asked. Some of the four-wheel-drive vehicles the Patrol used out in the more desolate areas were equipped with night vision, but he'd never been in one. He knew there weren't any lights on that side; you could barely make out the iron and steel of the Black Bridge on a night like this. Ryan grunted in affirmation.

"Not Starlight—this is infrared, NightSight technology. State-of-the-art military equipment on loan to us from the local base—"

"Fort Bliss."

"Yeah. Anyway, you can see in zero available light with this setup, and it can't be blinded by headlights or flares, so we'll have a good view of anybody coming across."

"What's that?" Pete's finger painted the parallel lines of white on the screen. One of Ryan's agents adjusted the screen slightly to focus.

"The tracks," he explained. "They've retained more heat than the wood or the surrounding metal. It's only been about half an hour since the last freight train came through. If we rotated the camera, you'd see warm tires on the van, anything retaining a heat signature."

"Heads up," Ryan broke in. On the monitor pale ghosts bobbed as they came into view on the bridge. "Shit! They're early!" He reached down to key his headset mike, but Pete held out a hand to stop him.

"We're looking for men with backpacks, right?"

"That's what your guys said."

Pete leaned closer to the screen. "Those are three

kids and a woman. Jesus, the resolution on this in incredible."

"Hartman?" Ryan asked, tapping the DEA agent on the shoulder. "He right?"

"Yes, sir. Looks like a woman and three kids. No— four. That's a baby in her arms. It's hard to see because it's wrapped up."

They watched the silent procession cross the bridge and make it safely to American soil, where they stopped. The mother knelt down on the ground, and Pete had a flash of how cold it would be there by the river, the humid chill blowing in their faces. The river had a dead smell, too—more like a lake than running water. Too much waste dumped in, from both sides.

"What are they doing?" Hartman asked.

Pete rested his chin on his fist. "Praying. Thanking God they made it alive."

After a few minutes they stood up again and walked out of the camera's range. The imprints they left in the ground, the marks of knees and feet, glowed brightly as lost souls.

"There's more starting across on the other side," Hartman said softly. "Jesus. How many can make it before the next train? Don't you people stop this kind of thing?"

"Periodically, but we don't have enough man-power to cover it all the time. The border leaks like a sieve. We try to cut off the most dangerous access points, like this one, but we still lose a lot of people in the river every year. Mostly kids. They get swept away in the current." Those were the worst. Their parents were afraid to call for help and just tried silently, desperately, to find them. By the time they screamed, it was too late.

"When's the next train scheduled?" Ryan asked.

Pete checked his watch. "Another hour and ten minutes. But sometimes the Mexican side makes changes, and we don't always get the word. Neither do they." He nodded at the ghosts on the screen making their careful way over the river.

"Christ, this is a mess. Any sign of your guys yet?"

"No."

"Okay, keep your eyes open. Hartman, watch for anybody coming over with a backpack. We may not be able to wait on all three of them if we spot one and it looks like he's moving, so stay alert. Ross, any way to contact Sanchez or Grivaldo?"

"Not now."

"Shit." Ryan chewed his lip, staring at the screen. "What a cluster fuck. I guess we wait."

Four long hours passed. Pete kept a silent count— sixteen people passed, but none of them fit the description they'd been given by Sanchez. Ryan griped about the cost of his five-man team and all the equipment. Pete worried about the absence of Sanchez and Grivaldo. A train passed, thankfully grinding no one under it as it sped over the tracks; it left behind rails that gleamed hot silver on the screen.

A voice in Pete's earpiece said, "Post Two, we've got a car coming from the north. Black Cadillac sedan."

The picture on the screen jerked as the camera panned in that direction, up the gravel road, then tilted to follow the car's progress. No headlights showing, but the car showed up clearly, the tires silver donuts, the hood glistening with heat.

"Two men inside," the voice continued. "Okay, the doors are opening."

"No way to tell if it's Sanchez and Grivaldo?" Ryan asked. His agent operating the NightSight screen shook his head.

"We can differentiate general characteristics—facial hair, that kind of thing—but the faces aren't going to show as distinctive enough. They're both armed, though." He indicated a non-glowing area at one man's waist. It had the shape of a gun, probably an automatic. As the man turned, Pete caught sight of another dark blur on his other hip.

"Two guns," he said, and stared hard at the second man. Something wrong with this picture . . . "And no hair. These aren't my guys."

"Shit." Ryan's voice dropped low with tension. "Okay, listen up, everybody, this may get ugly. Treat the two at the car as hostile, repeat, hostile. These are probably not our contacts. Post One, any sign of foot traffic on the bridge?"

"We've got a family coming across, looks like two adults and three children."

On the screen the two men got back in the car. Headlights flicked on and quickly off.

"No sign of a single man?" Pete keyed his mike and asked. Ryan flashed him a look that said, *Stay off the air*.

"Nope," Post One replied. "Just the family."

The camera whirred back to focus on the bridge. Focus shifted, a blur of grays and whites, and the family stepped off the railroad trestle and onto dry land. No praying this time—the woman grabbed the hands of two of the children, the man the third one, and they headed in the direction of the parked Cadillac.

"Aw, shit," Ryan said. "That guy's got a back-pack."

"He's also got the kids for cover," Pete said. "Back off. Let him through."

Ryan tapped his fingers on the console, staring at the picture, and keyed his microphone. "Post One, Post Two, observe, do not move. We still have to more coming, if our information is—"

Pete saw it a second before Hartman did, but the words stuck in his throat. Hartman seemed to have trouble getting them out, too.

"Sir," he said, and swallowed. "I think two of those kids have backpacks. It may be nothing—"

Pete thought, *Oh, Christ,* and it was half a curse. He looked up at Ryan, and their eyes locked.

"I don't have a fucking choice," Ryan said, his lips tight, and keyed his mike. "Post One. Post Two, move now, repeat, now. Isolate the family, keep them away from the car. Maybe we can use the darkness before it's too late."

"No!" Pete yelled, but it was too late, and they weren't going to listen to him anyway. On the screen glowing figures with dark torsos—thanks to the vests—sprinted in toward the family from both sides.

The children would scream. Didn't Ryan know that?

On the screen one of the running men staggered and went down. Pete's earpiece crackled.

"We're taking fire!" someone screamed. "Jesus!"

On the screen one of the small figures fell.

Ryan and Hartman snapped on helmets with night-vision goggles and bailed out of the van. They hadn't given Pete the equipment. He'd be a hazard out there, a sitting duck. He dialed Ryan's abandoned cellular phone one-handed and got backup rolling, ambulances, the police, anybody close.

He couldn't move the camera to follow the gun battle. It stayed focused on the two bodies lying on the gravel road, one large, one small.

"You bastards," he said, and his voice was unsteady and tasted of ashes and vomit. He checked the clip in his gun and bailed out of the van, running in the smothering dark as shots exploded to his right. Muzzle flashes marked positions, but everything was confused. There was no telling who was where, who was in the way. He dived for the ground and crawled after he'd made it within sight of the starlit gravel road.

The DEA agent he reached first was breathing shallowly. His eyes were open, but there was a hole in his right temple, no exit wound Pete could find. He left him and crawled to the child.

She couldn't have been more than ten, a thin little thing, wild black hair curling around her shoulders. Pete felt for a pulse and found one. He ran his hands over her, searching for the wound, and found it in her shoulder, blood pumping warm over his hands.

All he could think of was that she'd bleed to death before the ambulance could find them, the victim of this stupid, useless screw-up, and he looked up and saw it just a few blocks distant, a gray, dingy building like all the other gray, dingy buildings around it. *La Clínica Libre.*

His breath came out in a puff of steam—not quite Ana's name, not quite a prayer—and he took the girl in his arms and started running.

Chapter 7

October 31, 1996
Dr. Ana Gutierrez

Ana passed the day in a state of nervous denial; she kept her mind on each thing in turn, *Stitch this cut, treat this fever, counsel about his social disease.* Halloween, even more than most days, was passing in a whirl of blood and bandages and crying children. Rafael wore rabbit ears and had a fluffy homemade cotton tail stuck to his lab coat. He was the one who soothed the frightened children, gave them candy treats, and was generally better liked. That was the way things fell out. Ana, for all her skill, was not warm and comforting; she'd long ago accepted it.

Which was why she went to pains to find assistants who made up for her shortcomings.

The day ended, as days will. As the last of their patients shuffled out into the darkness, Rafael leaned against the wall next to her, closed his eyes, and asked, "You want to talk about it, Ana?"

Was she that obvious? The thought of confiding in him was very tempting. She flashed on the empty bed upstairs, saw the same thing reflected in his eyes, and looked away. Her fingers nervously pulled on her stethoscope. He had removed the bunny ears and cotton tail, and in some way she missed them. It was easier talking to him when he'd looked so—unthreatening.

"I'm just—tired, that's all." No, that was the wrong thing to say; it led them back to the bed again. "I'll snap out of it, I promise."

"Let me buy you a cup of coffee." He poured her one out of a thermos, lukewarm and of mediocre quality, but she accepted it with a smile. "Bar's open, Doctor. Tell me your troubles."

"Well, it's—" However much she trusted Rafael, she couldn't tell anybody about Rámon Cruz. "I just get lonely sometimes. I look at all these children, all these families, and I think, *I could have had that kind of life.* And I don't know if I did right or not."

He nodded, poured himself coffee, too. They settled themselves in two of the waiting room chairs, facing out toward the empty street. A pale lemon moon had risen over the Rio Grande—a ghost moon, Ana's grandmother would have said, to guide the spirits. As she watched, it passed behind an unexpectedly dark cloud.

"Forgive me for saying this, but you don't really seem like the motherly type, Ana. You're a good doctor, but you're a little obsessive, too."

"Yes." She remembered the bitter arguments with Pete over that very thing, over his need for a home and her need for a cause. They'd been far too different, and not just in skin tone. "Obsession doesn't keep you warm at night."

She couldn't believe she'd said it, but there it was,

out between them. Rafael put his coffee cup down without quite looking at her.

"I heard you had to leave Dallas because somebody threatened you. That true?"

She was actually relieved to change the subject, though this one was no better in the long run. "Yes, that's right. I worked for a women's clinic, and the people there—we were targeted by an anti-abortion group. I started receiving hate mail. Somebody threw blood all over the door of my house one night." *Our house.* Pete had been so afraid for her, but the fear had come out as anger. He couldn't understand why she was devoting herself to the women's clinic, and she knew how he'd felt about abortion. "My husband and I were in the process of getting a divorce, so I moved here. Back home."

"You're Catholic, right?" Rafael asked. She nodded. "How'd you reconcile that with performing abortions?"

It was a good question. She smiled bleakly and said, "What makes you think that I did?"

The silence grew longer. She slowly reached over and put her hand atop his, and the touch of their skin made him draw in a deep breath and look right at her, hunger in his eyes, endless and dark, and she felt like she was falling into him, sucked in by the casual brush of their fingers. Her heart pounded so hard it hurt.

"I should—" He cleared his throat. "I should get back to work. Restocking. In the supply room."

The supply room didn't have a camera.

He stood up and went that way, not looking back. Ana felt the absence of him on her fingers like frostbite, and she thought, *What are you doing?* but didn't really care what the answer was. Better to make a mistake than never again *feel*.

She stood up, deliberately casual, and adjusted her lab coat. She gathered up the empty styrofoam cups and threw them away, tidied up the meager, tattered Spanish-language magazines.

She walked through the treatment rooms, one after another. Everything was in place, ready for the next day.

The open door of the supply closet loomed large as she approached it.

She froze just inside, closed her eyes and thought, *I can't*, and as she drew breath to tell him, his hands closed around her shoulders and he kissed her, and her knees went weak at the shock of flesh on flesh. She hadn't known she was so *hungry*. He tasted startling, hot and spicy and delicious beyond words, his lips soft and so very gentle.

She pushed him away, knew she was shaking and her cheeks were red, knew he could tell how much she wanted him. Her hands stayed on his chest, as if glued there.

"Ana," he whispered. "Come on. You don't have to fight it."

She remembered Pete saying that. *Let go.* The slow, exquisite rhythm of his body, his breath in her ear. *Let go*, querida. *Let if happen.*

The memory shamed her.

"Not here," she said. "I can't. I'm sorry."

He didn't say anything, but she saw the regret in his eyes as he murmured an apology. He brushed past her, out of the supply room. She heard him gather his books and papers, stuff them in a backpack, and leave the clinic.

You're a damn fool, Ana.

The stairs to her apartment seemed longer than fifteen steps tonight. She flicked on Univision as she passed the couch and went to Gabriel's room. He was asleep, snoring lightly, still sitting in his chair at the monitors. She turned off the pictures, one by one, and kissed him on top of his head.

"Ana?" He started awake as she straightened, caught her hand. "Sorry. I think I dozed off."

"It's okay." She brushed his cheek with her fingertips. "Sleep well."

She let herself cry, silently, on the couch, until she was exhausted enough to fall into a restless, lust-warmed dream.

She woke to the sound of distant banging. Gunshots, a lot of them. Not unusual in this part of town, but the quantity disturbed her; she dragged herself upright and rubbed sleep from her eyes, fumbled on her discarded shoes, and went downstairs into the chill.

She had just reached the front window of the clinic when she saw a man stagger into the watery light of the ghost moon. He looked half ghost himself, too pale, and in his arms—

Oh, God. She turned the key on the door and flung it open as he lurched toward it, grabbed the child in his arms, and carried her to the nearest treatment bed.

"Ambulance is on the way," the man gasped in English. There was bright red blood smeared on his hands, on the crumpled white of his collar. He was wearing a bulletproof vest.

And then she recognized his face, as if a camera had suddenly spun him into focus. No time to feel anything. She dismissed the problem of Pete and focused on the child she was holding. Her pulse was good, but there was too much blood. She worked in silence, putting pressure on the wound from the front and stripping off the girl's blood-smeared backpack when it got in the way. It slapped to the floor, too heavy for a child's body. She kicked it aside to give her room to work.

Pete reached down for it. She nailed him in place with a look, took the backpack, and moved it out of his reach.

"It's heroin," he said. "They were using her for a mule."

"I guess you taught her a lesson she'll never forget," Ana said grimly. In the distance sirens screamed. "If she lives."

She sat by the window in the clinic, watching the aftermath with exhausted fascination—so many police cars, so many important-looking Anglos brought out of bed in the middle of the night. Reporters, too. She'd tried to give a statement to a reporter from the *El Paso Times*, but a cop had chased him off. She didn't know how many cops had been inside the clinic—ten? Twenty? More than had ever entered it since it opened, she was sure. Mostly they'd looked around with that secretly pleased gleam in their eye, noting the old curtains, the well-kept but worn floor.

No, it isn't the Mayo Clinic! she'd wanted to scream.
Whose fault is that? Who keeps cutting our funding?

Pete hadn't said a word to her since the child had
been taken away in the ambulance. He was standing
outside next to a black van, arms crossed over his
chest, head down. A red-faced Anglo with a pot belly
was talking—no, shouting—at him. Ana felt a second's sympathy, quickly shattered as he raised his
head and looked in her direction.

Dragging a child into their broken lives, a painful,
obvious cycle. She stood up and left the window to
pull the bloodied sheets from the treatment bed, pile
them in the bio-hazard container, dispose of the bandages and her bloody gloves. She'd have to clean her
sweater, too; she shrugged it off and put a lab coat
on instead, buttoned up to conceal her lack of a shirt.

The clinic door pinged for attention. She pulled
back the curtain to tell whoever it was to leave and
saw Pete standing there, his hands hanging limply
at his side. He looked lost.

"What do you want?" she asked, not too welcom-
ingly.

"I'm sorry to drag you into this."

"A little late for that, Peter. Thanks for the apology. You can leave now."

Past him, the police cars were pulling out, strobes
dying away into darkness.

"Your friends are leaving." She nodded in that direction. "You should go with them."

"Jesus, Ana—" Suddenly, startlingly, he was crying, his shoulders shaking from the force of it. "Oh,
Jesus."

As she went to him, she saw a photographer outside aiming his flash through the open window; she hit the lights and plunged the clinic into darkness, locked the door, and drew the shades with a vicious yank. With a doctor's impersonal kindness she led Pete to a chair and let him sit, brought him a tissue and waited until the storm calmed.

"Better now?" She kept her voice as neutral as possible. The sight of him so vulnerable hurt her deeply, in places she'd thought safely cauterized. "I'll get you some water."

"Ana, I'm sorry. I know you don't believe it, but I am. So sorry. There's something I need to tell you—"

"Not now." The idea of sharing anything with him made her break away and get to her feet. She filled a cup from the water fountain and started back to him, checked herself as the telephone rang. She caught it on the third ring.

"Ana?"

Rámon's voice. She'd forgotten about *it*, about him, about the thing that had made her so desperately nervous all day. But it was a new day, wasn't it? All Saint's Day now, the devils put to rest, the spirits gone back to heaven and hell.

He was sending a man to her, he'd said. But the man had never arrived.

"Yes," she said cautiously.

"I can't get to you. What's happened?"

"I don't know. Shooting, lots of police. There was a wounded child."

Rámon said, "There's a package in the backseat of your Pinto. Go outside and get it, take it upstairs and hide it. If someone's with you, don't let them see it. Ana, this is important, truly important. Do this for me."

She wished she hadn't turned the lights off; the darkness disoriented her, made it seem that Rámon's voice issued from the air over her shoulder, like the voice of a whispering angel. He sounded stronger today. Well enough to walk? Well enough to put something in her car?

"I don't know if I—"

"Do it, Ana." All the warmth vanished from his voice. "I don't have time to let you think. If you don't go, people will be hurt. Maybe a lot of people."

"What?" Her hand went cold, as if the phone had given her frostbite. "What do you mean?"

"I've put myself in danger trusting you, myself and others. We could end up in jail or dead. Please, Ana. I swear to you, I won't forget."

She knew he wouldn't; Rámon was the kind of man who kept his word. She hesitated only a few seconds before she said, *"Bueno,"* and hung up the phone.

"Ana?" Pete's voice in the darkness, warm and close. She sucked in a startled breath and saw his tall shadow against the white gleam of a curtain. "Anything wrong?"

"Nothing," she said sharply. Rámon was a wanted man, and here was Pete, too close for comfort. She had to get rid of him, no matter what she might have felt for him. "You can go out by the side door. They won't be waiting for you there."

"I needed to talk to you. Please. Give me five minutes."

An invisible clock ticked behind her, a stopwatch

in Rámon Cruz's hand. "I don't have the time now, Peter. Maybe later."

"This is impor—"

"It's always important when you want it!" she stormed, and the anger she'd felt at seeing the wounded little girl flung itself out of her and into his face. "That *child* was important. What did she do to you? Take a job from a hungry Anglo? Get out of my house! Get out!"

She pushed past him, shaking off his outstretched hand, and opened the alarm-rigged emergency exit; bells exploded into clamor. A dry, cold breeze ruffled her hair and brought her the smell of ripe garbage and alley wastes.

"Get out," she repeated, loud enough to be heard over the alarm.

He left. She averted her face as he passed, slammed the door behind him, and gulped in deep breaths as the bells shivered to silence overhead.

He didn't deserve that, she thought miserably. But among all the hurts they'd done to each other, that was insignificant. What had he called their divorce? *The death of a thousand razor blades?*

She pushed away from the door, took the stairs two at a time. Gabriel was in his chair, wheeling anxiously from one window to another; he spun it in a tight circle at the sound of her approach, relief spreading over his face.

"Man, I've been waiting—"

"Later," she said. "Call the police, tell them it was a false alarm. Everything's fine."

"You're sure? What was all the shooting—"

"Later!" She used her keys to turn on the freight

elevator and waited while it jerked and ratcheted its way down to street level. No one waiting outside in the dark; she hurried over to the Pinto and opened the door. The dim overhead bulb showed her a plain cardboard box, reused many times, with the flaps folded instead of taped. It was about the size of three shoe boxes stacked high, and unexpectedly heavy. She squirmed backward, arms laden, and almost dropped the box when she saw a man turn the corner and come toward her. Not Pete, thank God. The reporter from the *Times*—Hector? Hector Arridondo?

"Busy night," he said pleasantly. "Any comments, Doctor? I know you saw at least one of the victims—"

"No comment." She stepped into the elevator and brought the gate down. Her desire to make Pete look foolish had passed.

"Not even about Peter Ross being involved?" He had a coyote's smile, and he smelled blood. "Your ex-husband, right?"

"He's a *pendejo*. You're a *pendejo*, too," she said, and pushed the button for the second floor. "And you can quote me on that."

He was laughing as she pulled down the steel door.

As the elevator struggled upward, she looked down at the box in her arms. Heavy. Heavy like the girl's backpack had been. Rámon hadn't told her not to look inside. Maybe he'd assumed—

Before she could talk herself out of it, Ana unfolded the flaps of the box and looked in. Another box, this one sealed with strapping tape. She'd have to cut it open to take a look.

I should, she thought. *I should find out why this is important to him.*

Instead, she folded the flaps back in place, ducked out of the elevator, and went to the other side of the second floor, where the supplies were stored. She tucked the box behind piles of old medical records and put a carton of latex gloves on top.

It looked so innocent, sitting there.

Rámon wouldn't put us in danger.

She was sure of that.

Chapter 8

November 3, 1996
Esmeralda Sanchez

She woke up before dawn, with the sure knowledge that she was going to die. Her heart pounded hard, her skin sweated cold. She wrapped herself more completely in thin blankets and a handmade quilt handed down from her mother, and tried to remember the dream, but nothing came back except fire and fear.

Don't cry, Mama. A whisper touched her hair, soft as thought, and some of her trembling eased. Jaime was here, watching over her. *You'll find a way to stop it.*

"Stop what, Jaime?" She spoke aloud to the darkness, to the fading dream. In the distance a dog barked; a pickup truck with a bad muffler chuffed up the hill toward the bridge. "Help me do this. I can't do it alone."

It might have been a draft from the window, or the brush of a child's lips on her cheek. A promise, she thought. Or an apology.

She hugged a pillow close to her stomach and

wished she was stronger, older, wiser. Other *curanderas* might have been able to unravel the dream, or to listen more carefully to Jamie's words. Perhaps she was not yet ready.

A bone ached in her hand, that phantom bone that Jaime's spirit had placed there. It pointed out sickness of body and spirit; it pointed to another world of knowledge and wonder. She wasn't sure why she'd been chosen by the bone, but all the *curanderas* were chosen like that, unexpectedly and decisively. If she'd been given a choice, she would have turned away from it. Her power. Her knowledge.

Her life.

And who would have seen the stain on Pete's spirit? Not an Anglo doctor, for all their machines and medicines. They could treat the effects, but not the illness—they didn't even acknowledge that such a thing as *susto*, the disconnected soul, existed. But she saw it in Pete's eyes, felt it in his touch. He had lost his way.

She would help him as long as she could, while they both lived. She and Jaime owed him that much.

Though she waited until after sunrise, Jaime didn't come back, and the dream slipped away under daylight like a guilty shadow. She waited until eight o'clock to brew the coffee Peter liked, lit the candles, and waited for the sound of his knock at the door.

He didn't come.

The candles burned low, the coffee soured. Esmeralda tried to tell herself nothing was wrong, but she couldn't forget Jaime's warning the last time Peter had visited—*great trouble, many dead.* At the center of it Ana Gutierrez, who held Pete's heart still, though he didn't want to admit it.

She had no telephone. She dressed warmly and walked to the bridge, where glassy-eyed *touristas* crossed into crowds of trinket sellers and beggars. She knew most of the people selling fresh vegetables and crafts, and spent time talking and watching passing Anglo faces for one she knew would not be there.

Late in the afternoon, she returned home and unlocked a battered metal box and took out the day pass that Peter had given her in case of emergency; it was still good for the rest of the year. She had never used it, never set foot on the American side of the border since she'd seen Jaime buried in it. The land of gold had become the land of graves.

The Mexican border guard passed her with a bored glance at her papers—she was carrying nothing with her, not even a shopping bag, and so could hardly be considered suspicious. She slowed her steps as she came near the halfway point of the bridge, the mysterious seam where lives fractured and countries warred.

She felt no different when she'd crossed it.

The man in the uniform of *la migra* on the other side waved her through the steel cage of a turnstile, and she was in the land of the free. The land of her son.

She didn't know where to go. Fear almost made her turn back, but she forced herself to walk off the bridge and into the cold street. Cars were parked up and down both gutters, new cars with Texas license plates. The Americans hesitated to drive their expensive toys into Mexico, where they might be stolen or vandalized, though that wasn't as likely to happen as they wanted to believe. So they left them here to be stolen and vandalized. She saw two teenage boys prying a license tag free from a glossy black pickup truck; the younger one gave her a hostile, blank stare, and they didn't hurry as they left.

Peter's phone number was written on a card in her pocket; she put an American quarter in a telephone booth near the corner and dialed it. After four rings a machine asked her to leave her name and number; she hung up on it, confused, and rocked back and forth in the chilled-metal silence. She had only a few dollars American, and not many more pesos, not enough to call a taxi. She might be able to take the bus, but she didn't know how to get to the address Peter had given her.

The telephone wouldn't give back her quarter, which she thought was strange—did it make you pay to talk to a machine? She found another coin in her pocket and dialed again. This time when the machine beeped, she said, in halting English, "Pedro, I miss you this morning, I fear—"

The telephone popped and crackled in her hand, and then a weary man's voice said, "Esme? Where—where are you?"

"I—at the bridge. In America." Tears burned in her eyes at the sound of his voice. "I was so frightened."

"Stay there," Peter said. "I'll come get you."

It seemed an agonizingly long time to wait, but she did as he said, stayed next to the telephone booth, rocking back and forth against the cruel slap of wind. There was no color on this side of the border; everything was gray and brown and weary.

Only the cars glittered. The few people who walked were either Anglo *touristas* who watched her with frightened eyes or, at the corner, an angry-looking man with a bottle in a brown paper bag. A police car drove by, and the men looked at her with the blank disinterest—not seeing *her* at all, but only her skin, her clothes, her behavior.

She thought of Jaime, and sadness overwhelmed her. She'd left him here alone, no one to talk to him, to remember him. No flowers to brighten his grave.

Está bien, Mama. She could almost feel the warmth of his breath on her cheek, the heat of his small fingers wrapped around hers. *You remember.*

She opened her eyes as a brown car pulled to a stop at the curb. For an instant she didn't recognize the man inside, so pale and unshaven. He leaned over to unlock the passenger door.

"Peter?" She took a tentative step forward. *"Dios mio."*

In all the years she had known him, she had never been to his apartment, but she was not surprised by what she found. Peter was a man caught in limbo, and the small rooms reflected that. Nothing permanent, nothing hung on the walls, boxes still hiding in the corners like sad, neglected children. He had a big leather chair, a lamp, a television, a stereo. In the bedroom, a small, unmade bed just wide enough for one.

It was the home of a man with nothing to hope for.

"What happened?" She turned on him as soon as he had shut the door. Her fingers itched to touch him, but she could tell he wouldn't welcome it. "I in fear for—"

"*En Español*," Peter said wearily, and dropped into that language. "You shouldn't have come, Esme."

Manifestly true. Instead of arguing, she went around the half wall into the kitchen. She felt sick at the bleakness of the counters, the blank stare of the cabinets. A kitchen was the heart of a home, and his was empty. She opened doors until she found some tea and a pot and put the water on to boil. The warm glow of the burner cheered her a little, and the burble of the teapot reminded her of better times.

"You shouldn't have come," Peter said again. He was standing behind her, very close. "Thank you."

She turned and put her arms around him; she felt relief tremble through him, and his head rested against hers, fever hot. He needed a shower and, she thought, a long, dreamless sleep.

They stood that way until the kettle screamed for attention, and she turned away to put tea bags in to steep. He found a forlorn bottle of honey hiding in a nearly empty cabinet, two mismatched mugs in another. She fixed the tea and commanded him to drink it down, all of it, then poured him another cup before allowing him to retreat to the barren living room.

There was only the one chair. She pushed him down in it, set her tea mug aside, and put her newly warmed hands on his head. So much darkness in him today, so much anger. She closed her eyes and tried to draw it out of him, but it was stubborn as a root.

"Headaches?" she asked him.

"No," he said. "Heartaches."

And then he told her about the dark, dark night, and the Black Bridge, and the wounded child. *Not again,* she thought, stricken. Hadn't Jaime's death been enough?

"She is not—"

"No, she's going to be okay. Time, and therapy." Pete's voice did not seem lighter with the knowledge. "But it shouldn't have happened, Es. She shouldn't have been there, it the middle of that. And we shouldn't have moved with her in the cross fire. You should have seen the headlines today—'Mexican girl critically wounded in government gun battle.' I was told to stay home, keep my head down. That's what I'm doing."

"They mentioned you?" she asked. "In their article?"

"Articles, plural. I'm on the national wire services. Pete Ross, one-time civilian hero, gunning down a defenseless child—"

"Peter," she said sharply, and tilted his head up to stroke her fingers over his brow. "You know that isn't true. Why let this hurt you?"

"Never mind me. What about my friends? What about my family? I hate to sound stupid, but I joined the Border Patrol for a *reason*. I wanted to keep what happened to you from happening to other Esmeraldas, other Jaimes. This—" He struggled for words and finally gave up. Esmeralda continued to gently rub his temples until his eyes closed. There was a troubled frown on his face that would not smooth away.

Unexpectedly, she felt Jaime next to her—not the sweet and loving child who was her spirit guide, but another Jaime, sterner, unsettlingly angry. His touch burned. She let her hands fall away from Pete, startled, and began speaking words she did not recognize as her own.

In English, in which she was not fluent—but Jaime was.

"You almost saw," she said. Peter jerked upright, startled, and turned to stare at her. Whatever he saw made him go pale and still, his eyes all pupil. "The Black Bridge. The child. *Fire.* You didn't stop it. Now there will be death."

It should have been a frightening sensation, losing control so suddenly, but Esmeralda felt numbed and insulated from the fear on Pete's face. *Jaime*, she tried to say, but the child was not hers now, he was God's.

"I tried—" Peter began.

Her voice cut him ruthlessly short. "The dead won't care how you *tried*. It will be harder now, but you must stop it."

"Tell me!" Peter almost shouted it at her. He stood up and put his hands on her shoulders, the crush of his fingers distant and unimportant. Esmeralda stared deeply into his eyes and saw the frightened, angry child he was, the one who took on the weight of the world. *Eh, bien*, if he wanted the guilt of the world, he would have to be its savior, too. That was Jaime's message.

"I have told you as much as I can," Jaime said tonelessly. "I can't tell you more."

And then he was gone, melting away from her like an outgoing breath. She reached out blindly to hold him close, and her hands touched Pete's.

She said, in Spanish, "I'm afraid."

Though he didn't answer, she felt it in his fingers,
like a chill at the edge of winter. She gently massaged
his hands, feeling the bleak tension melt, the skin
grow warm, and she was not innocent; she knew
what he was thinking as he looked at her, what he
was dreaming. She let herself think of it, too, a brief,
hot moment of possibility, and saw his lips quirk in
a smile.

She did not have to move far to kiss him, and their
lips melted against each other, hot as blood, sweet
as the honeyed tea, an undertone of seriousness to it
that made her heart pound and her legs grow weak.
Pete's hands traced lines down her back, slid down
to her waist, drawing heat down between her legs.
She swayed against him and opened her mouth to
his tongue.

The telephone rang. Though they continued the
kiss for a few more seconds, she knew he would
have to pull away, and he did, with a sad, sweet
smile, and turned away to speak rapid English to
someone on the other end. When he was finished, he
put the receiver back and stood in silence, head
down, a new tension in his shoulders.

"What?" she asked, and took a step to him. Something told her to stop.

"I have to go," he said, "I'll take you back to the
bridge, Es. I'm sorry."

Something cold and gray under the words, completely erasing the heat of their kiss. She swallowed
hard and tired to pretend it didn't mater.

By the time she returned across the bridge to Mexico, she felt weary and wilted, drained by Peter's

empty grief. So much broken in him, depths she couldn't fill no matter how hard she tried. *Susto.* She had heard about it all her life, from her *curandero* grandfather, from friends, even from her priest. Children and women were the most vulnerable to *susto*, having a closer connection to the spirits; when they became badly, deeply frightened or shocked, they lost their way. Physically, *susto* might take many forms—physical illnesses, like cancer and heart attack, or sickness of the mind. Peter had been severed from his spirits for a very long time. The longer it went on, the worse the risk—the common people knew that, though the bright, shiny American doctors did not. They spat on ideas like *susto* and its more fatal form, *espanto.* They called the healers frauds and witches.

But the people still believed. *Esmeralda* still believed.

There was a thin young man and a little girl sitting on her porch when she came up the gravel walk; he rose respectfully and nodded shyly to the girl. She was a quiet, earnest-looking child too grave to be pretty, and her eyes took in Esmeralda without interest. Perhaps twelve, and small for her age. One hand clutched a much mended rag doll, the colorful cloth faded and stained.

The young man started to speak to her, but Esmeralda stopped him with a shake of her head. She knelt down on the cold concrete beside the child, stripped the gloves from her hands, and put her palms on either side of the child's face. Such big, empty dark eyes. Esmeralda did not like what she saw there.

"You are welcome in my house," she said gently. "Come inside. You're cold."

The girl's coat was new, brightly colored. Esmeralda took it from her and laid it aside on the couch, stopped at the shelf under the crucifix to light the row of votive candles. It was cold in the house. She turned on the electric space heaters Peter had given her two years ago, and the smell of baking iron stung her nose, warring with the vanilla of the candles.

The child stood where she'd been left, staring down at the floor. The father gently urged her to the big oak table and sat her in a chair that nearly swallowed her. Esmeralda took a clean white taper from a box and put it in the holder beside Jaime's picture. She closed the girl's fingers around a match and helped her strike it. The two of them held the flame to the wick as it sputtered and whispered and finally burned steadily.

The girl said, hesitantly, "I'm not supposed to play with matches."

"We're not playing with them, *querida*, we're honoring my son. This is Jaime, do you see? He's a little older than you, but not that much. He's a very good boy, just as you're a good girl, and he's going to help you get better. You feel sick, don't you?"

The girl's satin hair rustled as she slowly nodded, once.

"The doctor says there is nothing wrong with her," the father said anxiously. "But he doesn't know. He doesn't understand."

Esmeralda reached over and warmed his hand with hers. She smiled at him until he hesitantly smiled back.

"I'm Victor," he said. "Victor Carrasco. This is Angela."

Esmeralda nodded and reached over to hold Angela's hand—such an unresisting little hand, limp as a corpse's.

"Did Angela have an accident?" she asked. "A shock? Anything like that?"

"Her—" Victor looked reluctant to continue. In the flicker of candles, his face was drawn and unhappy. "Her mother. She passed."

"Recently?"

"Seven months ago. But—Angela found her." His voice lowered. She had to lean close to catch his words, which crept away on the cool air. "She hanged herself."

Suicide. No wonder there was so much rage in the girl's placid eyes, so much blackness in her small, fragile heart. If her mother had died in grace, she might have become a spirit guide for Angela, the way Jaime had returned to Esmeralda. But Angela's mother was gone, and whatever spirits Angela heard now, they were not spirits of light.

"She—hurts herself," he continued haltingly. Angela seemed not to hear any of it; her eyes were focused on the crucifix on the wall, the candles glowing beneath. "I gave her a kitten. She drowned it. I think she—I think she is cursed."

There were still a few who believed in the *mal de ojo*, the evil eye, and Esmeralda had no doubt that a powerful will could bring ruin to a weaker one. But there was no need to blame evil on anyone else; this, she felt, was from a wellspring in Angela's soul, fractured at its root.

"Angela," she said, and squeezed the girl's hand lightly. The solemn brown eyes turned from Jesus' face to hers. "I'm going to say a prayer. Will you pray with me?"

Angela's shoulders lifted ever so slightly in a shrug. She didn't resist as Esmeralda took her other hand and began to pray to the Virgin for the repose of the lost soul of Angela's mother.

She was only halfway through when the girl tugged at her hand, trying to free herself.

"Stop," Angela said. "The Blessed Virgin doesn't want to hear about her."

"Why not?"

"Because she—she—" Angela's eyes suddenly sparkled with tears. "She was a coward. She ran away. The Virgin wouldn't have anything to do with her."

"God forgives all things to those who approach him with a true and contrite heart, Angela. Don't you think your mother went to God sorry for what she'd done?"

Angela's cheeks reddened. The fury Esmeralda had sensed under the ice of her false placidity exploded. She came at Esmeralda, small hands curved into claws, surprisingly strong. Esmeralda fought to keep the girl's fingernails away from her face while her father leaped up and came to subdue her. As the child struggled, Esmeralda opened a chest of stoppered bottles, removed a vial of rosemary oil. She smeared the oil on Angela's forehead in the shape of a cross; Angela let out a piercing scream and pitched forward, dragging at her father's arms, fingers clawing now at her own face instead of Esmeralda's. Between the two of them they held the child until her struggles subsided. Esmeralda left her in her father's care and mixed up some strong hot tea, dosed with soothing herbs, and had Angela drink it. There was no further resistance, but tears ran down the girl's cheeks, steady and heart-true, and her father rocked her like a baby as she fell asleep.

"She hasn't cried before," her father said as he set the cup on the table. The girl looked utterly peaceful as she slept, but that was deceiving. It would have been good to tell the man his child was healed, but it wasn't the truth.

"It will help," Esmeralda said. "But the wound goes deep, Victor, very deep. You must talk to her, every day. Let her tell you how it happened. Let her release the anger if she can; if not, it will shatter her, too."

"Will you—" Victor took a deep breath and looked away. "I have no money, *señora*. I can bring you bread. I make bread at the factory in El Paso; they let me have the old loaves."

"I didn't ask for payment," she said as she closed up her box of herbs. "Bring her again, when you can. But not soon. Let her heal a little."

The girl was still asleep when he carried her out into the gathering darkness, the brightly colored coat a spot of cheer in the dull twilight. Esmeralda watched them go until the coat disappeared from sight, then sat down at the big oak table and put her head down on its cool surface.

"Did I do right, Jaime?" she asked. "It's so hard to know."

But Jaime was silent tonight, and when the chill grew too much for her, she blew out the candles and went to bed.

Chapter 9

November 3, 1996
Dr. Ana Gutierrez

Ana woke up well before dawn, restless and heavy with exhaustion, and her first thought was of Pete's anguished face as he handed her the wounded little girl. Her second, oddly, was of the box sitting so innocently in the storeroom down the hall.

Pandora, she reminded herself. What a wonderful world it might have been if Pandora had been able to keep her curiosity in check. Then again, that was an Anglo fable, and it had nothing at all to do with her. In *Indio* culture curiosity was a trait of the Trickster, friend of mankind and sometimes his enemy, too.

She debated theology and legend for about an hour before she got up, threw on a housecoat, and went down the hall. The storeroom was cold, and the light from the naked bulbs harsh to her tired eyes. She pulled the box out of its hiding place and slowly folded back the cardboard flaps.

Why two boxes? Because he'd known she'd look? She examined the tape and took down a roll of brown mailing tape from a hook nearby. It matched almost exactly.

They'd never know she looked, would they?

She told herself they wouldn't, and used a box knife to slice open the tape.

Inside the box was a small, colorful bag. No, a child's knapsack, decorated with happy dinosaurs in bright Day-Glo colors. She started to reach in, but stopped as she heard something behind her.

No one there. She put a hand over her heart to calm its frenzied beating and unlatched one of the plastic catches, just enough to peek inside.

Toys. Plastic dinosaurs, badly molded, poorly painted. Cheap plastic dinosaurs. Why smuggle them? They were like pesos lying on the sidewalk— too cheap to bother with. Frowning, she clicked the latch shut again and resealed the box, folded the flaps again, in the order she remembered they'd been.

She went back to the kitchen to make coffee and fix breakfast for a yawning Gabriel, who looked worse than she felt. And then she started the day.

The knapsack festered at the back of her mind while she went through the motions of another workday. It was a busier day than she'd anticipated, because most of the patients, even after two days, still wanted to gossip about the shoot-out at the Black Bridge, and what it meant. Omens flew like blackbirds in the fall. The government was going to sweep through the *barrio*, wholesale arrests, deportation to barbed-wire camps. The government was going to issue another blanket amnesty. The government was going to reward the cops who'd shot the little girl. No, they were going to fire them.

Ana tried to do her work without answering any questions at all. They all knew, of course; she saw it in their shiny, inquisitive eyes. They'd been told about her ex-husband. *Why did you marry the Anglo?* That had been Rámon's question, but it was a question they would all have asked, given the chance.

She had remembered why as she watched him with that child, his rage and horror naked on his face, his hands covered with blood. Pete had always loved children that way, with unstinting passion. He would have thrown himself off the bridge to save that girl—thrown himself in front of the bullet if there'd been time. And that was the root of their fracture. No matter that she was the saver of lives, the one dedicated to healing—she was not the passionate one. The motherly one.

But she admired that in him, unconditional love. And she knew she did not deserve it.

"Doctor." The nurse today was Yvonne, a plump earth mother of a woman with a round, plain face. She peered around the edge of the curtain into the treatment area where Ana was methodically, mindlessly sewing stitches on a five-inch-long gash in a teenage boy's arm. "There's a man in the waiting room to see you. He says to tell you he's come to pick up something."

The package. Ana completed the stitch, breathing deeply and evenly though her whole chest ached and felt like bursting. A hiss of blood in her ears startled her. *My blood pressure's up.* She'd have to remember to check it later.

"Tell him I'll be right there," she said. Yvonne, an indistinct white and brown form in the corner of her eye, bobbed away. She finished the stitches more quickly, less meticulously, and tied it off before looking up at the boy, who was trying hard to look stoic.

"You're done," she said. "My nurse will give you a tetanus shot, and you're free to go."

"Don't need one," he said, and started to slide off the table.

"Do," she corrected, and pushed him back up. "Stay. Give me any trouble, and I'll tell your *amigos* out there you're scared of needles."

His face darkened, but he stayed. Ana stripped off her latex gloves and handed Yvonne the chart as she passed her. In the waiting room, nearly empty at the end of the day, stood a man in a battered straw hat, his face creased by wind and sun.

Miguel. She'd been afraid it would be him.

"Hello," she said, and tried to smile. She offered her hand. When he shook it, she felt thick scars and calluses ridging his palm. "Why don't you come with me? I think I know what you're looking for. Somebody dropped it off."

He followed her out of the waiting room and past the treatment areas, to the door marked NO PASEN. She let him in and closed it behind herself, turned to lock it, and was unprepared for the harsh crush of his hand on her arm.

"Don't talk too much," Miguel said. "It's a bad habit, Doctor. Upstairs?"

"Yes," she said faintly. He moved quickly ahead of her, light and quick, taking the stairs two at a time. "That way."

She pushed past him at the top of the steps and led him to the storerooms. She retrieved a box from the back and started to open it.

"Stop," he said. It wasn't a loud command, but it froze her in place. "Give it to me."

She handed it over. He opened the flaps and looked inside. She couldn't tell anything from the expression on his face, couldn't tell if there had been some way she'd betrayed her interference. If there was, she knew Miguel's answer to that. Even though Gato wasn't around, it would be a bullet in the skull. There was only one penalty for treason.

"*Excellente,*" he said. "Thank you. I know the way out."

He showed her that he did, a disturbing familiarity that made her shiver in the chilly hall as the elevator creaked down to street level.

What have I done? There was no answer to that, but the question was a biting, angry fly. *What have I done?*

She could only pray that whatever she'd done, it was the right thing.

Gabriel, of course, had the security-camera footage from Thursday evening. She found him rerunning the video on a separate monitor when she came back upstairs, workday done. She recognized her own distressed, professional face and the child's blood-stained figure.

And Pete, of course. Gabriel stopped the tape, freezing Pete in a cage of horizontal lines, his face blood-spattered and wretched.

"Thought he was gone for good," Gabriel said.

Nothing in his tone at all—it was just an item of mild interest.

"He is," she said. She couldn't help it; the sight of Pete made her feel sick and helpless. "What do you want to eat?"

"Frog guts." It was a joke from their childhood days, when Gabe couldn't understand why sheep guts were all right to make *menudo* out of but frog guts, it seemed, weren't good for anything except the frog. "Took a lot of nerve for him to bring her here. How is she?"

"Alive." The last thing Ana wanted to talk about was Pete and the girl. "Look, if you don't want to eat, I'll just make a sandwich and go to bed."

"Sandwich sounds good." Gabe wheeled his chair around and came toward her. The wheels made a breathy hiss on the wood floor as he passed her, heading for the kitchen.

He left Pete frozen there in time. She had an irrational urge to play the tape, release him, let him go into the dark. But she turned and followed Gabe to the kitchen, where she made them bacon and tomato sandwiches that they ate with tortilla chips and Mama's homemade guacamole, and cold bottles of Tecaté beer. In due course, Gabe got around to what he was really thinking.

"Funny," he ventured, "how it took both you and Rafael to restock the supply room the other night."

She almost spilled her beer. She'd virtually forgotten Rafael, though Gabe's words brought it all back with a not unpleasant rush—the smooth, hot feel of his lips, the pressure of his body against hers. She looked away from Gabe to something else—the bull and matador salt and pepper shakers Mama had given him—and knew her cheeks were turning red.

"There was a discrepancy on the count of syringes," she lied. "We had to do it three times."

"Three?" Gabe's eyebrows rose dangerously high, as if they might float off his face. She felt her cheeks burn hotter.

"You know what I meant!"

"Yeah, I know *all* about it. 'Bout time you got something on the side, you ask me. I was thinking Teresa was converting you or something. Or—" He deliberately did not look at her as he said it. "Or you were still maybe thinking about Pete."

"Pete?" She forced scorn into the name, disdain into the tilt of her chin. "Since when did you become such close personal friends?"

"Since he ran off with my sister and made her happy," Gabe said. His eyes came back to meet hers. "For a while, anyhow. Best anybody's ever done I know of."

"Shut the hell up, Gabe. You don't know anything about it."

He tipped his bottle back, drained the Tecaté, and shrugged. "Whatever you say, *chica*. Listen, good food, gotta run. I got a date tonight."

"A—a date?" She didn't mean to sound so surprised. "Sorry. With who?"

He gave her the darker version of his charming smile. "Don't worry, you won't need to recognize her again. I pay her by the hour."

"Gabe!"

"I'm joking, I'm joking. Her name is Carma and she's a physical therapist at William Beaumont, you know, the army hospital. And she's picking me up in fifteen minutes, so I got to go."

"Where—" Ana bit her lip. She would *not* sound like Mama. "Have a good time."

"Count on it." He waved as he wheeled back toward his bedroom, navigating expertly around the furniture with casual swipes of his hands. "Oh, and it's the movies. You know, moving pictures, they project them on a wall. Maybe you've heard of it. I hear they even got sound and color now."

"*Cabron*," she said under her breath, and drained her beer.

After he left, carried off in a van that had, she was relieved to see, a handicapped parking sticker, Ana decided it was time to take a long, hot, luxurious bath. She'd been thinking about it for weeks, and with Gabe gone and the clinic closed—what better time? She did a thing she had not done in years; she turned off the lights and lit scented candles, arranged them around the tile bathroom to give it a warm, peaceful glow. Hot, steaming water, scented with rose bath salts. She eased into it with a sigh of utter relief and closed her eyes. The whisper of water lapping at her skin lulled her into a calm so profound it was like sleep, but her mind continued to wander.

Why had Rámon asked her to keep the package if it was nothing but a child's backpack? Rámon had always been in trouble, all his life. Drugs, fights, shootings, stabbings, protests—he was a bad man, she knew that. And yet there had always been a white-hot core of truth in him that she envied. Rámon was a man who knew what he loved, and he let nothing stand in the way of that.

And what did *she* love? Gabe, Mama, severe, wise Sister Teresa—maybe Pete, once—maybe Rafael, someday. Herself, never.

Quite unexpectedly, she remembered Pete's face the day she'd told him she was performing abortions. The horror and the grief in his eyes. The rage, quickly gone because Pete was not a violent man, whatever his faults. She had been ashamed to see herself the way he saw her.

I don't have to be ashamed. I believed in the cause, and I still believe in it. What Pete believes means nothing to me.

She heard something.

She snapped back to the present with a gasp and a flinch, and water sloshed loudly in the quiet. Or was it quiet? Had Gabe set the security? Of course he had, he always did. But she'd heard—

Maybe it was Gabe coming home early. Maybe the movie had been bad, or the girl obnoxious, or—

She heard, very clearly, the creak of a floorboard. No sound of wheels.

Not Gabe.

She didn't dare move, not even to find a weapon. It was too quiet. The noise of the water would draw an intruder to her immediately. Maybe she could— what? Scream? Who would hear? *You liked the solitude.* Ana eased slowly, carefully up to her knees in the tub, water gliding down her skin like beads of oil, and removed the cover from the toilet tank. It was startlingly heavy and awkward, and her hands were slippery. She almost dropped it, moved too quickly to catch it. Water sloshed.

A shadow moved outside the bathroom door.

And then the shadow stopped moving and stood right in front of the door. Ana heard her breath rasping in the silence, tightened her numbed fingers on the ceramic lid, and almost screamed when she heard the polite, measured knocks at the door.

Tap. Tap. Tap.

Then silence. She got her feet underneath her and stood up, not caring anymore about the noise, caring only to be out of the tub and on firm footing. She grabbed a towel from the rack and wrapped it around her body, gasping with lungs that felt singed from the effort.

Incredibly, she heard herself asking, "Who is it?"

A man laughed, a gentle, quiet laugh.

"You got guts, Ana, I'll say that for you. It's Miguel. Get dressed. Rámon wants you to take a ride with us." She recognized the voice, and her knees went weak with—what? Not relief. What was it Pete used to say, *Better the devil you know than the devil you don't?* Miguel was the devil she knew. Or was that Rámon? *You talk too much, Doctor,* Miguel had said. *Bad habit.*

She put the toilet-tank lid back in place with a grate of ceramic and shrugged on her fleece robe, belted it tight. She turned the lights on and blinked in the glare, then snuffed out each candle and drained the tub before she opened the door.

Miguel lounged against the elevator down the hall, arms folded. He was alone. He looked at her and smiled.

She shoved past him into the living room, then to her bedroom, where she locked the door and yanked on clothes as fast as she could. She considered calling the police, Pete, someone—but what good would that do? She didn't know what she would tell them that could help.

She'd have to hope things didn't turn bad.

On the way out of the living room, she looked into Gabe's room to check the security alarms.

All the lights still glowed red. The alarms were all on.

So how had Miguel gotten in?

He never left. He'd been in the storeroom all day, waiting. Or in her bedroom. Somewhere. Watching her?

She felt sick, but she didn't let any of that show on her face as she got into the elevator with him and he pulled the cage closed with a bang.

"Let's go," she said, and punched in the code to allow them to exit.

"He's running a fever," Miguel told her in the car—a sedan, something completely forgettable, painted a sun-dulled white like half the cars in El Paso. "High. I don't know how bad it is, but he needs you, Ana."

An American car, maybe a Chrysler. She'd tried to get a look at the license plate, but the streetlights had been too dim. If they were stopped, would Miguel have a driver's license? Insurance? A gun to shoot the officer with?

She forced herself to focus on medical matters. "How high?"

"Hundred and four."

"Sweating? Or is his skin dry?"

"Dry. And his leg looks swollen."

She nodded and checked her seat belt, an automatic reaction from someone who'd worked far too many auto accidents. As she looked up, a police car rocketed toward them, then past, sirens and lights wailing. Miguel didn't even flinch, though she experienced a moment of blank panic. *No killing. Please, God, no killing. I just want to heal the sick!*

"Why didn't you see Rámon when he was in the hospital that night?" Miguel asked, too casually.

"It wasn't safe."

He smiled and lit a cigarette with a snap of a lighter. "For who?"

"For you," she shot back. "Did it occur to you that *la migra* was in the building? *Policia?* Who knows who else? I was trying to keep away from you because I thought that would keep him safer."

"So you were doing it for him. That's good." Miguel stopped at a light; she realized they were stopped next to the old Sears store at Five Points; it was now police headquarters. Traffic crept by from the crazy-quilt intersection, up toward the mountain or down into the valley. She swallowed and turned her eyes back front. Miguel didn't seem at all worried. "I thought maybe you were doing it because you saw your husband there."

She almost snapped *ex-husband,* a reaction without thought, but then she realized that he'd seen them together, and that was bad. Especially since Rámon probably knew Pete had been at the clinic, too. He didn't trust her. How could he?

"I saw him there," she admitted. "I didn't want him to know Rámon was anywhere nearby. So I left. Rámon got the note, then."

"From *La Bonita?* Yes, he got the note." Miguel grinned again; he was full of amusement tonight. It took her a moment to remember that Maria's high school nickname had been *La Bonita;* she'd had it sewn on her letter jacket. "Quite a woman, your friend. She could make a dead man rise."

He lifted an index finger slowly off the wheel, leaving no doubt what he meant. Ana looked away.

The light turned green, and Miguel turned the car left. On the dark outline of the Franklin Mountains a huge white outline of a star glittered. They traditionally lit it for the holidays; it had a stark beauty, like the mountains and the desert and the clear night sky. She was still looking at it when Miguel parked the car and turned off the engine and said, "Inside."

She didn't recognize the building, and there was no sign outside. Miguel led her around the back and up a flight of creaking iron stairs. He tapped the door three times before unlocking it, held it for her to precede him.

Five or six men sat around a table, playing cards under the light of a single buzzing fluorescent, but there must have been twenty in the room, most of them lying on the floor wrapped in blankets. They were quiet sleepers; she heard only one or two snores as Miguel led her through the room and the mine field of sleeping men to another staircase, this one built of narrow wood planks like an attic ladder. Farther down the hall, two men in blue jeans sat in folding chairs, guarding a closed door. One of them stared at her indifferently, flexing a tattooed hand; the other one offered her a quiet smile. She made her way up the stairs, feeling her way in the dim light, and came out in a tall, angled room that still smelled of fresh-cut wood.

"*Señora*," a man said, and offered her a hand up; she accepted with relief. She felt disoriented and oddly weightless in the dark.

"*La doctora.* So, you found her for me." Rámon's voice was weak but full of good humor. A light was switched on, and she saw him lying on a cot, blue and magenta blankets tucked neatly around him. His color was better than the last time she'd seen him, but not the healthy tan she remembered from his youth. "Ana. It's good of you to come."

She didn't debate whether or not she'd had a choice; it seemed petty. He gave her a sweet smile and nodded for his guard to pull a chair beside the bed. Miguel came up the ladder and stood in the shadows, hands behind his back, as she sat down and took Rámon's hand.

"I hear you're not well." His hand burned with fever. She put her palm on his forehead—dry, as Miguel had said. And very hot. "Not so bad. A little fever maybe."

"I'm not one of your *barrio* children, Ana. I know I have an infection. The question is, how bad?"

"You remember when you were seventeen and you had the fight with that boy from Ysleta, what was his name—" She folded back the blankets; he had on only a pair of boxer underwear. His thigh, even bandaged, looked swollen. She donned gloves and cut the bandages, then began unwrapping them.

"Juan Leál," Rámon put in. He hissed in a breath as she pulled the sterile dressing free. The wound was clearly inflamed, leaking pus. "Well? Will you saw it off with a dull knife?"

"I'll sharpen the knife," she promised, but her heart wasn't in the humor. She found Betadine and washed the wound a dull yellow-brown, gave him an antibiotic shot and asked him the usual question about tetanus boosters. When he shrugged his shoulders, she gave him that shot, too. "What happened with Juan, then? I never heard."

She rewrapped the wound. As she fastened the gauze in place, he said, "How much truth do you want, my *doctora?*"

"What do you mean?"

"Juan Leál. How much truth?"

She suddenly knew from the coolness in his eyes what he would tell her. Juan Leál was dead, vanished, his life erased. No wonder she hadn't heard the outcome of the fight.

"Maybe not so much truth as all that," she said quietly, and felt like a coward. Worse, like a guilty conspirator in a killing. "Miguel, I'm going to give you two different kinds of pills, one to bring his fever down, one to make him sleep. And a prescription, I'll make it out to you."

Miguel exchanged a look with Rámon; Rámon reached over and took her hand again as she checked his pulse. His eyes were fever bright, but there was something else to them, something she almost recognized.

"Ana—" Rámon simply stared at her for a few seconds, then moved his gaze back to Miguel. "Leave us."

"*Jefe*—"

"Vamanos," he said. "You, too, Carlos."

Both men left, boots clunking on the stairs. There was no door to shut, but she understood his desire for privacy. In wrapping his thigh, she couldn't help but notice the effect her presence had on him in more private regions.

"Ana," he said again, his voice softer now. "I need you to stay. You understand?"

"You're sick. Of course I'll stay for a while—"

"Not for a while."

"Rámon, I can't. The clinic—"

"No." His fingers tightened on hers. He guided her hand to his mouth and kissed her fingers gently, one after another. "I need you, Ana. Not just for the fever. I know you won't believe this, but I've been thinking about you for a very long time. All these years."

She had always been attracted to his danger and promise on some deep level, and that brought heat to her cheeks as she said, "I'm your doctor, Rámon. And I have other patients. I need to go back to the clinic."

As if she had a choice. Rámon had brought her easily enough, and he controlled the way out. But she sensed that if she really wanted to go, he wouldn't stop her.

She hoped she wasn't deluding herself.

"Let me tell you a story," he said, and closed his eyes. "There was this girl in high school—a wild girl maybe, a *cholla*, didn't take shit from nobody. Smart, good grades, but attitude so thick it was like a second skin. You know this girl?"

"I know her." It could have been Ana or any of

her friends. She fought to keep her voice level and professional.

"She broke my heart, this girl." His eyes opened suddenly, burning into hers. "I never could tell her what I felt for her, what she meant to me. She was the one clean thing in the world, and I couldn't speak to her because I wasn't worth her time. She was smart, and she was going to be something good. A lawyer. A doctor. Someone to pull her people up from the *barrio* and into the light."

She couldn't say anything. She swallowed hard.

"There was this boy, Juan Léal, he spoke disrespectfully of this girl. He bragged of fucking her, and I knew he was lying. We fought, he pulled a knife, and I had to defend myself. He almost killed me, Ana. In the end it was him who died, but it was very close. Do you understand?"

She felt frozen. Unable to feel. Rámon's hand lifted and traced her cheek gently.

"I pray to God every day that he forgives me for that." Rámon smiled slightly, a wounded, fragile smile. "I pray that you do. I never meant it to happen, Ana. I hope he lied, but it doesn't matter. It wasn't worth his death. I understand that now."

She searched for words, was unable to put them in order.

"I kept track of—this girl—after that, when she went to college, then to medical school. A long road. Hard. I knew she would be true to her people—and then she broke my heart again." His hand caressed her lips. "She married an Anglo. All these years I have waited for her to find her way again. And here you are, Ana. Here you are."

She felt almost feverish with the conflict. "What do you want?"

"A kiss. One kiss, *querida*, for the boy who almost died for your honor. Please."

She leaned down until their lips met and melted. His were hot with more than fever. She hadn't been kissed like this, with so much promise, for so long—not even that hurried groping in the supply room with Rafael. This woke something so strong in her that it brought tears to her eyes. He tasted smoky and sweet, and she wanted to taste him forever.

"Sweet Ana," he breathed as their lips parted. "You see? Stay. Stay with me."

"You're ill," she said, a weak protest, almost inaudible. "Wounded."

"An inconvenience," he said, and kissed her again. "A dying man's request."

Somehow his hands were inside her blouse, sliding over her skin, leaving trails of unbelievable heat behind. The kiss was open-mouthed this time, and she met it with a sensation of falling, falling toward something, away from something else.

Later as she bit back her moans, she heard him say in Spanish, "Let go, Ana. Let go."

And she did.

Chapter 10

November 22, 1996
Peter Ross

Two weeks later, they were still trying to figure out who was to blame.

He tossed his Border Patrol identification on the table and laid his gun on top of it. There was silence in the room, even from the six men who had, for the last hour, been debating what to do to clean up the mess.

"I'm tired," Pete said quietly. "You want a scapegoat, feel free to tie the horns on. I'm sick of the bullshit anyway."

Senior Investigating Agent McDonough looked at the badge and gun, then back up at him, with no perceptible change in his expression. McDonough was a tough old Irish bastard, the kind who would have been cracking heads on a beat in Chicago in the old days; he wasn't liked, but he was feared. The one who commanded respect in the room sat to McDonough's right. His name was Tito Nueves, and he had three different degrees hanging on his office wall, social science, criminology, and law. He was the kind of man who could buy a suit off the rack and make it look tailored, and he was also the kind of man you trust with your life.

So Pete had always thought. But Nueves hadn't opened his mouth so far. Now he sat looking cool and relaxed, his eyes half-closed in thought, his fingers laced together on the table in front of him.

There were two other administrators in the office. Pete hadn't caught their names and didn't much care. The other two were DEA agents Joseph Ryan and the man who'd run the NightSight monitor that night at the bridge, Hartman. Hartman looked extremely uncomfortable. Ryan looked bored.

"Don't be hasty," McDonough said, and shoved the badge and gun back to him. "You heard what I told you—ballistics tests couldn't confirm whose bullet ended up in the girl. No need to overreact, Ross. Let's just sort this out."

The ballistics crap was a damned lie, and he knew it. He knew that one of the DEA agents had shot the girl, or Hartman would have looked him in the eye.

"Any word at all from Sanchez or Grivaldo?"

"Nothing." It was the first words Nueves had spoken, but he made them count. "I don't want to count them out, but the other side must have smelled something wrong. Otherwise, why change the plan? The two men you described in the Cadillac sound like the brothers who were supposed to drive the car carrier over Copia Bridge on Friday. That never showed, either."

"Why aren't we working on that instead of sitting here talking about this crap?" Ryan asked rhetorically. He stared at a gold-nugget ring as he twisted it around one thick finger. "Because the Border Patrol wants to dump the crap on us, that's why. It was you guys' show, your operation. Things went wrong, you guys get to handle that, too."

"Now, *wait* a minute," McDonough thundered.

"He's right," Pete said, and once again got ripples of silence. "This was our operation. We asked them in on it. It was my call. I could have asked for a bigger setup from Border Patrol on this, but in my judgment"—the word hurt to say—"the DEA had plenty of men and equipment on-site to handle the situation. So it's my blame. I'll take it."

Nueves opened his eyes. "I don't think so. I'm not about to let you do that. Not only did you not have control of the situation—"

"And that's my problem! If I'd been in charge of it instead of letting Ryan cowboy his ass out there—"

"Then you would have been pulled off the case!" Nueves interrupted before Ryan had a chance to respond. "Whatever DEA says about it now, it was their show and everybody knew it. Okay, here's my proposal. Stay low, keep quiet, everybody goes home and takes a week's leave until things cool off. There'll be an interdepartmental investigation later, but this is just an interim measure to keep the press from blowing this further out of proportion. Also, to keep the Sons of Aztlan from another march."

The Sons of Aztlan were a growing political and social faction up and down the California and Texas borders, the new, harsher cousins of La Raza. And they were gaining in popularity all the time. No violence from them, but plenty of rhetoric and political demonstrating. It was just the sort of thing Ana would be involved in. Pete wondered if she was a member. No, she was too much of a feminist to join anything that labeled her a *son*.

"That's the plan? Go home? Don't talk to the press?" Ryan snorted and heaved himself to his feet. "Shit, you could have phoned that one in, didn't have to pull my ass down here."

"Ryan." McDonough's voice was soft, and that was trouble. "Not only did you drag our name through the mud again, you also didn't even put your hands on any of the principals in the deal. All we've got is a nameless kid in a hospital. That does not make me happy with you, so you better not think you can pull crap in here with me. It'll be a cold day in hell before you see support from us again, and I mean that. Not just cold. *Frozen.* The devil on ice skates. You get my drift?"

"I think so." Ryan jerked his head at Hartman. "Gentlemen, it's been informative. Hope y'all have a real nice day."

The door clicked shut behind them. Nueves let out a sigh. Pete rubbed his temples, but his fingers were no substitute for Esmeralda's. He felt the gravity-sucking pull of nausea in his stomach, and when he opened his eyes, Nueves' face was framed in slow-moving black sparkles.

Oh, Jesus. He knew this headache.

"You okay?" Nueves asked. Pete nodded, too numbed to really be afraid. "Pete, take your badge and gun and go home. Relax. We're okay here, and I'll let you know first thing if we get any word from Sanchez or Grivaldo. Consider yourself on leave until after Thanksgiving, okay? Paid leave."

Pete slowly picked up his badge and replaced it in his inside jacket pocket. The gun made an annoying, comforting weight in its holster.

"Thanks."

He left the building without incident, drove out of the secured lot, and almost made it home before he had to pull over and throw up at the side of the road, to the shocked fascination of a couple of elderly ladies at a bus stop. One of them offered him a tissue and told him not to drink so much, dear. He made it the last seven blocks, feeling as much under the car as in it, and escaped into the blessed darkness of his apartment, the sweet silence.

The migraine had a rhythm in time with his pulse; with each beat of his heart he felt a vise squeeze tighter on the right side of his head, a blinding pressure that robbed him of anything but the need to make it stop. He found the pills he still carried in the pocket of his jacket and popped two Midrin, washed them down with a cup of water, and staggered to his bed to wait it out. Thirty minutes later, more Midrin. The third dose left him floating and disconnected, an observer of suffering rather than a participant, and he was finally able to curl up into a protective ball, still fully dressed, and collapse into a drug-heavy sleep for the next six hours.

He woke to the shrill ring of the phone, a sound that sliced right through his head and made him whine in pain. The Midrin worked only when you were calm and quiet; any exertion woke the monster again. He had to cross the room to get to the phone.

" 'Lo," he said. His voice sounded slow and dull in his ears.

"Pete?" He knew the voice, a man's voice. A torrent of Spanish followed. Oh, God, he couldn't think in Spanish right now.

"Slow down," he whispered. *I'd kill for an ice pick right now, put it right in there, right where the pain is. Or a drill. Right into the skull.* "Damn it, slow down!"

"*Amigo*, I can't stay on the line, man. We're screwed. We need help, man."

It was Sanchez; his drifting brain finally made the connection. He tried to fight off the mustiness of the drugs. "Where are you?"

"This ain't what we thought it was, man, it ain't drugs. That was what they told us, but they were bringing across something else—"

"Sanchez?"

Silence on the other end of the phone, but he could hear breathing.

"Tap the phone if you can't talk," Pete said. "In his ear he heard two gentle taps. "Okay. You hang on, man, hang on. Talk when you can, I'm waiting."

He had no idea what it was like on the other end of that phone, alone and terrified, with death breathing down the line. He couldn't think of anything to do. The migraine woke up from its drugged coma with a fresh pounding at his skull, and his stomach twisted with disorientation. *Not now. Oh, God, please. I have to focus now.*

"Okay," Sanchez whispered. "It's clear. Listen, we need to bail. Pick us up, man. Now."

"Where?"

"You know where Lopez Ironworks is? Close to Five Points?"

"Fifteen minutes. You be careful."

"You know it."

Sanchez hung up. Pete stood in the dark, fighting back despair. He wasn't supposed to drive under the influence of Midrin, or the migraine, for that matter. The sun was going to eat his eyes and melt his brain.

Didn't matter. All that mattered was getting his men out alive.

He dialed the number for Border Patrol headquarters, then asked for Tito Nueves.

The drive was fifteen minutes of hell, generously spooned; the sun was bright enough to inject pain straight into the back of his neck, where it rose up to bury fangs just above his right eye. That side of his head throbbed with a continuous, sick, nauseating rhythm. The Midrin made him taste ashes and sweat, and he drove with perfect, thin-lipped concentration, reactions lagging a second or two behind events, the way his vision lagged behind the merciless dagger of light.

He didn't kill anybody. Didn't even run over anybody. By the time he pulled the nondescript brown sedan to the curb a block from Lopez Ironworks, he no longer cared about that. All he cared about was turning the car around and slamming it head-on into a concrete abutment, which might shock the pain into silence for a while.

He was watching for Sanchez and Grivaldo, but wasn't surprised that he didn't notice their approach. They were ghosts, those two, when they wanted to be. Sanchez took the passenger side of the car, Grivaldo the back, and Sanchez nodded at him to get moving. There was a sweaty shine to Sanchez's face that didn't bode well.

In the rearview mirror Pete noticed that Grivaldo was staring back toward where they might have acquired a tail.

"How bad?" he asked. It was a huge effort to speak, and more to care about the answer. The words tasted faintly like blood.

Sanchez turned to face him, and a frown dug itself in on his face. "You look like shit, boss. What's up?"

Nothing much. My brain is exploding. I have cancer. How's that for a laugh?

"Headache," he said. "Bad. Listen, man, can you drive?"

"Huh, can I drive. You kidding, right? Yeah, man, I can drive. Pull over."

He did it with relief, changed places with Sanchez, and fumbled on a pair of dark sunglasses that had somehow found their way into his glove compartment. They helped a little.

"You're screwed up, man," Sanchez said in a different voice. "You good to go with us, or you want to go home?"

"I'm good to go," he said, swallowed a mouthful of acid and pulled himself upright. "Tell me what's happening?"

"I think we better wait until we can talk to Nueves, man."

"It's that big?"

"It's pretty big, we think, but we don't know. That's why we wanted to come in."

It was too hard to watch someone else drive; the world moved in unexpected lurches and slides. Better to close his eyes and pretend there was an ice pack on the back of his neck. The migraine made him uncommonly sensitive to smells, and he realized one of the other two men had eaten onions for lunch.

"Why call me, then? Why not call Nueves, have him pick you up?"

"Yeah, well, there's a reason, boss, and it isn't so good, you know? Hey, you still with me?"

"Yeah," he said. He'd been drifting a little, but he was holding on with both hands. "Go on."

"You sure?" It wasn't like Sanchez to be this solicitous. He really had to look like death. " 'Cause you know, it can wait—"

"Spit it out, man."

"It's your ex," Sanchez said, almost apologetically. "I mean, I'm not absolutely sure—"

From the backseat Grivaldo said, clearly, "Shut up, Sanchez."

Pete opened his eyes to catch the look that passed between the two men; their eyes locked through the rearview mirror.

Sanchez sighed. "Yeah," he agreed. "Better do that. Sorry, man. You know."

He didn't. But he didn't have the energy to follow the possibilities, all unpleasant, that spun out in front of him like spiderwebs.

Time drifted off for him until the car jerked to a stop and he heard the rattle of the security fence retracting. They were at Border Patrol headquarters.

Tito Nueves met them in the hallway on the way to Pete's office and blocked the way. He wasn't looking at Sanchez or Grivaldo, except for a brief welcoming glance. He was looking at Pete.

"You're supposed to be home," he said, and hesitated. "Besides, you look like—"

"Yeah," Pete said, slow and tired. "I know. But this is important."

"Not important enough to get you back in these doors right now. Listen, I want you to listen to orders for once, go home and rest. I'll call you with an update. Good work bringing the guys in, but I'll take it from here, okay?" Tito's face was stone. The question wasn't a question.

"Yeah." Easy enough to give in, to agree to anything. *Want a bullet in your head, Pete? Yes, sure. Forty-five caliber, please, that ought to fix everything.* "I'll wait for your call."

He started to turn away, but Sanchez caught his arm.

"You remember what I said in the car," he said. "I meant it."

About Ana? He hadn't actually said anything. But this wasn't the time or place to talk about it; he knew that from the cautious look on Grivaldo's face and the grim look on Nueves'. He nodded and walked away.

As Pete Ross disappeared through the double doors leading to the parking lot, Hector Sanchez looked after him and said quietly, "So what happened with him?"

Nueves said, "He's on leave. A week."

"Yeah? For what?"

"For the screw-up at *El Puente Negro*, but you already figured that out. Why weren't you there?"

Sanchez looked at him calmly, raised an eyebrow at his partner, Grivaldo, who shrugged as if to say, *What the hell?*

"We weren't there because they told us not to go. What you think? We're going to play hero and blow the job because plans changed? We figured things would go down okay. Not our fault they didn't."

Tito Nueves was smooth, all his edges rubbed off, but he still had a killer's gleam in his eyes. Word was he came up from the *barrio;* looking at him now, Sanchez believed it.

"In my office," he said, and turned to lead the way.

Nueves' office was in a whole other universe from the Formica and institutional green of the rank and file—deep blue carpet, dark wood furniture, silky American flags with fringe. He nodded to two leather chairs positioned opposite his desk, and Sanchez sank into one, careful not to scratch anything. Grivaldo didn't seem impressed. He didn't seem impressed when someone shoved a shotgun in his face, either. That was just how he was.

"So tell me the story," Nueves said. He sat down behind his desk and steepled his fingers. Behind him sunlight chewed through partially closed blinds—old aluminum blinds, dusty, just like on the other side of the building. Some things never changed.

"Cruz's lieutenant Miguel got wind of something—maybe he checked for us while we were here setting up the bust, I don't know—but he figured something was up. He sent somebody else in our place and told us to hang around and guard his office. We took a look inside, and we see just what you'd expect to see, lots of heroin, lots of cash. Only there were some boxes there that didn't look right."

"Boxes of what?"

Sanchez exchanged a look with Grivaldo. Grivaldo grinned and said, "Dinosaurs, like from *Jurassic Park*."

"Toys?"

"*Si*. About so big. Grivaldo held his tattooed hands about four inches apart. "Ugly mothers, too. Cheap."

Nueves took this in silence, considering. After a couple of moments he said, "Did you open one up? Anything inside?"

"Solid," Sanchez said, and shook his head. "I don't know what they are. Just dinosaurs, I guess. But that isn't the weird thing."

"What is?"

"Agent Ross' ex-wife, Ana. You know, the doctor who works at the free clinic? Well, she's been sneaking around, coming in real late, staying until real early. I thought they were bringing her in to fix up his leg, but—"

"A prisoner?" Nueves demanded. Because that was the thing they were all afraid of, deep down, that their families would get caught in the cross fire. Sanchez didn't know whether to be relieved or nervous about his answer.

"Looked pretty free to me."

Nueves shook his head and rubbed his forehead. "So you're saying that Agent Ross' ex-wife might be involved with Cruz and his crew. Maybe covering for them, maybe even acting as a mule for the heroin?"

Grivaldo said, staring down at his tattooed hand, "I don't think we got to worry about the heroin so much. I think we got to worry about the other stuff."

"The dinosaurs?"

Grivaldo nodded.

"Why?"

Grivaldo shrugged. "Just a feeling, you know? I don't know. We didn't get a chance to take one. They caught us in the room, and we had to make shit up about hearing a noise. Then we got the hell out and called Pete."

"So they'll be gone by now."

"Oh, yeah, they'll be gone. Question is, where will they go?"

Nueves picked up the phone to call DEA and let them know how well and truly screwed the case was, and as he did, his eye fell on a bright pink backpack with shiny plastic straps. His daughter had been in the office yesterday, she'd probably left it.

He reached down for it one-handed as he waited for somebody to pick up on the other end.

The world

Ended.

Pete was just starting his car when the bomb went off.

It was a noise so huge that it wasn't a noise; it was pressure and white-hot pain. The world went utterly dark for a few seconds and he was weightless, floating, and thinking absurdly, *This is a really bad migraine*, when the sound finally caught up with the blast and he went deaf. His car was tossed end over end through the air to slam against a pale green Border Patrol bus, and as he opened his dazed eyes he saw a spray of bright orange glitter everywhere he looked, shimmering, and it was glass, broken glass, and the orange was fire coming from the shattered ruin of the Border Patrol headquarters building. The whole west half of the building had been severed and destroyed. Smoke hid the rest of it, but he saw girders twisted like putty, water spurting like blood from broken pipes, steam boiling where it touched superheated metal and stone.

It was all eerily silent, and he realized that the blast had stunned his ears. Maybe destroyed them, the way it had destroyed tons of concrete and steel and human flesh.

He stared at the orange stars until they slowly went black in his vision, and he fell away from the pain, into a quiet church with warm rainbows of color, and Esmeralda was praying at the altar, her face wet with tears.

Please, he heard her say, but his ears heard nothing, it was his heart. *Please live.*

Chapter 11

November 22, 1996
Esmeralda Sanchez

She was standing in the dusty parish church seven blocks from her house in Juárez, one hand holding a bag of herbs she was going to give Father Nani for his fever, when she heard Jamie say, very clearly, *Mama!*

She stopped talking to Father Nani, who was a good and kind man but had no sense at all of the spirit world, and turned to look toward the alter. Jamie was standing there, her son, as real as he had been that last morning when she'd bathed his face and combed his hair and put on his best shirt and short pants for the trip to America, the land of freedom.

He looked at her with huge, tragic dark eyes and said, *It's time to go.*

And she heard, in the distance, what sounded like a rumble of thunder. The bag of herbs she'd been holding thumped to the cool stone floor, crushed leaves and preserved flowers whispering out over her feet, and she turned back to Father Nani with tears in her eyes.

He frowned, puzzled. She couldn't speak, couldn't breathe for the sudden terrible knot in her chest. She ran, leaving the startled priest, ran into the street and to the border crossing, her papers in hand, every muscle burning. On the El Paso side a thick column of black smoke rose toward heaven.

"Reason for visiting?" the Mexican guard grunted. She stammered something she couldn't understand herself, but he let her go, called sharply after her to stop running when she was free of the turnstile. She came to a frustrated halt behind a line of other people, some of them Americans, all being held on the American side while the American guard spoke into a telephone. She saw the ruddy skin of his face turn the color of old paper.

He pulled a lever inside the booth. A red light began revolving, and he lifted a microphone to his lips.

"The U.S. border is now closed," he said. "Please go back to the Mexican side of the border until further notice."

"No!" Esmeralda screamed it, pushed through the crowd and battered the guard's booth with both fists. "No, you have to let me cross, you have to, he'll die—"

The guard opened the door, grabbed her wrists, and slammed her forward into the glass. She blinked back tears of pain at the impact, tried to stop him from jerking her arms behind her. Cold metal snapped around her wrists.

"Anybody else makes any trouble, you all get the same treatment," he yelled. The others who'd surged forward after her stopped, milled in confusion, and began trickling back to the other side of the bridge. "You, *señorita*, you shut the hell up. Shut up!"

She heard the shaken rage in his voice and stayed still. Tears tore at her heart, but she couldn't give them voice. *Peter. Oh, no, Dios no.*

"What happened?" she whispered. She didn't think he would answer her, but like all people stunned by tragedy, he had to speak of it.

"They blew it up," he said hoarsely. "Somebody blew up Border Patrol headquarters with everybody in it."

His eyes were red, his hands shaking. He was just a man, as she was just a woman, and she longed to reach out to him, but the stupid difference of skin prevented that. She closed her eyes and felt tears slide down her face.

A child's hand touched her cheek, reminding her of something. She turned her face toward the guard without opening her eyes, and listened to Jamie's whisper.

"Your brother Erik. He's alive. He was—in the back storeroom when the bomb went off. He's trapped, but he's alive."

"How—" It was the question they all asked. She felt Jamie's presence melt away from her like smoke.

"God," she answered. "Let me go, Carl, and I'll tell them where to look to find him. I'll tell them where to find them all."

"How did you—"

"There isn't time!" she almost screamed. "Please! Let me go!"

He fumbled the handcuffs off and pressed a button

to buzz the gate. She slammed it open, stiff-armed, and ran.

She didn't remember how she convinced a taxi driver to get her close to the scene of the disaster, but she had the vague impression she'd told him something about his wife's health; she had no money to pay him. She slid out of the cab as it stopped at the intersection of Montana and McCommas; there was no point in trying to drive farther. It was a grid-lock of cars and flashing lights and, in the distance, the flashing blades of helicopters.

She ran on foot, dodging police and firefighters when she could, gasping out explanations when she couldn't. The last line of police held her back in spite of everything she could do, and she collapsed in a heap on the hot road, shaking, praying, watching the black smoke of a funeral pyre rise into the air.

Bus loads of illegal immigrants were being taken out of the secured buildings behind the headquarters complex. That part had not been targeted.

Jamie's vision had come true. The fire had come, and it had swallowed up everything and everyone. Even Pete.

She went up to a firefighter who had the dazed, smoky look of a man who'd seen hell, and said, "I can take you to the wounded. Let me help."

Chapter 12

November 22, 1996
Peter Ross

He didn't remember climbing out of the ruin of his car, but he found himself standing dazedly next to the bus he'd crashed into. A dead man lay on the ground at his feet, a smoking carcass black on one side, fresh-pressed khaki on the other. There was no knowing who it had been in life.

It was so very *quiet*. He couldn't even hear himself breathe, though he knew he was breathing because he started coughing at the smell of cooked meat. His shirt was bloody. So was his head. He left the body and wandered toward the smoke, no particular reason, just a sudden dazed impulse to *know*.

There were people in the detention bus; he saw them pounding at the cracked glass of the windows. Their mouths were open, and he thought they were screaming. He went to the dead patrolman and found his keys, unlocked the door on the detention bus, and let the prisoners out, dazed and weeping, men and women and children, most cut and bloodied, some just disoriented.

One young woman continued to sit on the bus, staring straight ahead. She had blood spattered along the side of her face from a network of glass splinters, but was otherwise unharmed as far as he could tell. He tried talking to her, but couldn't even hear himself and knew she couldn't hear him, either. He took her unresisting, warm hand in his and made her stand, led her outside and let her go.

She stopped, like a rundown machine, where he left her. He doubled over, coughing, as some acidic fumes erupted from the wreckage of the building. Gravity dipped over on its side, and he found he was lying down, the universe of glowing orange stars spread out at eye level now.

The girl leaned over the body of the dead patrolman and unsnapped the holster at his hip. She pulled out his gun.

"No," Pete said. He felt his lips move as she turned to look at him, the gun in her hand, held casually and almost thoughtlessly. "Please don't."

She walked to him, her bare feet stepping on burning orange stars and leaving them dull and red behind. She handed him the gun, sat down beside him, and rocked back and forth, back and forth, as smoke closed them in an invisible cocoon and the stars died into ash gray around them.

She was afraid. She wanted to be safe.

It was like being a ghost, Pete thought. He saw people moving in the smoke, caught what sounded like whispers. Two firefighters in smudged yellow slickers loomed out of the smoke, grabbed the girl, and hustled her away; one of them came back presently for Pete.

He didn't remember being carried out of the parking lot. The next thing he remembered was sitting in the middle of a street—Montana? It seemed so *different*—surrounded by flashing lights and smoke and running figures, the firefly dance of television cameras and lights, an oxygen mask flooding him with air and making him light-headed.

Funny. His migraine was gone. He decided that meant he should help, so he stripped off the oxygen mask and wandered into the smoke, looking for someone to help, anyone, and ended up on his hands and knees in front of a pile of smoking, burning rubble that looked like the gateway to hell.

He had friends here.

With tears making white trails down his smoke-blackened face, with his hands trembling, he began to dig for them.

Pete uncovered six men, all dead, made faceless by the effects of explosion and collapse, before he found anyone alive—a patrolman, young, probably no more than twenty. His arm had been crushed, but he was alive. He got the young man's head and shoulders free, but his foot was trapped somewhere down in the rubble. Without any thought at all Pete crawled into the hole and worked by touch, easing the leg free, boosting him up out of the hole and into the smoky daylight.

Two firefighters appeared at the hole to lift another man out. One of them reached a gloved hand down to Pete, and he stared stupidly at it. He was too tired to think. He had a distant ringing in his ears now, and a growing sense of exhaustion in his arms and legs.

Beside the firemen a woman knelt at the edge of the hole and held out her hand, too. Smoke-smudged and tear-stained, Esmeralda looked down at him with love and anguish in her eyes.

He thought he had never touched anyone before the way he touched her hand in that moment.

Without any warning, the rock underneath him shifted and fell away. He clung to her hand, found the fireman's, and was dragged up out of hell into Esmeralda's arms. They folded together like one person, collapsed shaking on the shards of concrete and metal and glass, and rocked each other as the firefighters went on to others.

He looked at Esmeralda's face, both of them stripped of everything that had separated them, and saw her lips say something he recognized. In English.

I love you.

Chapter 13

November 22, 1996
Dr. Ana Gutierrez

She came awake almost instantly, aware of the presence of someone else in the room, of her nakedness and the blanket wrapped awkwardly around her body. Rámon was still asleep; she put a hand on his forehead, a doctor's reflex, checking for fever though he'd been doing better for almost a week now—a week she'd spent at the clinic, in light, in his arms in the shadows.

A hint of fever, but nothing dangerous, she judged.

"Ana." It was Miguel in the shadows. She couldn't tell if that was judgment or approval she heard in his dry voice. "How long before he wakes?"

"He took painkillers. Hours. Six, maybe seven."

Whatever the news, it wasn't good; she glimpsed the dark expression on his face as he stepped forward.

"Get dressed," he said. "We have to leave. Get him ready."

"What's—" She was cut off as he grabbed her arm and squeezed, hard.

"No questions, Doctor, not now, not ever. Do what I say. Go."

She waited until he'd disappeared back down the ladder before dropping the blanket and stepping into her underwear, then her blue jeans and shirt. Dressing Rámon was more time-consuming; he was almost completely relaxed, deep in sleep. His eyes opened and he asked muzzy questions, but slipped back into dreams as soon as she let him. She stripped the cot and folded the sheets and blankets. Miguel reappeared with two other men, who carried Rámon tenderly downstairs. Miguel folded the cot and handed it down, then the lantern.

The room was bare, as if they'd never been there. Ana realized, with a crushing sense of panic, that she was now somehow on the run. A fugitive.

But what was she guilty of?

In the van, packed in with twenty men, Rámon's overheated weight across her legs, she had time to wonder where they were going, and to ask Miguel. She got silence for an answer. Someone offered her an open bottle of fruit juice; she took a sip, for politeness, and almost spilled it as the van finally pulled to a stop.

"Nobody moves," Miguel said softly. There was utter silence as the driver's-side door opened and closed. Wherever they were, it was dark, and there were no windows in the cargo portion of the van. Ana swallowed back a deep sense of claustrophobia and thought, *This is what it's like to be illegal, to be packed in a small metal van, with fear on every side—*

Footsteps outside. The van door slid open with a

metallic hiss, letting in cool, fresh air, and she gasped it in relief. Men jumped out into the dark, and someone helped her ease Rámon's weight to a limp standing position. Supported on both sides, he looked drunk.

Two quick steps from the van to an elevator, all of them crammed together in it. It was late, and she was tired, and it took her a few seconds to realize where she was, because she didn't expect it.

She was at *La Clínica*.

She was home.

"What are you—" she began, but Miguel hissed her to silence as the elevator shuddered up two floors to the living quarters. She shut off the security alarm with shaking fingers before sliding up the steel gate. Men flowed past her into the hushed sanctity of her home, and some of them turned left toward the living room. "No! Miguel, stop—"

He put his hand over her mouth. Someone took Rámon's weight from her, and Miguel put an arm around her throat. She felt the promise of choking and subsided to frightened silence.

A man ghosted back out of the dark to say, "One man, *jefe*, asleep. *Incapacitado.*"

Miguel took his hand from her mouth a bare inch; she inhaled the sweaty smell of his skin, the warmth of it, and said, "My brother, Gabriel. He's no threat to you."

"*¿Incapacitado?*" he asked. "He's crippled?"

"*Sí.*" Anything that would make him seem less a threat. She could salve his ego later. "There's no one else."

He didn't, of course, take her word for it. Men

reported back to him like an army of scout ants, detailing food in the refrigerator, facilities, the storerooms that could be emptied to make room for them.

Miguel finally released her.

"You want to save your brother's life?" he asked before she could speak any of the hot, angry words that boiled at her lips. "Do what I say, Doctor. Do your work, go about your business. Pretend we aren't here and your life doesn't have to change. The men won't harm you, and no one will interfere with you. *Eh, bien,* this is better, yes? Because now you can get to your medicines and give Rámon what he needs."

She thought, *What have I done?* but she didn't know. She really didn't know.

Her help for the day was not Rafael, thank God; she didn't think she could have given enough of a performance to fool his sharp eyes. It was one of the other rotation nurses, this one a cheerful young girl, not very clever, who didn't know Ana well enough to see her distress. Ana tried to concentrate on the patients, and succeeded for a time, until she heard the nurse, Beatriz, cry out just after two o'clock in the afternoon and turn up the radio she kept playing in the reception area.

Ana heard just one word, *bombing,* and her heart turned cold. She left Beatriz and went upstairs, taking the steps at a run, arriving breathless, grabbing up the television remote and clicking the power switch. Miguel sat on the couch, watching her, a magazine open on his lap. As the television warmed up, she said in Spanish, "What did you do?" and then she saw.

She did not immediately recognize the wreckage, only the scale of the destruction. She sagged against the back of the couch, suddenly weak, and her eyes finally left the jerky helicopter-fed picture of the bomb site to focus on the white letters at the bottom of the screen.

BORDER PATROL HEADQUARTERS, EL PASO TEXAS

Pete.

She began to cry, helplessly, hopelessly, and was surprised as someone grabbed her by the hair and pulled her head up again. She screamed and tried to twist free, but he was stronger. She was humiliatingly helpless.

"Look, Ana," Rámon said in her ear. She blinked back tears, her eyes burning with rage and shame. "There is no going back for us now. Aztlan is rising. They are listening now. Believe me, they are listening, and it is we who have the voice."

"Murderer," she whispered. Tears shivered down her cheeks as he kissed her neck, a benediction of hell.

"We are all murderers now, *querida.* Do you want to be a murderer again?" He spun her around to look at the doorway, where Gabriel sat in his wheelchair, face gone pale, muscles knotted with fury. There was a gun to his head.

She didn't know the man who held the gun, but she was sure he would fire if Rámon gave the word. She had never felt so humiliated, so completely betrayed. What she had imagined was betrayal from Pete, that had been a child's disagreement.

Rámon had *used* her. Whispered the words she wanted to hear, taken her trust, taken *everything*. And she had let him, like a stupid schoolgirl.

"Speak a word to anyone about us, give any sign you know anything, and you are guilty of your brother's murder. Believe me, Ana, I don't want this to happen, but I can't take a chance for you. Stay with us."

She wanted to curse him, but the fear in Gabriel's eyes stopped her.

"Stay alive," Rámon said, and let go of her hair. The relief of pain made her begin to cry again. She was shaking uncontrollably. *I thought I was strong.* "I don't want to lose you, Ana, but I've gotten used to losing people. Generals have to."

She closed her eyes and said, with as much composure as she could manage, "All this to kill my ex-husband? How brave you are, Rámon. Like the bully you always were."

He slapped her—probably a mild slap, but she had never been slapped by a man before, and it hurt. She raised a shaking hand to her hot cheek as he turned away from her, limping on his wounded leg, firing rapid instructions to Miguel. She meant nothing.

She'd made the error of thinking that it was Miguel these men followed, Miguel who was the true killing soul. But now she knew. She'd embraced that darkness, loved it, called out to it.

And now she was lost in it.

And Gabriel, too.

Chapter 14

He didn't remember much of it later, just a confused jumble of explosion and fire and the orange stars glimmering on pavement. They told him he saved lives. He remembered television cameras staring and lights blazing, voices shouting questions, but he didn't remember answering.

He had a flash of memory of a car, of Esmeralda in her fumbling English telling the driver his address.

And now, somehow, he was home. That didn't give any comfort.

"Peter, please, you have to clean up now," Esmeralda said; it came through his recovering ears distant but anguished. She reached across him to take the television remote. CNN was running footage of the building again, the smoke gone now, the destruction clear. Smashed concrete looked like exposed bone. "Let go. Please."

She was speaking English, which he thought strange until he remembered he'd asked her to speak it. Too tired to think in Spanish. Too tired to move.

He still smelled of smoke and filth and death, his clothes bloody, but he couldn't move.

"Help," he whispered. It was something he'd rarely asked for before, but it was all right to say it to Esmeralda; there was no shame in it. She got an arm around him and helped him to his feet, steered him in the direction of the bathroom. As he sat on the toilet seat, she ran a hot bath, murmuring words under her breath he thought were probably prayers. He wondered what she would have put in the bath as a *curandera.* Herbs probably. Something that smelled sweet and soothing.

Her touch startled him. She stopped tugging at his shirt as their eyes met, and her cheeks blushed warm. She looked away.

"I am your nurse," she said. Her fingers trembled on the buttons, so he helped her with them. His shoes were bloody and caked with dirt. When she had everything off but his pants, she paused and sat back on her heels, looking up at him. "Take them off."

He found it surprisingly difficult; his brain was simply shutting down, refusing to cooperate anymore in this struggle to stay awake. He was too exhausted even to feel embarrassed as he stripped off his pants and underwear both and stood up. Esmeralda helped him step into the tub.

The water broke the trance of shock nicely, because it was *hot.* He gasped out loud and almost stepped out again, but she held him there, finally persuaded him to sit down in the tub as steam wreathed around both of them. The heat didn't seem so bad now. He leaned against the cool porcelain and his head touched the wall, and it seemed like the softest pillow he'd ever felt.

He might have gone to sleep right then, except that something touched his body, soft and smooth, and he opened his eyes to see Esmeralda leaning over him with a washcloth and soap. She blushed again when she saw him watching her, but he didn't say anything, and her embarrassment faded. He watched her as she squeezed hot water over his chest, rubbed soap over it, rinsed it clean.

"Lean forward," she said. He obeyed, closing his eyes, and hot water spilled over his head, washing away crusted black dust and smoke, washing away blood, washing away the past. She rinsed his hair again and again, worked shampoo through it with her gentle fingers, rinsed it clean.

Words came to him out of nowhere, and he said, "Ritual bath." Her hands stopped scrubbing his back.

"*¿Qué?*"

"I remember—they used to give knights ritual baths. To make them pure." For some reason that struck him as funny, and he started to laugh. "Probably the one time they bathed in their lives."

He kept laughing until it threatened to turn to tears, and she kept washing him, washing away the sorrow and the guilt and the fear. The bath water turned a muddy gray, the soap bubbles oily. Esmeralda drained the water and turned on the taps again, cooler this time, more soothing. They sat in silence as the tub filled. When the level was halfway up his chest, she shut it off and sat back, watching him.

"You knew this was going to happen," he said.

She shook her head. "You were there, Es. How else could you be there?"

"I knew when it happened, but I did not know it was *going* to happen. I think Jamie—" She bit her lip. "Jamie tried to tell us, but we couldn't understand. I came because I knew if I wasn't there, you—"

He remembered the rock sliding under his feet, carrying him down into the darkness. Esmeralda's hand holding him to life. He reached out with one wet, clean hand for her now, touched her cheek and saw pain in her eyes.

"No," she said softly. "Don't do that, Pedro. Because we both know it isn't me you love, it's a dead little boy you never even knew. You keep trying to make it up to me, but it wasn't your fault, don't you see that? It was never your fault."

She pulled away from his hand, stood, and had to catch herself as she swayed. She was tired, too, hours out in the cold wind, working as hard as he had. Smoke still smudged her face, and her eyes were red and swollen, but she was the most beautiful thing he thought he'd ever seen.

It might have been exhaustion, but he didn't think so.

Not anymore.

"Es," he said, "I love you."

Her breath caught sharply, and she turned her face away as if he'd slapped her. He found the strength to stand up, reached for a towel, and tied it around his waist before he stepped out of the tub and put his arms around her.

She had been strong for so long. Strong for Jamie,

then for him, for every person who came to her door
with a sick child or a broken heart.

She sagged against him, finally able to be weak,
and he sat her down to pull her sweater over her
head. He undressed her as she had him, economi-
cally, had her down to brassiere and underwear before he hesitated.

She opened her eyes and, moving slowly as a
dream, unfastened her bra. She stood up to let him
slide her underwear down, and for a second they
stood there, staring at each other as if they'd never
been naked before, as if they were the first people in
the world to take the risk.

He reached out and traced the line of her cheek
with his damp fingers. She turned blindly into the
touch and fitted her cheek to his palm.

"Your turn," he said, and put her in the bath
he'd left.

They slept together like children, twined in a lover's embrace that exhaustion rendered innocent, clean
skin against clean skin, and her hair smelled like
flowers in the sun, and he thought he had never had
such a moment of peace in his life, and it lasted all
through the long, cool night.

In the first light of morning Pete opened his eyes
to find her looking at him, her black hair spilled
under them like a memory of night, and it was such
a small move to touch her lips with his, such a sweet,
warm reward for the effort. The innocence might
have vanished, but the wonder of it remained like
the smell of flowers in her hair, and he realized they
both knew exactly what they were doing when she

rolled him over on his back and, without a single word, took him in and made love with him, silent in the still morning, her skin the color of dawn, and he never thought of Ana, not once.

He knew the exact moment she climaxed, and the sight of her face and the feeling of her ecstasy set him off, too, the first time that had ever happened together, and they both forgot about being quiet and laughed, wrapped together, laughed like children. Esmeralda said, in between giggles, "I like—your—ritual baths. My white—knight."

He was unreasonably touched. "White knight," he said, and smoothed back her hair. He saw the map of the fine scars, the lines of tragedy, and he realized he'd been looking at the scars all this time, and never really the face. "I'm not a knight."

"No," she agreed. Her eyes were full of mischief, and he realized she was speaking Spanish again. "Not yet. But you will be, when I need you."

"Oh, yeah? And when will that be?" He kissed her where she liked it, right below the ear, gently nibbled her lobe. "Soon?"

"Soon," she agreed. "*Very* soon."

He realized she'd unplugged the telephone from the wall, and plugged it back into the jack as he reached for the teapot; the phone started ringing before he could finish the motion. He picked it up and held it to his ear, watching Esmeralda brush out her long, dark hair.

"Hello?"

"Mr. Peter Ross?"

He didn't recognize the voice. "Yes?"

"Cynthia Gale from *Eyewitness News*—"

"No comment," he said, and hung up. Ten seconds later, it rang again. He looked at Es, who shrugged and kept on brushing her hair.

"That's why I unplugged it," she said practically. "They all wanted to talk to you. I wouldn't let them."

He answered four more calls, Channel 7 news, CNN, *Hard Copy*. The fifth call was from Agent Evan Miller of the FBI, who wanted to see both of them at the downtown FBI office without delay, and offered to send a car. Pete peeked through the sun-stiffened mini-blinds of his patio door to see the parking lot full of television vans. Some of the more prepared reporters had either brought or stolen patio furniture, and most of them were sitting around chatting as if it was a coffee klatch instead of a stakeout.

Then again—he looked around at Esmeralda. He hadn't exactly been in mourning. He decided he'd have plenty of time to feel guilty about that later.

"That might be a good idea," he told Agent Miller, and hung up. When he hung up, the phone rang again; he turned the ringer off. "Es, you know we've got to answer some questions."

"I know," she said. "Will they make me go back?"

She meant to Juárez; he hadn't thought of that. "No. No, not yet. Unless you want to go."

She cocked an eyebrow at him, plainly telling him, *Why would I?* and he had to laugh and lean over to kiss her again, a warm, lingering comfort that he was sure they were going to need when the door opened and the real world came charging for their throats again.

Before the car arrived, the reporters apparently got

tired of waiting for him to come out and started knocking on the door. He kept Esme away from the windows and turned the television up loud, couldn't find a channel that didn't have continuing coverage of the bombing except for MTV. He was surprised to see someone was interviewing Joseph Ryan of the DEA, and remembered that Ryan and Hartman had missed being in the building by just a day.

He himself had missed it by minutes. That thought still had the power to make his stomach turn over. The death toll, according to the CNN anchorwoman, stood at a surprisingly low sixteen, mostly Border Patrol employees, some civilians, and some illegal immigrants who had been in the processing center at the back of the building. There were more than forty injured. He couldn't help the thought that somehow they'd gotten off lightly, given the destruction, but the next sentence the anchorwoman spoke put that out of his mind for good.

"As we reported earlier this morning, a militant group calling itself Libertidad de Aztlan has claimed responsibility for the bombing. In a written statement, the Hispanic group said that they considered themselves 'at war with the hostile government of repression' and had struck at the center of what they believe to be the enemy of the Hispanic people of the United States and Mexico. Existing political groups such as the Sons of Aztlan, La Raza, and others have been quick to respond denouncing this action and disavowing all knowledge of the group."

"My God," he said, sinking down to the couch. Esmeralda sat next to him. "They're not going to stop here."

They were both startled at a fresh volley of knocks at the door. Esmeralda put a hand on his shoulder. "Ignore them. Maybe they'll leave."

"No. If they want a quote—" He was too angry to think about how it might come across on television; he yanked open the door and glared at the shorter man who stood there, fist still upraised for another knock. Neatly dressed, a dark suit under the Burberry trenchcoat. An intelligent, mobile face; he was African-American, which was a little unusual in El Paso.

"Mr. Ross, my name is Zack Walters. Agent Zack Walters, FBI." He smiled—not much of a smile, but then there wasn't much to smile about, outside. "I'm your ride downtown, sir. Ma'am."

He nodded to Esmeralda as she joined Pete at the door. Flashbulbs popped. Agent Walters sighed and shook his head.

"Circus time," he said. "Keep your heads down and don't say anything. Walk quickly."

Pete locked the door, took Esmeralda's arm, and followed Walters through the corridor of lights and voices; it seemed weirdly like the corridor of well-wishers at the end of a wedding, only these were throwing questions, not rice. Agent Walters, who'd obviously done this kind of thing before, opened the back door and got them inside the dark sedan before he ducked into the driver's seat.

"I'm locking the doors," he said, and hit a power button; the click of locks engaging sounded a second before the rattle of one of the reporters trying the handle. "Okay. All clear. You folks okay back there?"

"Fine," Pete answered. "As much as can be expected, I guess. Why us?"

"Why you?" Agent Walters sounded amused as he drove the car slowly out of the crowd of flashbulbs. "Gee, I don't know, maybe the fact that you two have been in the news before? They do love a good follow-up story, and from what I hear, you guys are gold. Is it true you rescued her out in the desert?"

He hadn't thought of that, but he should have. Of course they'd know. And now they'd just watched the two of them stay together at his apartment all night. No wonder *Hard Copy* was calling.

"Want the worst news?" Walters asked, still cheerfully.

"Why not?"

"They're calling your friend there 'Our Lady of Miracles' because she found seven victims still alive. They want to know what kind of psychic she is. Some border guard says she told him his brother was still alive two minutes after the explosion, from the other side of the border."

He looked at Esmeralda, eyebrows asking a silent *Did you?* that her slight shrug answered.

"So," Agent Walters said, still in the same light tone. "Uh, did you?"

"*¿Que?*" Esmeralda asked.

"Did you have a vision or something?"

"*No hablo ingles,*" she said. Her hand gripped Pete's tightly, and he realized that she wasn't joking, she was frightened. Maybe this was against the rules, what she'd done. Maybe she'd have a price to pay for it.

"Oh," the FBI agent said. Pete could tell he didn't

believe a word of it. "Okay. Well, Agent Miller's eager to talk to you, and he knows Spanish, too. Hey, want some coffee? My treat."

Coffee didn't delay the trip nearly long enough; they arrived at the FBI office downtown and parked in a guarded underground lot. He supposed it was shared between a lot of federal agencies, who were probably all nervous after yesterday's events.

On the seventh floor, an agent in a blue suit and striped tie met them at the elevators and greeted Pete and Esmeralda with a quick handshake and no smile. Evan Miller looked at Agent Walters, who abandoned his puppy-dog friendliness and said, "She says she doesn't speak English."

"Yeah, tell me another one. Come on, let's get inside." Miller was a middle-aged man, strong but running a bit to fat around the middle. He had lost a battle with male pattern baldness, and his head looked sleek and hard, his eyes harder. As they walked down a paneled hallway, Agent Walters took Esmeralda by the arm and pointed her toward an open doorway. When Pete tried to follow, he was headed off by Agent Miller.

"Separate interviews," Miller said without apology. "You were, we think, the last man out the door to the parking lot before the bomb went off. You're our freshest set of eyes. I want to know everything you saw, by the second, while you were inside. Go."

It was a long day. He hadn't seen anything, but they didn't like that answer, and there didn't seem to be anything he said that could convince them differently. He went back to Sanchez and Grivaldo and Nueves, and was told that they were all three dead, identified from fragments. They'd been nearly at ground zero.

He was finished two hours before Esmeralda, and there wasn't much to do in the FBI waiting room. Back issues of *Popular Mechanics* and *Washington Week in Review* didn't do much to pass the time, and he realized that he was actually afraid for her, afraid they'd frighten her too much, or she'd say something they wouldn't understand or believe, because they damned sure wouldn't believe any story about Jamie's spirit and visions and the calling of a *curandera*. It was in her absence that he realized how much it hurt not to have her, and he closed his eyes and remembered the absolute purity of her joy as they'd moved together, the slide of her skin on his.

"Mr. Ross?"

He realized that he'd actually fallen asleep, and stood up before he recognized the voice. The friendly Agent Walters again, smiling.

"Yeah." His voice sounded rusty. Behind Agent Walters, Esmeralda waited, both hands clasped; she was pale but composed.

"You're both free to go. I can't tell you not to talk to the press, but—well, you know. It'll be a lot easier on both of you if you don't stir things up more than they already are." Agent Walters shook hands with him and turned away. A few steps away he turned, one hand raised as if searching for a question in the air. "Oh, Mr. Ross?"

"Yes?" He had Esmeralda's hand in his now, and the touch of her skin made everything better. "What?"

"Sorry, I forgot to ask you something. It's about

your ex-wife, Ana Gutierrez. She's kind of an activist, isn't she?"

Agent Walters had learned his technique from Lieutenant Columbo, but that didn't lessen the impact. Pete sucked in a deep breath and tried to think clearly.

"Ana doesn't have anything to do with this."

"You're sure about that. Because we're looking for people with ties to extreme Chicano organizations, and I'd like you to think really hard about that answer."

"Why ask me? I haven't said two words to her since our divorce. Ask her yourself."

Agent Walters smiled again, winningly. "Well, I really don't need to, because we've got somebody watching her already."

Chapter 15

November 23, 1996
Dr. Ana Gutierrez

By the time two days had passed, she was able to get through a day without betraying her fear; the work helped, helped enormously. These people *needed* her, and she could not, would not let them down.

As she took advantage of a lull in the waiting room to gulp down a cold drink, Rafael looked up from the desk where he was preparing paperwork and said, "You've been different lately."

Her throat clenched, and she almost coughed. It was an effort of will to swallow the mouthful of soda, but she managed somehow, smiled, and said, "How?"

"I don't know." He studied her curiously, tapping a pen on a battered clipboard. "Just now, when you were with that girl—it was as if you really loved her, Ana. That's dangerous, isn't it? To care so much?"

She almost laughed this time, and restrained herself again. *Dangerous?* The last thing she had to fear was her heart breaking. She'd welcome that kind of pain.

"Yes, you're probably right," she said instead. "But she reminded me of myself at that age. I was a wild thing, you know. Angry."

"I never would have guessed," he said, and stretched. "Tell me."

"What's to tell? Fast friends, fast cars, guns, knives, drugs, the usual thing. Only I think I saw early that it was all going nowhere, all this running. And I decided I'd rather go somewhere."

"What about your friends? You left them all behind?"

She took another drink. It didn't taste sweet this time; it was bitter as gall. "Not all."

She was saved from further conversation by the arrival of a large and noisy family infected with lice, and it became an afternoon of cutting hair and shampooing crying children. As she was shampooing the mother's hair, the woman said in Spanish. "You hear about the bomb, yes?"

"I heard," she said, suddenly aware of the camera at the corner of the room, Rámon's unblinking eye.

"It's time someone did it," the woman said, and there was vicious satisfaction in her voice. "I was beaten by *la migra*, you know. So was my husband. They made us pay them money."

The story was a common one, but this time it froze Ana's heart. She had been so preoccupied with her revulsion for the murders that she'd forgotten how others might see it, as a just and justified action, a valid shot in an ongoing war. Whether any of the stories were true or not, the *barrio* people were terrified of Immigration, and hated them in equal measure. And everyone had a story. Everyone knew someone who'd been beaten, raped, allowed to drown as *la migra* laughed. No one knew Pete, or wanted to. No one had seen him carrying that wounded Mexican child in his arms.

It was terrifyingly easy to hate. She'd done it, and she *knew*.

"You don't mean that," she said aloud. "None of us wanted murder."

"No?" The woman tilted her head up to look at her, bleak, black amusement in her eyes. "Maybe not you, *la doctora*, with your fine education and money, but *my* people wanted blood."

And as easily as that, she was the enemy, rich, American, an Anglo with tanned skin. She worked her gloved fingers through the woman's hair in silence, her mind far away, until she heard a woman's voice behind her say, "How can I help, Ana?"

She turned and saw Sister Teresa silhouetted in the butter-warm afternoon light, her black buttoned dress and coif out of another age.

Once the initial shock had passed, she wanted to scream at her, tell her, *Go, run away from here, I can't protect you, they won't care who you are!* but some last sense of self-preservation made her walk to her aunt and kiss her smooth cheek, accept the blessing of her warm embrace, and say, "Pray with us."

"Pray?" Sister Teresa pulled back, either startled or amused; none of it showed on her face. "I thought you healed and left the praying to me, child."

"I think this is a time when there can't be too much prayer." She gulped in air, took Teresa's hand, and led her to the woman who waited, shampoo sparkling in her hair. "This is *Señora* Galvan, and we were just discussing the bombing."

"A terrible thing," Sister Teresa said softly. *Sra.* Galvan nodded, face slightly flushed. "I know many feel it might have been deserved, but it's God's place to judge, not ours. Don't you agree?"

She continued to talk in her gentle, persuasive voice, of peace and redemption, as Ana finished rinsing out the medicine from the woman's hair. When they were done and the woman herded her crop of shorn children out the clinic doors, Sister Teresa said to Ana, "You surprise me. I thought you'd say it was justified."

Ana blinked back sudden tears. "Is that what you think of me? That I want this kind of—murder? *Pete was in that building.* I never wanted this."

Sister Teresa reached out and eased a curl back from Ana's damp forehead. Her smile was sad and peaceful, her eyes dark as eternity.

"At least you know what you want now, child. Maybe you're finally listening to your heart."

"Too late," Ana said, and turned away to the next patient.

She should have expected, at the end of the day, that Teresa would want to see Gabriel, but the casual request caught her utterly by surprise, panicked her into a blurted lie. "He's not here!"

Teresa lifted her eyebrows a fraction, the only sign of surprise she ever really showed. "No? I thought he worked until you closed the clinic."

"Usually he—he does, but today he—I gave him

the day off. He had a date. With his physical therapist."

The clinic was empty now except for Rafael, still shuffling paper at his desk, a girl named Juana who swept up the trash, usually not very well, Teresa, and herself. The door was locked, the CERRADO sign hung face out, the evening peacefully dark outside.

"So late?" Sister Teresa said, and smiled. "You're certain it was therapy?"

"No," she said with an immense feeling of relief. "I'm not. Well, I think we're all done here. Thank you for your help today—"

"And what time tomorrow?"

Panic froze her dumb this time, and when she turned to look at Rafael—why, she didn't know—he raised his head and said, "Clinic opens at eight a.m. sharp, but any time you show up we'll find you something to do, Sister. It's a good idea, wearing the habit. Most of these people respect the traditions."

"Then I'll be here at eight," Teresa said. "I have nowhere else to go, except to cloister, and I still think my vocation is in the world for a while. If you don't mind, Ana."

"Of course not, I'd love to have your help." She accepted Teresa's kiss and saw her to the door. As she unlocked it and felt fresh, cool air stroke her cheek, she almost blurted out the whole story to Teresa, almost confessed her guilt, but there was Gabriel to think of. Gabriel, who might never go out with his physical therapist again if she didn't play Rámon's game.

"Good night," she said, and let her aunt out. She shut the door and locked it again, watched Teresa's

back as the nun walked down the street with brisk
confidence, watched until tears made a chiaroscuro
jumble of light and shadow.

Juana left soon after, leaving her alone with Rafael.
He finished his paperwork and sat back at his desk,
looking at her. What was he seeing? What was he
looking for?

"What's wrong, Ana?" he asked. She shook her
head. "Come on, I can see it on your face. Is it
Gabriel?"

She nodded, grateful for the misdirection. Rafael
came up to her and began rubbing her shoulders,
hard, almost painful squeezes of her tense muscles
that left sweet relief behind. She moaned and put her
head down as he worked. With him so close, she
could imagine she was safe, that everything was all
right.

If she spoke softly enough, the audio pickups
wouldn't hear. Rafael's body was blocking the
camera.

"He's in trouble," she said very softly. "I need
your help, Rafael, please. Just do what I say."

"Always." He pitched his voice to the same soft
murmur, and his lips touched her neck in a gentle
caress.

"No! Listen to me, please, there's someone watching us—"

"You told Teresa Gabriel was gone." He moved
his lips from her neck to her jawline, sliding his
hands around her waist. "He isn't, is he? What's
wrong?"

She opened her mouth to tell him, but froze as she
heard the unmistakable sound of feet on the stairs

that led from her loft into the clinic. Rafael heard them, too. He let go of her and stepped back, face unreadable, as the door marked NO PASEN swung open and a tall man in a straw hat came out. He had the face of a farm hand, leathery beyond his years. He took his hat off and turned it in his hands nervously, ducking his head, a peasant approaching landowners.

It was Miguel. Ana forgot to breathe.

"*Señora—Doctora*—I'm sorry to bother you at this time, but the package you said was important is upstairs for you. Is very fragile. I wanted to tell you right away."

"Oh," she said faintly. "I see. Yes, I'll be right up."

She didn't dare look at Rafael, who was busy putting books in a satchel, preparing to leave. Had he understood? Did she dare to hope?

"I'll lock up, Ana," he said, and there wasn't anything in his voice that gave her any hope of rescue. He brushed past her to the door, opened it, exited. She heard the click as the lock engaged.

Miguel stopped turning his hat in his hands. He looked straight at her and said, "That was very stupid, Ana. You be stupid again, you pay the price."

He reached over and took her arm, not harshly, and led her up the steps. At the top, waiting for her, she saw Rámon, his face unreadable.

"I want to trust you, Ana," he said, "but you keep surprising me. What happened to the girl I remember? The one who carried a switchblade and was ready to cut the balls off any Anglo who looked down on her?"

"The one who got stoned every night and drank

tequila and danced until dawn? The one you killed
for? She's gone, Rámon! She's dead! You see, *I'm* the
murderer, too, because I *changed*. I got myself straight
and I learned that not every answer is found in
Rámon Cruz's mouth!"

Miguel pushed her up the stairs. Rámon didn't
move. When she was a step away from him, she
stopped, daring him to move, and with a smile he
did, making it look like his idea, arm sweeping out
in an extravagant gesture of courtesy. She made sure
she didn't touch him as she turned right into the
living room.

Gabriel lay on the floor, moaning. His face was
bloody. She cried out and went to her knees next to
him, mopping his face with the tail of her shirt. His
face was swollen and discolored with blooming
bruises.

"*Pendejo*," she spat at Rámon, shaking with fury.
"Get my bag."

Rámon shrugged. "He'll live." He limped to the
couch and sat down, eased his wounded leg into position with a sigh. "An object lesson, my little Ana.
You want to play rough, things get broken. Maybe
something that can't be fixed, yes?"

She wiped the blood from Gabe's face, whispering
his name, and he caught her hand in his with surprising strength. He was angry, of course. Enraged. He
hated being helpless, hated being disabled, hated that
she saw him this way. She read all that in his bloodshot eyes.

But what he said was, "Do the right thing, Ana.
You have to."

"Don't think, either of you. Thinking will get you

killed. Just do what we say, eh?'' Rámon gestured, and suddenly there was something bright at Gabriel's throat, held there by Miguel, a white line she didn't understand for a few seconds was a knife. It trembled in time with Gabriel's breathing. "Miguel here understands how important this is, don't you, Miguel? He understands that one life doesn't matter. Twenty lives don't matter as long as they serve a purpose. That is the essence of politics, Ana.''

Rámon was laughing at her, at all her comfortable causes and her armchair rebellions. She watched the light move on the knife at her brother's throat and couldn't even be angry. Fear had too much of her soul.

"It isn't just Gabriel's life you will forfeit. What we did to *la migra* we can do again, and we will if you try to betray us. Look.''

It was hard to tear her eyes away from the knife, from Gabriel's bleak, angry, frightened eyes, but she did. She turned to see Rámon holding up a newspaper article, a grainy black-and-white picture of what she thought of as a typically Anglo building, white, hard columns lifting up to arrogant heights, the false gentility of Southern living.

"This is a private Anglo school," he said. "There are more than two hundred of the wealthiest white families who send their kids to this building every day. And we have it, Ana. We have the power to destroy it and every person in it, any time we want. Children ages seven to eighteen, teachers, everyone. *¿Comprende?*''

"*Cabrón*," she whispered. He let her look at the

newspaper a moment longer before he folded it and put it aside.

"Good. We understand each other. That's the price of silence, Ana. Not your brother's life, though that would be the start. The school is the price. Think about it."

She turned back to Gabriel, tears making the world a vague, soft-edged jumble of light, and blinked to bring his face back into focus. Miguel took the knife from her brother's throat, and she put her arms around Gabe, helped him to a sitting position, clung to him for strength. His muscles were tight with fury, but he said nothing. He wouldn't.

"I understand," she said finally. "Yes. I understand."

She understood better than she ever had before.

Chapter 16

November 24, 1996
Peter Ross

Three days later, he walked Esmeralda back across the bridge to Mexico, back to the house with aqua trim and the open palm painted in the window. The cardboard Halloween witch was gone from the front window, but everything else was the same, basil and cilantro, the clean smell of her hair as she held him close, everything except what he felt for her.

He was a little afraid of it, to tell the truth. He'd never felt this for Ana, this overwhelming love, this need to be with her and protect her. He wasn't sure if it was entirely sane.

"Go," Esme said, and gave him one last kiss. "We both have jobs to do, Peter. There'll be time for us later."

"Promise?" He held onto her for a second or two longer, holding the kiss, wanting to take the taste of her with him. She touched his cheek, her eyes smiling.

"To le promesar," she said, and tapped his cheek. "You go now."

She turned to the door and unlocked it. Mail was scattered over the floor; she gathered it up in an untidy armload and turned back to smile at him. He was about to leave when the smile faded, replaced by something dark and terrible in her eyes.

"Jamie," she whispered, and turned away from the door, mail falling from her hands, forgotten. She was staring toward the living room.

He took a step inside and looked with her. For an instant he couldn't see what was different—the couch the same, the crucifix on the wall, the massive table—

And then he saw that Jamie's picture wasn't on the table. It was lying on the floor, the glass smashed.

Esmeralda stumbled and almost fell. Pete grabbed her and guided her to the couch, sat her down, reached out to pick up Jamie's picture, but her cry stopped him.

"It's a message," she said, her voice trembling. "Oh, God—"

"It's not a message, Esme, the picture just fell off the table. It's no—"

"It's a message, Peter, don't you see that? How could it just fall? There was no one here." She rocked back and forth in distress, and this time when he reached down for the picture she didn't stop him. Pieces of glass slipped out of the frame and clinked together on the wood floor. He brushed them away and set Jamie's picture back where it had been, went into the kitchen for a broom and dustpan. He cleaned up the fragments in silence, making sure he'd gotten every sharp edge, and when he looked up Esmeralda was composed again, her hands clasped in her lap, her face distant.

"Es," he began, and started over. This wasn't Es, wasn't the woman who'd made love to him this morning on the other side of the border. "Esmeralda, this isn't a sign. The window was open, the picture blew over. There's nothing supernatural about it. It isn't a message from Jamie."

"Yes, it is," she said. "It's good-bye. There is a price for saving you, Peter, and Jamie has paid it for me. He has gone on. I have no one now."

She stood up and walked to the table. She picked up the picture and pressed it to her breast, head bowed, making a thin sound of grief that cut like shattered glass. Pete wanted to touch her but knew it wasn't the time. He was an outsider now.

He dumped the glass in the trash and put the broom back where it had been, made coffee and carried it to her. She stood where he'd left her, the picture pressed close, but her tearless crying had stopped. After a long breath she put the picture face-down, on the table.

He almost dropped the cup he'd brought her, set it down on the table with a slap of china on wood. He was sure he'd gotten all the glass out of the picture frame, but Esmeralda was bleeding through her shirt around a single, needle-sharp piece of glass that had pierced her skin where she had held Jamie close. He held her still and pulled it out—two inches of glass, razor-sharp, glazed with blood.

She smiled, but it was a smile of tragedy. Blood dripped down her shirt in tear-shaped patterns.

"He's angry," she said. "You see?"

*   *   *

She refused to see a doctor, and there was nothing he could say against the unyielding, gentle grief in her eyes, whether he believed it or not. He kissed her and left her alone with the shattered picture of her son, in a house that had seemed so warm and now seemed somehow hostile.

He went back to his own world, because that was what she wanted.

The bombing investigation had been established at a temporary command center on Fort Bliss Army Base—which had the dual advantage of being on government land and heavily guarded. He showed his identification to the extremely alert guard at the western gate and was passed inside to the small, neat white building with a perfectly manicured gravel parking lot. It wasn't easy to find a spot, but he finally did at the back, between a smoke-stained light green official van and a cream-colored Toyota he remembered.

There was another guard at the door, complete with rifle; he was shown in after presenting ID to another desk with another military guard, this one female, carrying a sidearm. She buzzed him through to a plain white hallway, clean linoleum floors, and temporary room names taped to the walls. He stopped at the doorway that said INFORMATION and saw Marilyn Carver, longtime administrative assistant to Tito Nueves, on the phone. When she saw him, she put the call on hold, came out from behind her desk, and enveloped him in a hard, anxious hug. She was a tall woman, padded lightly with extra pounds; she carried the weight and her over-fifty age with equal ease.

But today she looked older. Her eyes were red and swollen, and he saw by the pile of used tissues on her desk that she'd been crying.

"I'm on casualty duty," she said. "It's hard, you know? Pete, I'm so glad to see you. I'm glad you got out."

"I'm glad you weren't there," he said, and squeezed her back before letting her return to the phone. "Is there some kind of record available?"

She wordlessly passed it over to him. Every familiar name on the death list hurt him, and by the tenth he had to sit down. It didn't seem possible to lose so many people so fast. So young, most of them.

Tito Nueves. Hector Sanchez. Alberto Grivaldo. He'd been with them. He felt, somehow, that he should have stayed with them. Maybe if he had he would have seen it coming, would have been able to stop it. Esmeralda's presence had cushioned that guilt, made it seem bearable, but now, looking at the names, it was hard to push it back. He wanted to have those five minutes back. He wanted to—

—*die*, Esmeralda's voice whispered to him, not anything she'd said, just what he knew she'd say. *You couldn't have saved them, Pedro. It was too late.*

Maybe it was, but that didn't help the crushing weight in his chest. He couldn't stop thinking about the bodies he'd pulled out of the rubble, the ones pounded to raw meat by falling concrete.

"Yo, Pete, good to see you, man." He looked up to find a man in a Border Patrol uniform looking down at him. Not a friend, not anyone he knew well. He looked at the name tag—JORGENSEN—and back at the broad face, the blue eyes. "Glad you're okay."

"You too," he said, and shook hands. Jorgensen went to Marilyn's desk and got a copy of the list. Pete watched him go through the same process of raw grief and anger and had to look away. It was too painful.

The next person into the room belonged to the car he remembered from the parking lot. Joseph Ryan, DEA. The heavyset man had on sunglasses and a trench coat, and the combination made him look like a cartoon spy. Pete watched him scan the room, dismissing Marilyn, lingering on Jorgensen, coming to rest on his face.

He didn't know what he expected, but he was surprised when Ryan walked to him, extended his hand, and said, "I'm sorry, Pete. Damn sorry. Now let's figure this out and get these assholes."

Ryan, it turned out, was in it because he'd worked with Border Patrol on many occasions; he was also, it seemed, a confidant of FBI agent Evan Miller, who was in charge of the investigation. There were a lot of FBI. Bomb experts, who were busy putting together an explosive profile. Forensic experts, who were going over the bodies for evidence. Investigators, who were talking to everyone about everything. Most of the records had been destroyed in the blast, but the remote computer backups provided them with leads on open cases, not the least of which was the cross fire at the Black Bridge.

And that, it turned out, was why Ryan was *really* present. And, for that matter, Pete. They went through a step-by-step reconstruction of the case, using computer records pulled from backup of Sanchez and Grivaldo's reports. What wasn't there Pete added from memory, and Ryan contributed the rest. It wasn't until the end, when he described taking the child to Ana, that something happened which surprised him.

"You took her to Dr. Gutierrez because you knew the clinic was open?" Agent Miller asked.

Pete shook his head. "I knew she lived there, I didn't know whether the clinic was open or closed. I wasn't thinking, I was just trying to find help. I didn't think the little girl could wait."

"So you took the backpack off and left it at the site of the shooting, carried the child to Dr. Gutierrez—"

"No," he said. "I didn't take the backpack off."

Silence all around the table. Ryan looked down at some papers and tapped a pencil.

"Is somebody saying I did?"

More tapping. Agent Miller said, "There were no backpacks entered into evidence at the scene or later. We were operating under the assumption that you removed the child's backpack before taking her to the clinic for treatment. That isn't correct?"

"No, she was wearing it. I remember Ana taking it off." Remembered it hitting the floor, making a dull thud. "You mean it's missing?"

"I mean it was never found by anybody after you say Dr. Gutierrez took it off and put it on the floor. So the question is, Where did that backpack go, and what was in it? Your assumption was heroin, correct?"

"Yes, that's right."

"What if we told you that an analysis of the girl in the hospital revealed that there were traces of a highly toxic explosive, not heroin, on her clothing?"

He said, "I'd say I was surprised. We never had any information that pointed toward explosives. This was a purely drug-related case, that was our information. Ask Agent Ryan."

"We have," Agent Miller said, and leaned back in his chair. "And now I'm going to ask you about your relationship with Dr. Ana Gutierrez. Your ex-wife."

"I don't have a relationship with her."

"Your phone records show you've tried to call her. You had a long conversation with her that night after the child was taken away in the ambulance—in fact, you were the last officer on the scene, isn't that right? So you would have had a very good opportunity to see what happened to that backpack."

"I don't remember seeing the backpack after Ana took it off."

"You forgot about important evidence in a criminal investigation?" Agent Miller overacted his disbelief. "It was your responsibility to tag that evidence, Ross. Do you have any kind of explanation for why you failed to do that?"

"No," he said. "I don't."

Looking back on it, he didn't see how he *had* forgotten. Yeah, he was concerned about the girl, but—

The only explanation was that it had disappeared sometime after Ana had taken it off. He would have looked for it to tag it. In fact, he remembered looking for it and assuming one of the other officers had tagged it—a fatal mistake. Stupid.

"I think we're going to have to talk to Ana Gutierrez," said Agent Miller. "Get a search warrant for the clinic."

Chapter 17

November 25, 1996
Esmeralda Sanchez

She sat at the table, both hands touching the photograph of Jamie, her eyes looking at the crucifix on the wall. She had spent the morning praying, but heaven seemed very distant, as far as the American border, as far as Pete. She had never felt so alone. The cut in her left breast ached, a reminder of what had been severed from her, and she looked away from the suffering face of Jesus to the happy, smiling face of her son, frozen in time.

Jamie. She thought it kindly, warmly, lovingly. *Please come home. Please come back to me. I know what I did was wrong, I know you told me to tell him about Ana, but please forgive me, I couldn't. For the first time he looked at me with love, and I couldn't put Ana back in his mind. I'm sorry.*

Silence, vast and cold as the sky. It was cold in the house, too, but she did not want it warm. She wanted it as cold as her heart, as empty as her arms.

Jamie, she called more sharply, a mother angered by a child's disobedience. *Jamie Alberto Vargas y Sanchez, listen to me!*

It was so very quiet. She closed her eyes and waited for the warm brush of a child's fingers on her cheek, but all that came was silence, and the whisper of cold wind.

She was alone now. She was of no use to anyone, even to Pete. He hadn't confessed it, but she sensed the darkness in his head, a tiny pinprick of pain, a hungry monster of cells that would grow and grow until they consumed him. She could lay hands on him, but it would only be the hands of a woman, and that was not enough for Pete. He was *susto,* severed from his spirit, and he needed the touch of someone wise to guide him back to life.

You can make it right.

A whisper somewhere from the air. She turned her head, eyes still closed, searching for the voice. Not Jamie's voice this time. An older spirit, wiser, with a bitter undertone to its whisper.

"How?"

Make the wrong right.

"I don't know how!"

Silence now. She had received all the guidance there was. She opened her eyes and shivered convulsively in the cold, cold room, traced the line of Jamie's remembered face, and stood up to put on her coat. She'd go across the border. Talk to Ana. That was the way to make things right. There was trouble in Ana's spirit, and she was *curandera;* it was her business to heal the spirit. That was what God wanted from her.

Yes, surely.

She realized as she approached the international bridge that she'd lost her papers, or left them at

Pete's apartment; they were nowhere in her pockets, though she turned out every scrap of paper. Without a pass she couldn't get across, not as someone on file as illegally crossing before. They'd turn her back.

I should go home, she thought, discouraged and sad. It wasn't meant for her to make things right.

A small boy ran past her, bundled in a bright red coat, and for an instant she caught her breath and thought, *Jamie,* but of course it wasn't. There were a thousand boys that age at the border, and none of them her son. This one carried extra clothes in a rough sling on his back—a *mojado,* then, looking to cross the river. His parents might already be in the water, fording the cold, cold streams.

For no reason than the red coat the boy wore, because it seemed warm to her in the chill of the day, she began walking after him, down the hill, into the dusty industrial part of Juárez where the factories worked all day and all night, and smoke plumed into the sky like black offerings.

It was growing dark, and she knew it would quickly get colder as the night fell. The flickering figure of the boy ran ahead of her, past street vendors, past closing shops and parked, rusted cars. She began to walk faster, then run, her lungs hurting from the cold air, the ache where the glass had stabbed her a pure, cold anguish.

The boy turned up an alley, into the darkness. She burst into it, gasping in the stench of week-old waste and unwashed bodies, and found the boy looking at her. More than the boy. There must have been twenty of them, all staring at her fearfully. They were huddled in the shadows, blankets around their shoulders,

men and women and children. She knew, looking at
them, that they were all *mojados*, waiting for darkness
to cross the river.

No, not the river. On the other side of the alley a
gravel road ran next to the Rio Grande, and she knew
where it led.

El Puente Negro. The Black Bridge.

She sank down on her heels where she was, found
a wall, and put her back against it. She said softly,
"Don't be afraid. I need to cross, too."

Chapter 18

November 25, 1996
Dr. Ana Gutierrez

In the absence of sanity there was work, and she did it with a passion.

For the first time ever, Rafael wasn't on time the next day when the clinic opened. Sister Teresa was, dressed in her habit, and she took on Juana's job of sweeping up without complaint. Ana worked hard, wondering with half a mind where Rafael could be, busying herself with that thought rather than think about the men upstairs, Gabriel's bruised face, his angry eyes. *Do the right thing,* he'd said, as if she could stand there and watch him be hurt. He was the hero of the family; nobody had ever accused her of great moral courage.

She did not dare to think about the school, wherever it was. Did not dare think of gossiping teenagers together, or kissing in hallways, or looking forward to lives that might never be—and, oh, God forbid, the classrooms full of small children. *I will not let it happen,* she told herself. *Whatever the cost to me, I will not let that happen.*

She had set two broken arms—it seemed a holiday theme—and given three lectures on the hazards of AIDS to teenagers, complete with condoms, by the time Rafael finally arrived. He wasn't dressed for work; he had on a suit today, a very nice suit, and it made him look older than he was. She smiled when she saw him come in, turned away from stacking gauze in the supply cabinet, and said, "Ah, so that's it, you had a job interview—"

He cut her off coldly, completely, by showing her his FBI badge.

She blinked at it, her smile still in place, because she couldn't quite get her mind around the idea that this man—a man she'd trusted, a man she'd *kissed*—was a federal agent, sent to spy on her. She knew she should be shocked, angry, and betrayed, but his betrayal was in the same league with Pete's, unimportant before the huge offense of Rámon's.

She was relieved. The presence of the FBI meant that it was over. She could tell them—

The surveillance cameras. Rámon would see!

I can't let them die. It was all the conscious thought she could permit herself. She threw the gauze at Rafael, threw herself after, hands slapping at his face. It didn't take him but a few seconds to subdue her and handcuff her, but that was something. A small, costly victory.

She didn't recognize the men who entered after him, but she knew they were FBI as well. Police followed after that. Someone showed her a search warrant. Sister Teresa put down her broom and spoke with an Anglo man who gave her the paper; she read it thoroughly and gave Ana a look of utter help-lessness.

"Don't fight, Ana," she said. "Let them look. There's nothing to fear."

"Gabriel—" she said, daring to speak it aloud. "Please—"

"You want me to see to him?" Teresa asked, and confusion wrinkled her smooth brow. "Ana, he's not here. I saw him leave."

She stopped struggling against the handcuffs, her mind gone blank and dark like an empty house. She couldn't even ask *when*.

"He was leaving with some friends in a van when I arrived. Didn't you know?"

They had him. The message was clear. They'd known the raid was coming, and they'd taken Gabriel as a hostage. *Oh, God.* If she talked—

She stayed silent when they asked her questions, threatened her with charges of assault for striking Rafael, who still wouldn't meet her eyes or say anything to her. They opened the door that said NO PASEN and searched upstairs.

The didn't find anything. She'd known they wouldn't. Rámon wouldn't be so careless; he intended her to be silent, be cleared, and be obedient.

Gabriel's angry words came back to her. *Do the right thing, Ana.*

There were no right choices left.

They were, she could tell, disappointed with what little they'd found. They took her to a police station and tried to frighten her, but she stayed quiet, and in the end her silence and Sister Teresa's gentle, insistent pleas won her freedom.

Freedom. The word had ceased to have any meaning to her. There was no freedom now, not with the memory of Gabriel's bruised face, the knife at his throat, the picture of the school. She had nowhere to turn, no help in this world and no salvation in the next. If she stayed silent, she was guilty, and if she spoke—

Rafael was the man who drove them back to the clinic. Teresa sat next to her in the backseat, holding her hand, talking gently to her, but it was conversation Ana could neither understand nor respond to. She kept catching Rafael's eyes in the mirror, watching her. She turned away to watch the procession of people outside, walking in the cold, hurrying home this evening to warmth and laughter and family.

She did not know what would be there for her at the clinic; at best, there would be emptiness.

It surprised her when Rafael spoke; she'd grown accustomed to his silence. "Ana, it was an assignment. I hope you understand."

She almost asked if seducing her was part of the assignment, but the thought of asking that in Sister Teresa's presence made her acutely embarrassed. Instead she said, "I hope you understand that you're fired."

He laughed—a weak, uncomfortable laugh. "Don't worry. I won't file for unemployment. Ana, you were trying to tell me something the other night. I think you wanted my help. What's happening to you?"

She turned her face away, staring out the window as streets glided away from her. Lights were coming on in the twilight, a necklace of jewels at the throat of the mountains, and the sky was a lustrous, perfect dark blue, the sunset a glide of orange and red at the horizon. The star flickered into brightness on the side of the hill. It was, they said, the symbol of friendship between the two countries.

"You happened to me," she said. "All of you with a *side*."

"This isn't about sides anymore, Ana. It isn't about Tejanos and Chicanos and Hispanics and Anglos. It isn't about protests and marches. This is about *lives*." He sounded truly anguished. She kept her face still, her heart quiet.

"I know," she said. "Let me ask you a question, Rafael—as a man, not an FBI agent. Would you give your life for your cause? Something you believed in?"

He hesitated and then said, "It depends on the cause."

"You carry a gun, Rafael. Would you kill for your cause?"

Silence. He braked for a stoplight, but he didn't answer. She nodded as if he had.

"Maybe I would, too," she said. "I don't know. I just don't know anymore."

She knew one thing. It was now her and Rámon, locked together to the death, and there was no going back. No help.

She had to think what to do, and pray that she had the courage to do it.

The clinic seemed deserted when the car pulled up, the window blinds shut, the CERRADO sign turned in the window. But there were six people huddled outside in the cold, waiting. Ana sighed, her breath frosting the glass, and tried to get out. The car door wouldn't open—no, of course it wouldn't from the inside, it was some kind of police vehicle. Rafael came around back and opened it for her, courteously offered her a hand out to the curb. He did the same for Teresa.

"I need the key," she said without looking at him. "You have the keys to the clinic. I need them back."

Without a word he reached into his pocket and took out a separate key ring. She used the first one to open the door and let the weary, cold patients inside. The others were to the supply cabinet, the larger supply room, and the elevator. She dropped them into the pocket of her coat before she shrugged it off and put it on the coat tree.

Rafael stood outside, watching her through the closed door. Maybe he was hoping she would let him in; there was a sense of loss in his eyes, of abandonment. She wanted to, but she couldn't take the risk. Rámon surely had someone watching her, even if he wasn't upstairs himself. She could neither ask nor accept Rafael's help, or the FBI's, or even Teresa's.

She opened the door and said to Rafael, "Would you take Sister Teresa home, please?"

"Ana, I can stay," Teresa said. "You need help."

"No." She turned back to Rafael. "Please?"

He must have known it was the last favor she would ask of him. He nodded and opened the passenger door.

"Go," she said to Teresa, and kissed her gently on the cheek. "I need to know you're home safe. Please."

Teresa knew things were desperately wrong, but she had always kept her own counsel, always trusted to God. She put her hand to Ana's cold cheek and said, "God be with you, then," and got in the sedan. Rafael nodded to Ana, a simple, economical farewell, and she watched as they drove off into the dark.

She turned the sign from CERRADO to ABIERTO and began to ask her patients what was wrong.

It was more than two hours before she could open the NO PASEN door and go up the stairs, to darkness. No lights showing except for the glow of television monitors in Gabriel's bedroom. She flipped on all of the overhead bulbs, going from room to room, seeing the signs of FBI searches and fingerprint powder. She hadn't thought of fingerprints. Had they found Rámon's? Miguel's?

The storeroom was empty. The FBI had taken the boxes and left a piece of paper on the floor with an inventory. She wondered what they hoped to find among the gauze and syringes and Betadine.

They'd had the decency not to confiscate her operating supplies, at least. The clinic cabinets were still fully stocked.

She sat in the middle of the cold, empty storeroom and put her head in her hands, wishing she could think of something to *do*, some reason to *move*. All that came to her was the terrifying picture of the school, and the rubble of the Border Patrol building, and Pete's face.

But she couldn't trust, Pete, either.

Could she?

Chapter 19

November 25, 1996
Peter Ross

"She knows something," Joseph Ryan said. He and Pete stood behind a sheet of one-way glass, watching as FBI agents patiently asked Ana questions, over and over—questions about the girl she'd treated, the missing backpack, the headquarters explosion. "The bitch knows. She's in on it, Pete. Look at her."

He couldn't look at her, not for long. He'd known Ana a long time, but this was a different woman, and the stiffness of her face, the harshness of her eyes—this wasn't the woman he'd married. It wasn't even the one he'd divorced.

"Yeah," he agreed. He felt sick at the thought, but Ryan was right. Ana looked guilty, and she'd been a school friend of a man named Rámon Cruz—the one who had been smuggling heroin. The man who'd strapped explosives to the back of a child and sent her across the Black Bridge. There were too many lines connecting her to be ignored.

"So what do we do about it?" Ryan asked. "I'll tell you what the FBI glory boys in there will do, I know because I've seen it. They're going to let her go. They've got nothing concrete to link her to the bombing, and nothing linking her to drug trafficking, so they're going to let her go. Well, that's bullshit. Far as I'm concerned, she's the way in."

"Into what?"

Ryan winked at him. "That's the question, Petey. Word is she's a real firebrand, takes up all kinds of causes for illegals, Mexicans, migrants. She's a goddamn rebel. That's what we're looking for, isn't it? A rebel?"

"Not Ana."

"Bull*shit*. Look at her. What makes you think she wouldn't blow up a building? Especially one *you* worked in."

Against his will, Pete remembered her screaming at him in the hospital. If she didn't hate him, she at least despised him.

"No," he said again. "She takes her oaths as a doctor seriously. She wouldn't bomb a building full of people."

"Not people," Ryan said. He seemed to be enjoying this, his cheeks pink, his eyes bright. "*White* people. You're telling me she doesn't hate white people?"

He hadn't thought so, but he didn't know anymore. Ana had changed.

He turned away from the window as the door to the observation room opened and closed, and Agent Miller stepped inside. Miller looked tired, his suit wrinkled, his tie crooked, and there were blue smudges under his eyes; he'd lost the bout with insomnia.

"Okay, this is what we're going to do. We don't find anything on the surface to put her in this, but we're going to process samples from her apartment and the clinic, and if we find any traces of explosive, we're going to bring her in and shut the building, go over it inch by inch if we have to."

"That's your plan?" Ryan asked.

"That's the plan."

"Well, then, respectfully speaking, it sucks. What's to stop her from blowing out of here across the border in the next thirty minutes? If she's in this, she'll have backup plans."

"We can't hold her on nothing," Agent Miller said. "We'll have surveillance on her and the clinic, wait for something to turn up. That's our best bet."

"She's guilty," Ryan said again. There was a nasty edge to his voice, a hate Pete found familiar. He'd felt it himself, looking at the ruins of the building, the bodies of men he knew. "She's laughing at you guys. I'm telling you, you let her go and you send a message to those people that they can do anything."

Miller turned to the glass, looked at the room where Ana sat alone. She wasn't moving, wasn't crying, wasn't doing anything except staring down at her clasped hands.

"She's not laughing," he said. "She's scared. She's the wrong end of the chain, Ryan."

Ryan's eyes glittered. He looked at Pete and said, "Yeah, I smell fear, but it ain't coming from her. Come on. Let's get out of here."

"You want me to talk to her?" Pete asked. Miller looked at him a moment, then shook his head. "You're sure? She might talk to me."

"She might not. It isn't time for a full-court press right now." Miller sat down on a folding chair, chin propped on one fist, watching Ana. Ryan grunted in disgust and left.

After hesitating, Pete followed. Ryan led the way down the clean, sterile halls, pausing to exchange nods and looks with other FBI or DEA or Border Patrol.

"So," Ryan said conversationally. "You in?"

"In for what?"

"A little side surveillance. A second eye on the good doctor. Hell, Pete, they're not going to let you within a mile of her. This way you can keep an eye on everything, make sure it's copacetic."

He didn't trust Ryan's smile, or the shine in his eyes, but it was a way to be close to Ana, see what he could do to keep her safe. He nodded.

"Six o'clock," Ryan said. "Outside in the parking lot. Be on time or I go without you. Listen, I got to go, I'm late for a meeting. See you then."

He turned right at the next hallway intersection. Pete, glancing after him, saw the blond patrolman Jorgensen standing halfway down the hall, holding a door open. After Ryan was inside, the door clicked shut.

Pete continued on, intent on talking to the one person he could trust—Sister Teresa Gutierrez. Ana's aunt.

"Okay," Ryan said as the door clicked shut behind him. "We haven't got a lot of time, so let's get to it. Jorgensen, Stahlman, Waters, Kimball. Just us five, right?"

"Right," Jorgensen said. He nodded toward the other men in the room, all white, all about the same age. Three of them were Patrol, one El Paso police, and Sergeant Kimball was from the Army.

But none of that had anything to do with why they were here. This was unofficial.

Very unofficial.

"Okay," Ryan said. "How's the room?"

Sergeant Kimball held up a small electronic monitor. "Room's clean. We're okay here."

"Good enough. That thing check for wires, too?"

"Any outgoing transmissions." Kimball nodded. "I've identified every electronic signature in here, and I picked this room because it's soundproofed. Nobody's listening."

Ryan turned to Jorgensen. "They're asking questions about the backpack. You're sure nobody saw you pick it up?"

"I'm sure. I covered it up before I bagged it."

Ryan turned to Kimball. "You examined it. What's the verdict?"

"It's an extremely new kind of plastique, developed in Germany the last couple of years for the military. Pretty stable, but I wouldn't put a cigarette out in it. It's also carcinogenic, according to the Germans. Nice stuff." Kimball opened a pack of gum and offered it around; only Jorgensen took a stick. "Nice big boom, as you saw."

Ryan's lips thinned. "We saw. Cruz fired the first shot, but the question is, are we going to shoot back? Or are we going to roll over?"

Silence around the table. Jorgensen chewed his gum and finally leaned forward and said, "I don't think any of us would be here if we weren't prepared to hit them back, sir. Like you said, it's a war now. We've known it was coming, and some of us have been preparing for it. My group's ready to defend their homes and their neighbors against invasion, and we're prepared to take it to the enemy, too. They want to come over the border, we'll blow their asses away this time."

"Cruz doesn't have a headquarters," one of the other men put in. "He's a traveler. We can't hit him back."

"Yes, we can," Ryan corrected. "And I know how to do it. It's a surgical strike, not a lot of mess, and it'll get the message across, believe me. Best of all, I've got somebody to take the blame for it. It's all working just fine."

Kimball said, "I've got it rigged for a timer or a manual trigger. Which one do you want?"

"Timer," Ryan said. "I want us all to be visible when it blows. Alibis are very important now, gentlemen. But we have to stand together, because *they* damn sure are. It's time for a little patriotism."

"I want to be sure we're not going to be sloppy on this. No Americans dead. We want to hit the illegals only." Kimball again. Ryan eyed him, the crisp military posture, the fatigues, the cold blue eyes. A man who wouldn't hesitate to give his life for his country.

"Believe me, Sergeant Kimball, we won't take a single American life," he said. "And as far as the rest of them go, it's every wetback for himself."

Sister Teresa was sitting in the small, sparse waiting area under the watchful eye of two military guards, but relief spread across her face when she saw Pete emerge from the hallway. She stood up to greet him, and he was surprised by how small she was. She always seemed tall and strong to him, in memory, but maybe that was just the size of her will. He offered her his hand, and she gave him a warm, unreserved smile.

"Is that how you greet old friends, Pete?" she asked, and spread her arms wide. He hugged her, careful not to squeeze too hard. "I've wondered about you. How you were."

"I've been okay," he said, and pulled away to lead her to one of the two folding chairs along the wall. "As well as can be expected, I guess."

She reached out and brushed her fingertips across the cut on his forehead. "Stitches," she said. "Very dashing. Peter, I can only thank God that you survived. And I pray you can forgive whoever did this."

"They think it's Ana."

"It isn't," she said quite calmly. "You know that. Ana is sometimes thoughtless, and she can be cruel when she's frightened, but she isn't capable of this kind of atrocity. Killing—yes, she could kill if her life was in danger, or to save another. But she would not murder. She takes her oaths more seriously."

"Like you."

Teresa smiled again. "So far as I know, Ana is not a nun. But then I am only her aunt, not her confessor."

"I don't know whether to believe her or not. I know she hates the Anglos for what she thinks we've done to her people. It's personal to her."

Silence as she regarded him, her hands folded in

her lap. She carried a kind of stillness with her that always reminded him of deep lakes and deeper skies; she looked as if nothing had ever touched her placid surface.

"Would you like to hear a story?" she asked. "There was once a very young nun, and she was a very angry soul. She traveled to Central America with four other nuns to teach in schools—to teach about freedom, and patriotism, and injustice. She was very passionate. So passionate, in fact, that several of her students took up arms and were shot by the military as rebels."

Pete sat still, watching her, aware that he was hearing something that had always been in the back of his mind about her, some hint of old pain and rage. She continued to meet his eyes, and hers were very dark.

"She was summoned back to the chapter house with her sisters. Before they could arrive, they were arrested and put in prison. Prison was very hard, but what was harder was the knowledge that the other nuns were paying the price for her idealism. Two of them died. All of them suffered greatly. It took many years to learn to put that anger aside into God's hands, Peter. I think perhaps that anger runs in our family."

"I'm sorry," he said.

She shook her head. "Forgive Ana her youth and her rage. She came by it honestly, from an aunt who perhaps did not trust God enough to let him direct the world he made. She will learn, Peter."

"If she lives," he said. "I'm afraid for her."

Sister Teresa had a rosary in her fingers, he realized. She worked the beads absently, with a precision that showed long practice.

"Did you love her once?" she asked.

He felt uncomfortable at saying it to her, but he tried to answer honestly. "I did. I still care about her, I can't help that. And I want her to know—" He hadn't meant to use Teresa as a messenger, but the chance seemed too precious to miss. "I want her to know I never meant to hurt her. I did what I thought was best, and so did she. We should be able to agree on that."

"Yes," she said. "You should. Is there anything else?"

He thought about Esmeralda's warning, Ana's danger, but he thought maybe it was already too late for that. The darkness had already arrived, in the shape of a cloud of black smoke and the rubble of a mass grave. And whatever danger Ana was in, she'd earned.

"No," he said. "Just tell her—if anything happens to me, I want her to know I forgive her."

Teresa looked up at him, eyes suddenly very sharp, very focused. "Is something going to happen to you?"

He smiled palely. "It already has. But they say it's in remission now."

"Ah." It was a sound of pain, not a comment; Teresa abandoned the rosary and took his hand in hers. She squeezed tightly and he squeezed back. "Peter, I'm so sorry. But God looks after you, I know he does. Trust him. Live."

She didn't mean *stay alive*. She meant *live well*. He understood the message.

"I will," he said. "Her name's Esmeralda. You'd like her."

"I'm sure I would." Teresa looked past him as the military guard answered a ringing phone. "How much longer before they let her go, do you think?"

"Not long. They should be bringing her out soon. Listen, I'd rather she not see me here. It might be—"

"I know." Her smile took him by surprise, and he had to return it. "God bless you, Peter."

"You too," he said, and walked out the door into the cold, crisp air. The gravel in front of the building was a neat, even white, raked smooth, with larger gray border stones beyond. A line of soldiers jogged past on the road, chanting. Overhead, jets combed the blue sky, their thunder following late and distant.

It could all fall apart, he knew. All the appearance of unity, all the ideals. It would be so easy for them to turn on each other. There was so much blame to be spread around, like the gravel in front of him, a little piece for everybody. And with the blame, reasons to hate.

He wondered how Teresa had found the strength to give it up.

He didn't know if he ever could. He'd dug up so many reasons out of the rubble, and they didn't want to stay buried, no matter how hard he tried.

Chapter 20

November 25, 1996
Rámon Cruz

Rámon had many friends, and some of them worked for the government—not high in it, because they weren't the right color or the right class, but in positions where information passed through their hands.

And so he learned that the FBI was coming to Ana Gutierrez's clinic, to search for contraband. For him.

No one panicked. He let Ana believe it was another normal day, the kind of day she'd come to expect, and once she was downstairs he gave the order to evacuate. His men gathered their supplies in an orderly manner; many of them had been soldiers in one army or another, and they all understood the importance of planning. Miguel oversaw the loading of the van in the dim morning light while Rámon sat on Ana's couch, not a care in the world, flicking channels until Miguel sent word that everything was ready.

He turned off the television and looked around to see that Gabriel Gutierrez had rolled himself to the door of his room and was watching. There was cold satisfaction in the *incapacitado's* eyes. Rámon knew the boy wanted him dead, and he respected that. Gabriel was a lion—a crippled lion, but that made his teeth no less sharp.

"You're leaving," Gabriel said. Under the bruises on his face, muscles rippled at his jawline. "Good. Fuck you."

"You're going with us," Rámon said, and at his signal two waiting soldiers picked up Gabriel, wheelchair and all, and they didn't have any trouble pinning the boy's muscular arms to his sides. Gabriel raged curses until Rámon got up and took his blue bandanna from around his neck, knotted it, and shoved it into Gabriel's mouth. He held up a finger in front of Gabriel's face, and he saw a shadow of fear in the boy's eyes. "You don't have to die, boy. Just be quiet and follow orders, and you can come home to your sister again. Simple, yes?"

The boy was humiliated, his whole body trembling with the force of it. Rámon understood that, too. A man didn't surrender so easily. He nodded to the soldiers, who loaded Gabriel in the elevator. Rámon made one last circuit of the room, checking for any signs of their presence; they'd left fingerprints, but that didn't matter. He wanted them to know who he was.

They still had more than an hour when the van pulled away from the back of *La Clínica* and they disappeared into morning traffic, just another cargo van in a stream of metal. Rámon kept an eye on Gabriel, but the boy seemed resigned now, or biding his time. That was all right. *Wait*, he told the boy in his mind. *You'll have a chance.*

There was always a chance—that was something every good general acknowledged. There were no perfect plans, no safe retreats. A tire could blow on the van. A police car could cut them off for some minor traffic violation. But he didn't think it would happen.

It was a very short drive. They unloaded the van quickly, efficiently, paying special attention to the green foot locker marked PROHIBIDO FUMAR in block stencil letters; Rámon sat in the passenger seat, watching, kneading his injured leg. The wound still ached badly. He couldn't put his full weight on it, but his fever had gone down, and he thought the swelling was less. Ana was a good doctor. He'd have to thank her later.

Gabriel was still in the van, the last thing to be unloaded, when Miguel climbed into the cargo door and knelt down behind Rámon's chair to speak over his shoulder.

"What do we do with him?" Miguel asked. "Better to get rid of him."

"No," Rámon said. "He's Ana's brother. I don't want her to have good reason to hate us. As long as we have him, we control her. I need—"

Whatever it was he needed, it was driven from his mind as Gabriel Gutierrez lunged forward out of his chair, flinging himself onto Miguel's back. Miguel grunted and started to turn. Rámon turned, too, and saw Gabriel drawing Miguel's gun from the holster at his hip. Impossible. But that was all right. Miguel was fast, very fast. He'd simply grab the boy's wrist and take the gun back, no harm done, it was all under control—

Miguel whirled, grabbed Gabriel's hand, and pushed the gun wide.

As he'd thought.

But Miguel's other hand came up glinting silver, a blur, and Gabriel's eyes went wide and fixed, searching blindly for something Rámon could not see, and an instant later blood jetted out of his slashed throat, a thick red spurt that splashed over Miguel as Miguel held the boy at arm's length.

The gun fell with a clatter.

"Miguel!" It was too late now, but Rámon shouted it, and Miguel turned to look at him. The life was going out of Gabriel Gutierrez's eyes with each fading beat of his heart. There was blood everywhere in the van, the stench of it thick in his throat. And still the boy wasn't dead. "I said to keep him alive!"

"*Lo siento.*" Miguel shrugged. *I'm sorry.* He let go of Gabriel. The boy fell to the van's bloody floor, his body twitching as the last of his life ran out. "It was a mistake. I'll take care of it."

It was not conscious thought that guided Rámon's hand to his gun; he did not know he was making a judgment until he put the muzzle of the gun to Miguel's temple and pulled the trigger, one quick explosion in the silence, and Miguel's eyes were still trying to puzzle out what had happened when death caught him and laid him out in a sprawl next to the body of his last victim.

Rámon's eyes filled with tears. He was still weeping when the soldiers came back to the van to find out what had happened, but he told them to dump Gabriel's body neatly in some distant alley and to dispose of Miguel in another.

Perhaps that was right, after all. Miguel was a soldier. He would understand.

Lo siento, he thought and crossed himself as Miguel's arms were crossed over his chest, the weathered face slack and peaceful. *But I can't let anyone disobey me. Not even you. Not when I'm so close.*

Chapter 21

November 25, 1996
Esmeralda Sanchez

It was cold, but she slept in spite of it, lulled by the lapping of the river and the whispers of the families who waited with her for darkness. She woke up to feel a hand touching her shoulder, a tentative touch, light as a ghost's. She blinked back mist and starlight and saw the boy in the red coat standing in front of her. The others were gone.

He didn't say anything. She wasn't sure he *could* speak. He turned and ran away down the alley, toward the gravel road that glimmered beside the river.

"I'm coming," she said, and pulled her coat closer as she followed the boy out of the close stench of the alley into the fishy smell of the river, careful of her footing because her shoes were old and slick-soled. The boy ran like a rabbit, hesitating in the few shadows, then darted forward like a streaking comet to the next covering bush or rusting barrel. There were more lights, she realized—not on the Mexican side, but on the American. Fierce, bright lights—she could almost feel their heat on her skin. Across the river, behind the glare, she could dimly see the razor wire of the fence.

She hurried after the boy, her shoes sliding on gravel, certain someone was watching her from behind those lights. But surely the Border Patrol had more to do now than chase after lonely immigrants. The bomb had seen to that.

The thought struck her so suddenly it almost dragged her to a halt: what if that was the point? What if the bomb was supposed to draw attention away from the *mojados*? She heard a siren wailing on the Mexican side of the border and hurried on, too frightened to examine the thought in detail. Capture by the Mexican guards was worse than capture by *la migra*; the *mordida*, the bribe required to buy indifference, was very high, and while not all the Mexican officials were corrupt, many were, and didn't care about the consequences of rape, beatings, or even murder.

She hurried. It was a long way back to the bridge, stumbling from one precarious cover to the next, the boy's red jacket a hint in the dark rather than a sign. She had time to wonder if she was deluding herself—not only about the boy, but about the loss of Jamie as well. Maybe she wanted to be left alone, to punish herself for taking a lover after all these years of calm celibacy. Maybe it wasn't Jamie's anger, but her own, that had robbed her of a spirit guide.

She heard the hoot of a train before she saw the bridge—it was mostly unlit, its iron frame invisible against the night sky unless the moon shone bright. The boy was scrambling up the rough hillside, back toward the city and away from the river; this was because the Black Bridge was on higher ground than the depleted river. She began to climb, earning scraped hands and stinging bruises before she made it to the top of the hill and the fence that blocked off access to the railroad property.

It looked solid. Impassable. She looked at the silver chain of it, speechless, baffled, until she heard a thin, sharp whistle to her left. There, next to the tracks, the boy crouched on the other side of the fence. He worked the fence back and forth, showing her that it had been cut at the post; it folded back like an accordion. Even so, it was a tight fit for a grown woman, and she hissed in pain as skin scraped metal and she felt the heat of blood on her legs where her pants had been torn. She squirmed free, let the fence snap closed again, and sat looking at the dim industrial buildings crowding close. The railroad tracks were barely visible in the shadows, and the train's hoot sounded ghostly, both near and far away.

When she looked for the boy, he had vanished. She stood up, rubbed her stinging hands, and turned to look at the American side of the border.

It was simple enough, she told herself. One step after another. There was enough light to see the railroad ties, the separated road to freedom; it wasn't as bad as she'd expected. On the other side, the industrial area was a twin to Juárez's, hardly any lights showing except a few for security. The Border Patrol's lights did not shine here, either because of funds or because they had been destroyed by earlier *mojados*.

The others who had been waiting had already

crossed, she thought, or they had turned back. She couldn't see anyone else on the bridge, but it was very dark. She thought she could see the firelight glimmer of the boy's red coat far ahead.

Behind her a reminder, the train's whistle.

"Simple," she said aloud, and took the first step onto the Black Bridge.

It began simply, but it quickly grew harder, as land receded behind her and all she could see was the dim, rushing river beneath, fed by recent rains and, they said, a wetter than normal year. When she put her hand on the cold, sharp-edged iron of the trestle, she thought she could feel vibration, but perhaps that was her own fear. She was careful where she stepped, but it was easy to miss the wooden plank, and her shoes were not as reliable as they might have been. She missed entirely once, felt her foot plunge between the ties and into darkness, felt air suck her greedily and heard the river whisper its hunger. She pulled back too quickly and lost her balance, falling against the trestle, grabbing for support. The iron cut into her palms and was almost painful enough to make her let go, but she held on as she placed her feet more carefully.

She was, she thought, about a third of the way across.

At halfway, she heard one of the ties creak alarmingly under her. Three steps further, a tie was missing altogether, and she held to the trestle and inched slowly along its narrow iron frame, her shoes loose on her feet and sliding uncertainly. By contrast, the creaking wood felt like dry land once she was past the gap. She held to the iron a moment longer, drawing strength, and heard the train whistle again. Louder.

She tried to hurry, but hurrying was dangerous— too easy to miss a step, plunge a foot between the slats, twist an ankle, or become irrevocably trapped. She forced herself to move steadily, though her heart was beating too fast and she knew her hands were shaking from more than the cold now.

She almost collided with the man in black. She saw him only because he turned sharply toward her as she approached, and under the black ski mask he wore he was white-skinned, his eyes pale. He loomed like a ghost out of the dark, and she froze, a cry locked in her throat.

What was he doing here?

She tried a tentative "*Señor*—" and knew as soon as she spoke that there was no reason for this man to be here, so strangely, on a bridge frequented by illegal immigrants. He was not *la migra*, or he would wear the uniform, or at least show her identification.

He moved before she could say another word, slamming a hand over her mouth, throwing her back against the iron trestle. Now that it would do no good, she screamed, the sound bubbling against his hot leather glove. *Fingerprints*, she thought, but that made no sense to her. What matter if there were fingerprints on a bridge?

"Shut up!" he hissed in her ear, and she heard a click of metal, saw the gleam of a knife.

He was going to kill her.

Chapter 22

November 25, 1996
Peter Ross

He didn't know why he was thinking about Esmeralda, except that sitting in a car with Joe Ryan gave him a lot of incentive to think of more pleasant things. He hoped she was warm tonight in her lonely house. He hoped Jamie had come back to her, even though he still couldn't believe in Jamie the way she did. He hoped she was thinking of him, because he was thinking of her, the way she had looked in the soft morning light, her eyes wide and full of secrets. He knew he would never forget that peculiar feeling of safety while she bathed him, her hands gentle on his skin.

Even though he missed her, he was glad she was out of this. He didn't like any of it anymore, not the anger that surged under everyone's skin, not the hate that barely kept itself hidden under badges and uniforms and civilian clothing. Everyone hated now.

Even him.

"Guess she's in for the night," Ryan said. "Coffee?"

"No, thanks." The last thing he wanted was cold, bitter coffee to go with his cold, bitter fear. Ana was acting like a criminal. She hadn't spoken up, she had attacked an FBI agent, she'd done everything but spit in their faces and claim to be a political prisoner. He hoped Teresa was right about her. He wondered why Teresa hadn't stayed when the FBI agent dropped Ana off.

"They're all out of the building now, right? All the patients?"

"All out," Pete said. They'd kept careful tally of who went in and out. FBI surveillance was parked on the other side of the building, by the service elevator Pete knew Ana used as a private entrance. There'd be other posts, of course, and electronic surveillance. Pete wasn't particularly worried about it. The FBI hadn't bothered to throw them out of the area, though clearly they must have known who they were. He and Ryan weren't exactly unrecognizable, sitting as obvious as stakeout cops in Ryan's own car.

"There's no sign of the brother yet, either. He shouldn't be that hard to find in a wheelchair, but the APB's not picking up anything. You've met him. Is he a radical, too?"

Pete remembered Gabriel from the wedding, a strong, tall, smiling young man who'd looked uncomfortable in a suit.

"Not that I remember, but I didn't know him very well. He was hit by a drunk driver a few years ago. Lost his legs."

"Yeah, I looked it up." Ryan paused to sip his coffee, or for effect. "A *white* drunk driver. The asshole served a year. He's out on the street."

"I did a little checking, too," Pete said. "Gabriel Gutierrez registered Republican the last five years. He did fund-raising for the party. Sound like a rebel to you?"

Ryan didn't answer. Pete couldn't help thinking back on the last time they'd sat in a car together, on the way to what would be a disaster, that would end with a wounded little girl and a missing backpack filled not with heroin, but with explosives. What the hell had happened to the backpack? Had it ended up in Border Patrol headquarters, killing his friends? He hoped not. The thought made him weak at the knees, that he'd been so close to stopping it and failed.

"Why're you still in this?" he asked aloud. Ryan looked surprised. "It isn't DEA anymore. It should be an ATF matter, if it's anybody's. I understand the FBI coordination, but—"

"I was in it, I'm staying in. It's a courtesy from one agency to another. Besides, the Bureau needs all the help it can get, and the ATF—" Ryan shook his head. "God help us, they're a walking public relations nightmare these days. They're taking the low profile on this one—on the case, but not on the air, if you know what I mean."

Pete took a deep breath and realized that he had to piss, badly—too much bad coffee during the day. He popped the door. Ryan held out a hand to stop him.

"Where you going?" He sounded unaccountably nervous.

"Pit stop," Pete said, and shut the door. There weren't any convenience stores, not that they'd have let the pope take a piss in the middle of the night in this neighborhood; he chose an alley and walked into the shadows, not too far, and unzipped his fly. By the smell of the place, he wasn't the first guy to do it, either. He wondered if the FBI agents had some kind of portajohn in their cars, to avoid the indignity of whizzing on a wall.

He finished and walked back. The night was very quiet, and as he turned the corner, the brick wall bounced words to him. Ryan's voice, from the car. A trick of the acoustics—he shouldn't have been able to hear at this distance.

"Shit!" Ryan said in a harsh whisper. "Then get rid of her, damn it. *Now!* Take care of her and get the hell out of there! The Germans said the shit was unstable, for God's sake. Don't take the chance!"

Ryan was talking on a radio. Pete stood perfectly still, listening, but Ryan must have turned away. He caught only a mumble and a click, and then silence.

Her? *Ana?* Take care of her?

They were going to kill Ana. That was what all this was about. Killing Ana. Life for a life. *Payback.*

Ryan never heard him coming; the other man was still fumbling with a small portable radio, trying to get it back in his jacket, when Pete reached in the open window and grabbed his tie, jerked it tight enough to make a noose out of it, and opened the car door. He held the silk garrote tight as Ryan gagged and followed his tug outside.

Pete had never drawn his gun in anger, but he was angry now, and there it was, in his hand, glinting under Ryan's chin like a skeletal finger. He hardly recognized his own voice.

"How are you going to do it?" The words grated.

They tasted electrical. "A bullet in her head? A knife? Blow her up? That'd make sense. Send a message, right?"

Ryan tried to yell for help, but Pete pressed harder with the gun. After a second or two Ryan spread his hands out to either side, palms open. Surrendering.

"Got me," he wheezed, and grinned. "Yeah. We're gonna kill her. Your bitch of an ex has it coming, am I right?"

No time to kill him.

Pete slammed Ryan back against the car and ran across the street toward the clinic. The lights were all off, the sign turned to CERRADO in the window. He battered hard at the door, saw lights come on upstairs. Curtains twitched. He backpedaled a couple of steps, willing her to look down at him.

"Ana!" he screamed. "Ana, goddamn it, get out of there! Ana!"

No answer. He abandoned the front door and ran to the side street, slammed a hand on the hood of a parked black sedan, startling the two FBI agents inside. Man and woman. They froze in the act of sipping coffee.

"Bomb!" he yelled. "In the clinic!"

They jumped out of the car. Well practiced, they split up as they ran, the woman heading for the front, the man to the side entrance. Pete followed the female agent back to the front door and kicked in the glass, ignoring the razor stroke of splinters in his leg, reached inside, and turned the lock. Bells rang a raucous alarm. He slammed the door open and skidded inside, screamed Ana's name and tore aside gauzy treatment curtains until he found the door to her apartment upstairs. Locked. He kicked it in and took the steps two at a time toward the darkness at the top. He was dimly aware of the female agent's footsteps behind him.

Something came at him out of the dark as he reached the top step. He slipped trying to avoid it, went to one knee, and heard the hiss of disturbed air as something missed his head by inches. It slammed hard into the wall next to him, and he had a quick glimpse of the familiar shape of the weapon.

A baseball bat. On the other end of it Ana, dressed in a pale cotton nightgown, her hair wild over her face.

He lunged forward, the bat cracking painfully off his shoulder as she tried for another swing; he tackled her with bruising force to the floor, grabbed her wrist, and twisted her still.

"Ana," he said. "It's me. It's me! No time—"

The female agent had reached them. He heard the efficient metallic click of her weapon being taken off safety.

"Federal agent, ma'am, you're under arrest, for your own safety." The agent's eyes flicked to Pete. "Anybody else here?"

"No," Ana muttered. Pete tossed the baseball bat out of the way, let go of her and squirmed away, left her getting to her knees, her nightgown twisted crooked, her eyes wide in astonishment. He grabbed her and pushed her toward the steps.

"Outside," he said. "Go, damn it!"

Hell of a time for Ana to turn stubborn, but she leaned against his tug. The FBI agent put her weapon back on safety and holstered it. She grabbed Ana's other arm and boldly threw her toward the steps, where the other FBI agent caught hold. Very efficiently done. Pete exchanged a look with the female agent.

"You said bomb," she said, still eerily calm. "Where?"

"I don't know," he said. He was cut off by an explosion that rattled through the wood floor and shivered loose objects.

Outside the south-facing windows, the Black Bridge exploded in a fireball that turned night into day.

Chapter 23

November 25, 1996
The Bridge

He was talking to someone on a hand-held telephone, the words too whispered and rapid for Esmeralda to understand in English. She stayed where she was, frozen by fright and the dizzy surety that she was going to die here, killed by a man whose face she couldn't even see. She caught a glimpse of what the man held in his other hand—it looked like some kind of canvas bag. As she watched, he pitched it out onto the bridge behind her.

Behind, in the darkness, she heard the soft voices of *mojados*. The others hadn't crossed ahead of her; they were crossing behind. They had waited, but the train was catching up to them. She heard its whistle in the distance.

One of the children began to sing in a wavering, pure voice, a nonsense children's song of the *barrio* she remembered singing to Jaime when he was a baby; someone shushed the boy.

A child who sings. She remembered it with a physical intensity like a bolt of lightning. *Fire.* Jaime's warning.

She bit the hand over her mouth, bit hard enough
to taste the salty copper of blood through thick
leather; as soon as he let go, she screamed in Spanish,
"Jump! For the love of God, jump now!"

She twisted away from the man and ducked under
one of the iron X-shaped supports of the trestle, felt
emptiness below her and darkness at her back, heard
him curse, and knew the knife was coming. *Jaime*,
she thought, confused, because at the last he was her
only thought, and then she jumped.

The knife left a shallow wound in her back, almost
the size of the glass that had pierced her breast. The
fall felt surprisingly peaceful. She wanted to fall forever into this velvet darkness, no fear now, nothing
but love.

The world exploded in orange rage above. She saw
her own reflection rushing toward the water and
thought, *It's been a good life*, just as the water slammed
into her with the force of a punch and she knew
nothing else at all.

The female agent's face was painted a vivid bright
orange in the explosion, like sunset. Pete turned
away from her toward the glow and saw the Black
Bridge swaying, iron flying away from it in slow motion, supports buckling. The thunder of the explosion
faded and left the weirdly human scream of the
bridge collapsing in the sudden darkness. In the distance Pete heard cries of panic.

Ana came pelting back up the steps, grabbed Pete's
arm, and blurted, "What? What was it? Oh, God—"

"The bridge," the female agent answered for him.
She sounded dazed, still calm but not entirely by her

own choice. She shook it off and keyed her radio as
her partner stepped out of the stairwell behind Ana.
"This is FBI Agent Saletti, in position at the free
clinic. We've got a major explosion at the railroad
trestle crossing the Rio Grande, repeat, major explosion, we need fire and rescue."

After a short delay the radio crackled numbers
back to her, evidently confirming her message received; she looked at her partner and he said, "Tell
them to stop the train."

She conveyed the message with the speed of someone who hadn't thought of the possibility. The male
agent turned to Pete and said, "You're Ross, right?
Do you think they were trying to get the train?"

Pete thought of the night they'd watched all the
immigrants come across the Black Bridge, he and
Ryan, all those silver shadows inching along the
empty trestle. And he knew.

"It's not the train they wanted," he said, amazed
he could say it so calmly. "They wanted to kill
illegals."

And he was sure, without a doubt, that they'd
succeeded.

Esmeralda's lungs burned. She came back awake
with a startled cough that drew water in, gasped for
air and got more water. It was so black, so cold, there
was no way to tell where she was.

Above her, distantly, a fading orange glow. She
reached for it, remembering finally the fall, the explosion. It seemed so very far above her, as unattainable
as the sun.

She thought of Jaime, waiting for her on the other

side. Her father, her mother, both taken early. Her sister. With so much comfort waiting, the effort of climbing to the sun seemed useless.

Mama. Jaime's voice. She opened her eyes to stinging cold water. *It's not time. Not yet.*

Mijo. A single, loving word that rose out of her soul to him.

Whether she wanted to or not, she was rising toward the sun. Her hand reached for it, and she felt clear, cold air an instant before her head burst out of the water in a coughing, choking flurry.

Living *hurt*.

For a second or two nothing was more important than the sweet taste of air, and then she realized how cold it was, how swift the current. She was being pulled beneath the bridge. She began to swim for the nearest bank—the American side—with weakened, pain-heavy arms. Her lungs couldn't seem to hold breath.

Someone called for help in Spanish. She changed direction and swam blindly, listening between strokes. She knew she had little time before the water sucked all her strength away, and her coat was already weighing her down. She shrugged it off and heard the man call again, panic raw in his voice.

"Where are you?" she yelled, and coughed at the effort. The river tried to invade her mouth again, and she swam harder to stay above the surface. *"Señor!"*

"Aquí." A weak whisper, so close she could almost touch it.

She'd found him. He had a broken arm, but he was hanging onto the little boy in the red coat. She dragged them both laboriously toward the bank until the man, taller than she, got his feet under him and began to wade in the slippery mud.

Something groaned high above them. As her own feet finally touched the ground and lifted her shoulders out of the water, the child in her arms, she looked up and saw the dim shadow of something falling. The bridge was collapsing around them.

El Puente Negro was determined to have her.

Even the FBI agents forgot about the division between suspect and police, and ignored Ana's presence as she ran with them past parked cars toward the still burning bridge. She held Pete's hand in hers and wouldn't let go, though his long legs forced her to run fast to keep up; her house shoes were unequal to the demands of the street and then the gravel as they arrived at the road leading toward the railroad tracks. The female FBI agent was first to the fence; she yanked on it and nearly fell as it slid aside, neat as a curtain on a line. Her partner ducked through, taking the long hill down toward the river at a run.

Ana understood immediately. Victims, or survivors, would be down there, not up here.

The bridge was coming down, a hail of severed girders and broken ties. The whole center section dropped free with a huge tearing crash, sending water up toward the sky, throwing mist on her face as she slid down the steep hillside, her nightgown catching and tearing on rock, her skin burning. She made it to the bottom and realized that Pete was no longer with her. She didn't have time to look for him; she spotted someone struggling in the current and without any hesitation dove into the icy water.

The water was so cold it felt like a burn, and she immediately gasped for breath and got a mouthful of what tasted like oil. She spat it out and forced her sluggish muscles to work. The woman she'd seen vanished under the water, and Ana dove, her hands blindly reaching for anything she could grab.

Nothing. She came up for a gagging breath and dove again, terrified that she'd already lost the woman, terrified that she would never come up herself.

Her nightgown hooked on something sharp below the surface of the water.

She was caught. She twisted and tugged, her skin numb from the cold, felt the current drag at her, gave the fabric one frenzied jerk, and drifted free.

Her fingers brushed something else.

A cold, drifting hand.

She grabbed hold.

Esmeralda dove, pushed off from the mud, and arrowed for the safety of the bank, pulling the boy with her; something slammed into the water where they'd been and knocked her aside like a toy in a bathtub; she lost her grip on the red coat and the boy tumbled away, lost in the current, lost.

She came up with a raw scream and struck after him. Her arms and legs were aching with cold and weariness, but she would not give up. Could not.

Jaime, she thought. *Ayude me. Please, God, help me save at least one.*

She flailed into the dark, felt something cloth-slick and pulled. It slid out of her cold fingers. She lunged after it as it sank, found the child's arm, pulled him up like a rag doll. The current sucked at them both. They had been carried far from shore and now they were in the treacherous middle of the river, where the bottom dropped deep and it was impossible to wade against the current. They were being swept downstream.

God give me strength. God give me strength.

Agent Saletti was on her radio, shouting rapid-fire information as her partner stripped off his coat and shoes and dove into the rolling water. Another girder fell, this one from the other side; loose ties rained like thrown bricks, any of them heavy enough to smash a man's head like a melon. Pete scanned the water for bodies and located one, floating facedown; it was barely visible against the darkness, wouldn't have been visible at all except for the lingering orange fire on the ravaged bridge. He dove and was angrily shoved aside by the current; he stroked hard to where he remembered the body had been. How much time, if the man was even alive? Something hit the water with a huge splash, either a girder or a railroad tie, and his skin crawled with the nearness of the hit. No time to think of that. *Swim.*

The taste of the river was familiar. He remembered nights like this, cold water, futile dives into the water for missing children. God, how often—

His fingers touched the waterlogged bulk of a sweater. He wrapped an arm across the man's chest, got his face out of the water, and began to swim back for the bank. He couldn't tell if he was towing a corpse, but he knew he had only minutes before the chill sapped his strength and took them both.

There were floodgates downstream where the bodies ended up, smashed like toys between driftwood and iron grilles.

He couldn't see Ana anywhere. He swam for the only thing he could guide by, the FBI agent with her radio, standing on the riverbank.

He made it just as Ana heaved herself out of the water, towing a dark-haired woman.

The male FBI agent didn't come back.

The world narrowed to her will and the river. Esmeralda no longer thought of the child whose head she held above water; he was part of her now, and they would live or die together. She would not give him up.

They were far from the bridge, so far it was a glimmer of fire and a suggestion of twisted black metal, and the water roared in her ears like a crowd as it pushed her farther from shore. She tried to swim, tried with every muscle, but she was shaking with cold and exhausted. She floated, face straining to the sky, holding the boy close, and let the river take them.

"Hold on!" yelled a voice in English. She blinked foul water from her eyes and looked behind her, saw a pallid Anglo man in a white shirt and tie being swept toward them. No, he was *swimming* toward them. He slowed, treading water, and grabbed hold of her. His skin was icy, but hers was numb. "Hold on, I've got you!"

He began to swim for all of them, and she thought how strange it was to be saved by a man as white as the one who'd put her in the water, how very strange life was, and she knew Jaime was smiling at the joke, too.

They made the far side of the river—the Mexican side. They lay gasping on the bank, chilled beyond thought, but the thought of the little boy spurred Esmeralda to move. She stripped the boy's soggy red coat away and saw that his eyes were closed. When she moved him, muddy water flowed from his nose.

She screamed and rolled him onto his back and pumped his lungs with her hands. When she was sure the water was out, she began breathing into his mouth, fumbling at it because she had never tried before. The Anglo man moved her aside and checked for a pulse at the boy's neck, shook his head, and compressed the boy's chest, over and over, signaling for her to breathe.

She almost missed the boy's slight movement, out of rhythm with her efforts; she was very close to collapse, her vision gone gray from strain. The man looked ashen as she tugged on his arm and pointed down at the boy's face.

The boy was breathing. The man checked the side of the boy's neck and said something in English that sounded like a prayer.

Esmeralda put her arms around the Anglo man and said, "Thank you."

He seemed surprised. He was awkward at it, but his arms went around her and he hugged her in return, and they rocked together for a precious eternity over the body of the boy they'd saved together.

Chapter 24

The man Pete had pulled out of the water was still alive, but he had broken bones and a fractured skull, and his back was burned away. He was wearing what looked like paramilitary gear, and there were no tags in his clothes, no identification on his body. The female FBI agent, who Pete finally realized was named Saletti, rolled up his ski mask to reveal a slack-jawed Anglo face that Pete dimly remembered seeing at the temporary bombing investigation headquarters on base.

"Know him?" she asked. He shook his head and coughed, bringing up muddy water. They were all going to have pneumonia. "I think his name is Kimball, but I'm not sure. One thing's for sure, he doesn't work for Rámon Cruz."

Ana was shivering with cold; Agent Saletti took her own coat and wrapped it around both Ana and the victim she'd saved, a frightened Mexican woman who shook her head in answer to any questions. Even now she was afraid of *la migra*. There was no way to know how many had been on the bridge.

Down the bank, Pete found a man with a broken arm and two more women who'd somehow fought their way to shore; one of them was crying and asking for her husband. Pete looked out on the river and knew that if the man was out there, he was dead; there was no way he could go into the water and come out again. Agent Saletti couldn't swim.

"Did you find Garman?' she asked; she'd followed him down the bank. "My partner?"

"No." He had to stop and cough again, more water mixed with phlegm. God, he was cold. There were sirens above. Ambulances coming. He couldn't face the idea of being another news story.

Ryan. He'd almost forgotten. He turned back to Saletti, who was looking out at the river with dawning terror on her face.

"Look, he could be on the other side. Get back up to the top of the hill, tell them we've got survivors down here. And don't tell anybody I was here."

"What? I can't—"

"Yes, you can. If the newspapers get hold of me, they won't leave a chewed rag behind. Tell your superiors I'll talk to them tomorrow, but I've got to find Ryan right now."

"Joe Ryan? DEA?" Her face lit up with understanding. "You guys weren't supposed to be here."

"Something like that. Get up the hill. I'll wait until you come back."

Truth was, he couldn't have made it up the hill himself at the moment. Too cold, too tired. He sank down on his haunches and looked up at the twisted

wreckage of the bridge as she started climbing. Since
a train didn't come hurtling off it, he assumed they'd
caught it in time.

*I'm going to be answering questions for the rest of my
natural life,* he thought. But at least he had a few
more years to do it in.

Ana was where he'd left her, shivering in Saletti's
coat, trying to calm the *mojada* sitting with her. She
turned blindly toward him as he sank next to her,
opened the coat to let him have a taste of heat. She
smelled like the rotting river; they all did.

"Like your new perfume," he mumbled. She
laughed, but the laughter became tears.

"Why? Why do this?" she choked out. He
smoothed her short, dark hair.

"Because they wanted to send a message. Hurt us,
we hurt you. Death for death. I guess the only merciful thing is they didn't kill as many." He pulled back
to look at her. He could do it now without any con-
flicting anger, bitterness, or hurt. Whatever they'd
done to each other, it was past. "It's us on a larger
scale, Ana."

She coughed, deep, racking coughs that spilled
water out to the dirt, and he held her head until
it passed.

"I'm sorry," she gasped. "I knew how you felt
about abortion. I'm sorry I had one."

And there it was, out between them, after so many
years of misdirection and misplaced anger. He remembered her fragile, defiant harshness the day
she'd told him. *I know it's a sin, but I'm not going to
have the baby. You want to leave, you leave. I'm not carrying around a reminder of you.*

It had been the last thing between them, the very last. He'd hated her so much for that.

And now he knew how to forgive.

"It's past," he said, and held her close against the chill. "Please don't cry."

But she did, anyway. She cried until the paramedics arrived and wrapped her in blankets and hot packs and pulled her up the hill to the waiting ambulance. Pete watched them carry up the others, refusing treatment except for a warm, dry blanket and hot packs. Agent Saletti picked her way down the hill to put a hand on his shoulder.

"My partner's alive," she said. "The Mexican police found him and two survivors on the far side, a woman and a little boy. I think that's everybody."

He nodded. His shivering had abated, and he was starting to feel light-headed with exhaustion.

"Think you can walk up the hill?" she asked. He nodded. She cocked a cool eyebrow. "Think you can wear Agent Garman's trench coat and put on these sunglasses and pretend you're FBI until I can get you out of here?"

Ryan was gone, but the story unraveled surprisingly quickly. Agent Saletti, Pete discovered, had a taste for chewing ass, and knew how to do it constructively. Ryan was apprehended on his way to Sierra Blanca; he relied on his Fifth Amendment rights and refused to say anything at all. Lacking any pressure on him, they turned to the man in the hospital, Kimball, and when he regained consciousness, they got a few other names. Jorgensen, for one. Pete was sorry to hear that, but he remembered watching

Ryan go into a closed meeting, Jorgensen standing at the door. It fit.

It was the next day, and he was mostly whole again except for an all-over body ache and phlegmy deep-chest coughs that the doctor said was perfectly natural. His shoulder ached from tetanus and booster shots. Agent Saletti looked as perfectly composed and coifed as ever, but her partner—who had finally been formally introduced to him as Agent Garman— looked like death warmed over. It had been a long swim for him, followed by a brisk life-saving chest compression.

"They planned to incriminate you," Garman said over lunch—Mexican food, of course. He and Agent Saletti were enchanted with the local cuisine. Saletti had fallen in love with refried beans and green sauce. "Jorgenson found the backpack at the clinic while Dr. Gutierrez was busy talking to the paramedics and you were coordinating with the local police. He looked inside and showed it to Ryan, and Ryan hid it because he thought it was evidence of a complete DEA screw-up. Bad enough that one of them put a bullet in a ten-year-old girl when she wasn't even carrying drugs. Apparently he got suspicious about the contents of the backpack and had his lab run an analysis of a sample. They identified it as explosive."

"When was this?" Pete asked. He tried to take a bite of sour cream enchilada, but nothing tasted right. Antibiotics.

"Two days before the bomb went off. There's no way to tell if Ryan could have prevented the bombing, but if he'd shared the information, it's possible something might have gone right." Garman handed around a plastic basket of flour tortillas, took one, and smeared butter on it. "But he kept his mouth shut. Once the bomb went off, he was stuck."

"Why bomb the bridge?"

"This is where it gets strange," Saletti said. In the light of day, she was a slender young woman, fresh-faced, with thick, dark hair and a mouth that always seemed to be smiling. She took a bite of sauce-laden refried beans on a flour tortilla. "We think Kimball had ties to a paramilitary organization that was basically a front for white supremacists. We also think Ryan might have been a member. The others don't seem to have been, but they fell in line in the aftermath of the bombing. Ryan talked a good line of hate. He convinced them that striking back at what was known as an immigrant highway was a simple countermove against a militant Hispanic terrorist."

"Jorgensen lost a lot of good friends," Garman agreed. "The other guys, too."

"We all did," Pete said. "That's not an excuse."

Garman looked down at his place, pushed Spanish rice from one side to another. He reached for a golden-brown sopapilla and poured honey inside.

"Never had these before," he said. "I did two years at the field office in Dallas, but they make it different there. No sopapillas. I like these."

Saletti offered Pete a bite of cheese enchilada. When he shook his head, she said, "Phil and I worked the bombing in Oklahoma City. Believe me, no matter how much logic you apply, it's tough not to want revenge."

He looked up at them, her young face and old eyes, Garman's haggard, haunted expression.

"I know all about it," he said. "But if we don't stop this right here, right now, this whole city will come apart. More than ninety-five percent of this town speaks Spanish at home. More than a quarter of them don't know English at all. Almost thirty percent live in poverty, and ten percent of the Anglos control ninety percent of the wealth. You want to talk about revenge? If this city gets going, it's going to make the L.A. riots look like protest marches."

Saletti put down her bite of refried beans. Garman sighed and shook his head.

"So what's the answer?" he asked.

Pete considered the remains of his sour cream enchilada. "I wish to hell I knew."

That afternoon he went to see Esmeralda. He walked the familiar route, across the bridge, carrying a sack of groceries, down the hill and onto Calle Gavanza. He knocked on the door of her house, knocked again, shifted the groceries from one arm to the other, looked in the window. The living room was unchanged, the table in place, Jaime's picture still standing up.

Esmeralda wasn't home.

He left the groceries on the front porch and walked around through the gate to the back door, but she wasn't there, either. Her backyard was mostly dirt, though she had managed to coax a few pansies out of the hard ground near the door. A small chicken-wire pen held three hens, a magnificent dark red rooster, and a small wooden laying hutch. From the way the chickens were pecking the dirt, they hadn't eaten; he found the feed and scattered it for them, not sure he was doing it right, not even sure how much they needed. He wasn't a farm boy.

It didn't feel right. She should have been home.

At the corner of Calle Gavanza and Internacional, he saw the modest stone shape of a church. He went in without much knowing why, except that when Esmeralda was distressed he knew she liked to pray, and if she'd heard about the Black Bridge, she was probably very upset. He stood at the back of the small church for a few minutes, letting his eyes adjust to the dimness, before dipping his fingers in the font and crossing himself. There were a few women in the church, most wearing mantillas that covered their heads, but he didn't think any of them looked like—

"Can I help you?" asked a man in English. He looked around to see a cassocked priest standing next to him, surveying the church. "I'm Father Fernando."

"Father. I'm Peter Ross. I'm looking for someone— a friend—" He didn't know how to being to classify Esmeralda. "Someone I've lost."

"Who?"

"Her name is Esmeralda Sanchez. She lives—" He stopped because Father Fernando's face had lit up. He nodded happily and smiled.

"Yes, Esmeralda, of course. But she's lost? I thought she was at the hospital."

"Hospital?" Pete felt as if he'd missed a step. "Is she hurt?"

"Oh, no, they say she is all right, just very tired. But she's staying with the boy, the one she saved from the river last night when the railroad blew up. They're at Hospital de la Inocente."

"When—" Pete took a deep breath. "Never mind. How do I get there?"

Esmeralda was asleep in a chair next to the bed of a little boy who was asleep, too. He didn't really look like Jaime, but he looked very fragile, hooked to tubes. His eyelashes were as long as Esme's.

God, she looked so pale.

Pete took her hand as she slept and watched as she came awake. She raised her head from her arms and saw him without recognition at first. Then her eyes widened, and before she could say his name, he leaned in and kissed her, a long, warm, loving kiss that left them wrapped together. He held her tightly and said her name over and over until she winced and he realized that she was wearing a bandage along the right side of her back.

"I hear you're a hero," he said. "Again. Aren't you making a habit of this kind of thing?"

"I was there, Peter, I saw it. It was just like Jaime said. There was a child singing, and there was fire— oh, God, Pedro, all those people. I was so scared."

He smoothed her warm, curly hair back from her face to look at her again. *She was there?*

"You were where exactly?"

"On the bridge." She took a deep breath. "I was trying to get to Ana, because I didn't warn her—"

He had to close his eyes against the certainty of how close he'd come to losing her. "Why didn't you just come across the border?"

"My papers were at your apartment, I left them— I had to do it, Peter, I had to come. I don't know why." She pulled back a little to glance at the boy on the bed. "I *didn't* know. But I saw the man put the sack on the bridge. He tried to kill me. A white man."

"I know," he said. "I was there, too. I saw it explode. The experts say it went off early. Nobody knows what triggered it—"

If he'd known she was up there, he would have gone mad. Maybe that was why God had spared him the knowledge, to keep his mind on the job. He traced the line of her cheek with his fingers and thought again how lucky he had been, how incredibly lucky.

The boy on the bed opened his eyes and coughed. Esmeralda reached over and took his hand. She squeezed his fingers until the boy's roving eyes found her, and he smiled.

"*Pobrecito*," she said. "It's all right. *Esta bien.*"

"Who is he?" Pete asked. She smoothed the boy's hair back, let her hand drift over his forehead.

"No one knows. He can't talk. They call him Juanito. They think his parents died when the bomb went off."

There had been four bodies found, all drowned, none of them carrying identification. There'd probably been more killed, but it would take days for the bodies to be found, maybe weeks. He avoided thinking of that job, grateful that at least it wasn't his this time.

"How is Agent Garman?" she asked, and surprised him into laughter. "He saved my life, mine and Juanito's. I couldn't have made it alone."

"He's fine." *If he survived the hot sauce at lunch.* "Es—"

She turned to look at him, her smile a slice of teasing heaven, her eyes warm and glowing. "Everything's all right," she said. "It's over now."

But he knew it wasn't. Not as long as Rámon Cruz was out there, waiting.

Chapter 25

The room at the bombing investigation headquarters had not changed, and neither had the faces in it. Three FBI agents, whose names Ana did not remember, and someone from the Border Patrol as an observer. An El Paso police detective sat on a folding chair in the corner.

"Coffee?" the agent asked, the same one who'd questioned her last time. She took the cup black and sipped the hot liquid without tasting it. What she was about to do sickened and terrified her, but she had no choice.

Do the right thing, Ana, he'd said, her brother, the brave one. After watching the explosion last night, after seeing the death and the terror, she couldn't do anything else.

"Okay, Ana, we're ready to listen if you're ready to talk," he said. "I'm Agent Miller, these are Agents Simons and Galvan."

She nodded, automatic courtesy, and took a deep breath. She could still taste the foul green river when she swallowed.

"I know Rámon Cruz," she said. "He was at the clinic, but he left before you got there yesterday. I haven't heard from him since."

"Why didn't you tell us this yesterday?" he asked very gently. "Were you afraid?"

Her eyes filled with tears. "He said there's a bomb in a school. He said he'd blow it up if I said anything. Please, you have to find the school. It's a private Anglo school, it has big white columns—"

Agent Miller sat back in his chair, staring at her in shock for a second, then turned to one of the other agents and told him to get photographs of every private school in the city. The agent left at a run.

"He has my brother, too," she said. Tears had collected in her eyes, blurring her vision, and now threaded cold down her cheeks. "Gabriel. He's in a wheelchair. He said he'd kill him if I didn't cooperate."

She cried for a while in silence while they all watched. Agent Miller gave her some tissues, and she wiped her eyes and blew her nose, feeling foolish and empty. She was a little comforted by the compassion on his face, whether it was real or imagined.

"We'll find him," he said. "Ana, this is important—did you know he was going to plant the bombs?"

"He—" She felt something catch in her chest, like a pulled string. "He asked me to hold a package for him. I didn't think there was anything wrong with it. I—that was just before the first bomb. He hid it in my clinic. I didn't know it was a bomb."

It sounded pitiful. Stupid. She swallowed a mouthful of shame and looked away as Agent Miller judged her and found her wanting. After a while his chair scraped, and he got up to pace around the room. One of the other agents leaned forward and said, "Tell us everything, from the first moment you saw Rámon Cruz."

She did, pausing for breaks when they wanted clarifications. An agent came in with Polaroid photographs of schools; she put her finger on one of them, remembering the classic white columns, the smiling uniformed teenagers.

"Mount Olive Academy," Miller said, and handed it to the El Paso detective. "Close it. Get those kids out of there as soon as you can, and send in a bomb team to look for a device."

"Tell them—" She gulped hard. "Tell them to look for a backpack with toys inside."

The detective left in a hurry, with two of the three FBI agents. Miller stayed, sliding back into his chair across from her. The room looked very empty with just the two of them and the silent Border Patrol officer at the back, the glare of the one-way mirror behind Miller's back.

"I have some bad news, Ana," Miller said quietly. His dark eyes held hers. "They found your brother in an alley about seven blocks from your clinic. His throat was cut."

She sat very still, trying to put the words together with her last sight of Gabe. She'd told him good morning, hadn't she? She'd said something stupid, like *Don't get into trouble*, and gone downstairs to another day of work. She hadn't really believed, not *really*, that Rámon would kill his own people.

Her people. The loss didn't seem real. She kept waiting for someone to tell her it was a mistake.

"Are you okay? Can I get you anything?" Miller asked. She raised her eyes from contemplation of the table and focused on him.

"I want to see him," she said. "Before I say another word, I want to see my brother."

"He's already been identified. There's no need . . ."

She stared at him until he nodded and came around to take her arm as she rose to her feet. She didn't know why until her knees betrayed her. Why were her legs shaking?

The sunshine outside felt warm and strangely distant. Agent Miller and another man she didn't know took her off the Army base to a small gray building downtown. She knew the city morgue building, of course; she'd even sent people to it. But this—this—

It was a mistake.

She followed Agent Miller down a long hallway and into a small room with a curtained window. The air smelled metallic from the heaters but felt chilly, and there was the smell a medical student never quite forgets, the smell of dead flesh.

She held her breath, like a child, as Agent Miller stepped back away from her and the curtain slid open.

The subject is a young Hispanic male, approximately thirty years old, well nourished. Evidence of massive exsanguination— Her mind gibbered on in medical terms, a cushion to protect her from what she saw. He was too pale to be Chicano, his skin the palest amber, a completely unnatural color. His short, dark hair was still neatly combed. His face wasn't at peace, it was simply slack and empty, and his eyes were closed. The sheet was pulled carefully up around his neck.

His legs ended abruptly at mid-thigh. As she saw that pitiful detail, her breath exploded out of her, and it all focused for her. *Gabriel's face.* It was her brother's face.

Agent Miller put a hand under her arm, but she didn't need it. After a moment of listening to a silence that would never hold her brother's laughter again, she said, "Let me tell my family."

A new voice behind her said, "There's no need, Ana, I've told them." Sister Teresa. Ana turned blindly toward the voice, saw her aunt's kind, sorrowful face, and collapsed into her arms, resting her head against the stiff fabric of her nun's habit. Teresa let her cry in peace as the curtain rolled shut and Gabriel vanished forever from the world.

Teresa rode back with her in the FBI car, holding her hand, sensibly saying nothing. Ana watched the road ahead without any real interest. The road took them back to Fort Bliss. They parked in the same gravel lot, and she glimpsed her diseased old Pinto leaking oil on the pristine gravel. They would whisk that stain away, she was sure of it. No sign of her here tomorrow.

Tomorrow seemed a wearyingly long way off.

In the front lobby Ana passed four people, obviously waiting for someone inside the secured area. They were all Hispanic, and one of them spat on her. She stopped, astonished, staring at the man's furious black eyes until Agent Miller tugged her on behind the guard station.

"*Cabróna!*" the man sneered. "Traitor!"

"We brought in some of the Sons of Aztlan," Miller said quietly. "Don't take it personally. The opinion is that we're persecuting Hispanic activists."

"Aren't you?" she asked, and pulled away from his touch. "Rámon isn't one of them. He's insane, don't you see that? You can't blame the Aztlan movement for what this man has done. He doesn't speak for them!"

Teresa put a quieting hand on her shoulder.

"Dr. Gutierrez, you don't seem to understand the realities of the situation. Cruz has popular support in the *barrio*. He's a folk hero, like Billy the Kid. He brought down the Border Patrol. There are people out there, a lot of them, who maybe wouldn't set the bombs, but they cheer the results all the same, and those people are *dangerous*." Agent Miller almost hissed the word. "Those are the people who put money in the kitty for the 'relief fund' that ends up buying automatic weapons. This is Ireland all over again, don't you *see* that? If Cruz gets what he wants, this city will blow apart. He's just the fuse. It's people who believe in him who are the bomb."

She kept her voice quiet as she said, "And your answer is to tell us what to think."

Agent Miller sighed and looked up at the ceiling for help. "Ma'am, I wish I *had* an answer. I wish to hell I did. But all I can do is to keep an eye on people we think are the most dangerous elements and hope people like you can understand right and wrong. Can you?"

She bit her lip and said, "I'm talking to you. Instead of spitting on you. You tell me."

A man emerged from an office and handed Miller a piece of paper; he read it and nodded. "They've gone through Mount Olive Academy with a fine-tooth comb, Dr. Gutierrez, and there were no bombs. As a precaution we're also sweeping every other private school with a predominantly Anglo population, but I don't think we'll find anything. We think he was bluffing."

"Bluffing—" She was completely stricken.

"Don't blame yourself, you couldn't take the chance. There was no way to know, and he's crazy enough to try it. If he *had* targeted the school, though, I think he would have already blown it. He has to know you're here by now, if he didn't know we brought you in yesterday. There's no reason for him not to carry out his threat, unless it was a bluff. It's okay, Doctor. We won that round."

She stared at him, lost in the certain knowledge that she could have told Rafael the truth. She could have saved Gabriel's life.

"My brother's still dead," she said. "I didn't win."

They put her in a room with Sister Teresa and left them alone for an hour or two. Someone brought in drinks when they were thirsty, and promised lunch. She paced the room, full of a restless energy that she knew was really exhaustion, and asked Teresa about Pete.

"He's fine," Teresa said. Ana hadn't dared ask it of any of the FBI men; she dreaded seeing the speculation in their eyes. "He wanted me to tell you some things, Ana. It's what he was trying to reach you about, I think."

Ana turned toward her, frowning, and listened.

Chapter 26

November 27, 1996
Peter Ross

After getting Esmeralda new papers, Pete walked her home, and the trip seemed very short this time in her company. She laughed when he told her it was a long walk; for her it was a very minor distance. She walked everywhere she went.

As darkness fell, they arrived at her house and found the groceries right where he'd left them on the front porch, a minor miracle in this part of Juárez that Esmeralda took as natural. She sorted through the food he'd brought, smiling over the treats and rarities, and fixed him what she called a traditional Mexican meal of thanksgiving, brown sugar beans and hot dogs.

They made love in her bed, in the glow of thick vanilla-scented candles and the flutter of white curtains open to the night breeze. Her mouth tasted of brown sugar and her skin of rose and cinnamon, and she was the first lover he'd ever had that could laugh with him, laugh for pure joy, in the middle of it.

He never wanted the night to be over, but the

morning dawned bright and clear, and the rooster in the backyard made sure they knew it. Pete woke in her arms, warm and secure, and wondered how he'd ever managed to avoid this all these years of coming to this house, sitting so close to her. Had he been insane?

She burrowed closer to his warmth, murmuring in protest when he slipped away. The wind coming in the window was cold, and his skin pebbled with chill bumps as he dressed. Esmeralda watched him with sleepy, sated eyes, warm in her cocoon of blankets.

"I have to go," he said, and kissed her a long, lingering goodbye. "Stay safe, Es. At least for one day, okay?"

"I'm not going anywhere," she said serenely. "I have things to do here. Is safe, you see?"

Safe was a relative term, he knew. The Border Patrol building had been safe, too. He kissed her again and shrugged on his coat before leaving. He closed the door, tried the knob, and stuck his head back inside.

"Lock the door, Es!" he yelled. Her sleepy "*Sí*," followed him down the steps. He heard the click of the lock and started walking toward the Copia Bridge, unable to keep a smile off his face in spite of what he knew was waiting for him on the other side of the border.

His answering machine was full of messages from newspaper and television reporters, one from a reporter from the *Enquirer* who wanted to talk to "Our Lady of Miracles." The last one was from Sister Teresa Gutierrez.

He listened to the news of Gabriel's murder with a sense of claustrophobia; all he could think of was Ana, always so strong, and how she would be breaking under this weight. Teresa told him the FBI had allowed Ana to return to the clinic to gather some things, but that the building itself was closed for investigation. They were hoping for trace evidence, he assumed, left by Cruz or his men, but these men were soldiers; they packed their trash, policed themselves rigorously. Whatever they got would help convict, but it wouldn't help catch.

He sat in his apartment, looking out at the bright dry day, at the pastel stones that made up the rock wall outside. It had always struck him as strange that concrete and stones were such essential building materials out here; rock walls were a fixture of landscape design, as if chain-link fences or wood slats had never been invented. It was something that he'd always found weirdly charming about these people, that they thought a four-foot fence built of rocks would keep out intruders.

The fences weren't made to stand up to rain and snow. After every good rain half of them crumbled—like Ana, who was held together with cement and stone, a true child of the desert. Full of secrets.

His phone rang as he was thinking about her, and Agent Saletti said without preamble, "We're in the parking lot. Get your ass in gear, Ross, or you're going to miss the party."

Saletti and Garman were in a late-model sedan, not the same one they'd been driving the night before; he figured, rightly, that the FBI rented a fleet and interchanged them on an as-needed basis. Saletti was driving, and as Pete closed the back door he saw why; she could have worked for Hollywood as a stunt woman. He'd never seen a Taurus peel rubber like that before.

"We're late," she explained. "Agent Miller had a tip on a group of Hispanic men at an abandoned warehouse in the Lower Valley. It sounds like the right guys, and he's coordinating the roundup. I thought you might want to be in on it."

"Very thoughtful of you," he said, and grabbed for a handhold as she took a corner without bothering to brake. Garman placed a rotating bubble light on the dashboard. Pete hoped it had some kind of magic shield effect, considering the rate they were gaining on the cars ahead. "It's faster if you take the Ysleta cutoff."

He pointed to the right as they rocketed down Montana. The Taurus had better traction than he'd dared to hope. Now that they were on a straight-away, no cars in sight, Agent Saletti abandoned any concession to the speed limit.

"Keep it under eighty," Garman said, and glanced back at Pete. "She's the reincarnation of a dead stock-car driver. We proved it last year. No doubt."

"Yeah, you're the reincarnation of a turtle—" She cut herself off and started to brake as a stoplight loomed in the distance. "No offense to the amphibians, of course."

Pete tapped Garman on the shoulder. When the agent turned back to him, he stuck out his hand. Garman studied it, puzzled, then shook it.

"Thanks," Pete said.

Garman raised his eyebrows. "Want to tell me why?"

"Esmeralda Sanchez. When you saved her life, you saved mine. I mean it."

Garman studied him, then smiled. He had a startling smile, probably a devastating weapon on women, with a lot of real delight behind it. Pete got the feeling he didn't smile much, but when he did it was with his whole heart.

"Well," he said. "Always good to help a friend."

The car slid smoothly to a stop at the crossroads, waited a fraction of a second, powered on.

Garman had a map in his lap that he consulted as they left the cutoff and climbed the hill of Avenue of the Americas. "Right at the next light, Sal. Four miles on your left, turn on a street called Provado, and the warehouse is half a block up."

"I think we'll be able to see it before we get there," she said. She was right. As soon as they turned on Provado, they met a bristling forest of revolving lights—police, unmarked cars, ambulances, fire trucks. Saletti pulled in behind a car that had rental tags and shut the engine off. As Pete started to open the door, she stopped him.

"Wait," she said. "Phil, you see?"

"I see," Garman answered, and as Pete looked out the side windows he realized what the problem was.

Someone had tipped off the media, and the media had drawn a crowd. They lined the rooftops of the surrounding warehouses, pressed around the police barricades in a milling confusion. There weren't enough uniformed police to hold them all back. As Pete looked around, he realized he couldn't see a single Anglo face that wasn't on the inside of the barricades.

Garman said, "The natives are restless," and immediately got a look from Saletti. "Hey, I didn't mean it like that."

"Peter, stay here. I didn't exactly get an invitation for you to this party. Let's find Miller," she said to Garman, and he nodded. They bailed out of the car, walking quickly, and while the doors were open, the murmur of voices resolved into confused shouting. There were probably a couple hundred people gathered outside the barricades; he had no doubt it made a nice scene for the helicopter circling overhead. Film at ten.

He was at a bad angle to see the warehouse that was the center of all this attention, but he saw the shift in attention among the cops and spectators. Somebody was coming out. He caught a glimpse of a young Hispanic man, hands behind his head, walking out of a doorway before a cop blocked his view, gun drawn. There were a lot of guns drawn. That was understandable, but—

He never saw it happen, but he heard the first shot, crystal clear in the air like a broken lightbulb. *Pop.*

And then a volley of noise, too many shots to be separated out into separate sounds. Pete grabbed the door handle to get out and realized that Saletti had locked him inside. For his own protection.

The gunfire stopped as suddenly as it had started, and the cop blocking his view moved sideways enough for him to see that there were three bodies lying on the concrete in front of the warehouse. Three *vatos.* Young.

That was all he had time to see before the roar
started, building from the crowd, an anguished
scream of rage that echoed so loudly it broke through
the Taurus' soundproofing and raked shivers up his
spine. He looked at the faces beyond the barricade,
but they weren't individual faces now, they were a
confused blur of open mouths and wide eyes and
moving bodies.

The uniformed cops were swallowed whole as the
crowd rushed them. A bottle crashed against the
window of the car, leaving a frosted star crack and
golden foam of beer. Pete flinched back and ducked
as something else hit the car. It sounded like a brick.
A hammer of noises hit him, and he did the only
thing he could. He ducked down, covered his head,
and listened to the sound of the mob as they
slammed into the car, trampled over it. Some stopped
to beat the windows, but there were easier targets,
and after a few seconds the rush was past him, leaving the windows glazed with cracks. The hood was
pitted. The whole car looked like a hailstorm had hit.

Saletti. Garman. He looked for them, but they were
gone, lost in that tossing maelstrom of flesh. Nobody
had expected this. Nobody had understood the kind
of powder keg they'd put a match to.

He grabbed the radio from the dash and transmit-
ted an "officer down," gave a quick description of
the riot and got a confirmation that help was on the
way before he rolled over the head rests to the front
seat and went out the passenger door, not heading
in any particular direction, just looking for something
to do to help *somebody*.

Bodies. He stumbled over them almost immediately—a girl weeping on the ground, her arm broken, footprints on her back. An unconscious man with a skull fracture, an iron pipe lying next to him smeared with blood.

Agent Saletti, her clothes ripped, half under a car. She was shuddering but she was alive; her fingers were broken, and her gun was gone. The mob swirled twenty feet farther on, battling a thin, desperate line of cops. He helped Saletti back to the car, loaded all the wounded he could inside, and drove them to the nearest hospital.

All in all, there were the original three dead men shot by the police, two police, and one FBI killed in the riot, and twenty-seven injured.

The dead FBI man was Agent Garman, who'd been stabbed in the throat with a broken bottle.

It was the wrong warehouse. Rámon Cruz and his men were long gone. The police had shot three members of the *Perro Feroces* street gang.

And the war was on.

Chapter 27

November 27, 1996
Dr. Ana Gutierrez

From the flashpoint of the warehouse, riots spread across the Lower Valley and into East El Paso's predominantly Anglo neighborhoods; the rioters never made it as far as West El Paso, where most of the wealthier families lived, mostly because of geography. It was all uphill. The fighting was confined to easily accessible areas—Anglo-run businesses in the Lower Valley, Anglo homes in the golfer-named subdivisions off Lee Trevino and Yarbrough. By the time Ana saw the television reports, the death toll was up to thirty, with hundreds of injuries. They were talking about bringing in the National Guard, but popular wisdom was that the flashfire had burned itself out.

The *barrio* was strangely quiet. Waiting. She didn't seen any police cars, and supposed there wouldn't be any; they'd be staying at the battle lines, and it wouldn't be wise for stray police to show their faces in the *barrio* just now. She and Teresa loaded medical supplies into the Pinto—rusted and half scrapped already, it wouldn't be a target for vengeance. Her FBI escort infuriated her by refusing to leave them alone; he insisted that the building was still a crime scene, and he had to supervise the removal of all of the items.

"Get the syringes from the supply room," Ana said, busy with armloads of bandages. She tossed Teresa the keys, and the nun hurried away with surprising agility. Not so surprising, though; Teresa had been through bad times before. Ana loaded antibiotics from the main supply cabinet, then went back to the locked cabinet for narcotics. She remembered blood-pressure cuffs and pressure bandages and was on her third trip back for splints and braces when she heard the supply door shut and the lock rattle.

"We need to get moving," she called to Teresa. "Have you got everything?"

Her aunt didn't answer. Ana put down her armload of sterile-wrapped packages and brushed hair back from her sweating face.

A shadow flickered at the edge of her vision, and she spun to face it, froze as a voice behind her said, "Yes. I have everything now."

She turned to face Rámon Cruz, who was standing next to the locked supply-room door. He looked worse than before, his face pale, his eyes red, his beard an uneven stubble.

But he looked at her with the eyes of a man who was in control.

She took a step toward him, all her fury boiling up. There was a metallic click behind her, and she heard the scrape of footsteps. He hadn't come alone. Of course.

"Where is she?" she demanded, and her voice shook not with fear but with rage. He held up a calming hand.

"The sister is fine, Ana. I would never harm her. She's been detained, that's all. In there." As if in response, the supply-room door thundered under a volley of blows. "She's in absolutely no danger."

"Like my brother!" She couldn't say Gabriel's name, not without weeping, and she wouldn't give him that. He'd taken enough of her already. He looked away from her, down at his battered work boots.

"I didn't want him dead, I swear that on my soul. He chose that, not me." His face settled into grim lines. "And I punished the man who killed him. I might have cost you a brother, Ana, but I paid a brother's life, too."

"I spit on your *brother!*"

He crossed the distance to her in three unbelievably quick steps, before she could do more than raise a hand to stop him. He took a fistful of her hair and pulled her head around to face the television set mounted in the reception area, the one that showed the fighting. Her eyes teared from the pain of his grip, but it was more than that. She was heartsick at the faces on the news, the hate, the violence. As she watched, four white men beat and kicked a Hispanic woman.

"You spit on my brother?" he repeated. "You spit on yourself, Ana. Look! It's finally happening. Blood for blood, all these years of slavery and death. You see that? Out of the ashes we'll build something new. Something good."

"Aztlan," she hissed. "The city of blood. The home of killers."

"What's wrong with you? *Look!* You see that?" He shook her head for emphasis as the picture jerked and focused and showed the face of a dead young Hispanic man, his face misshapen from beatings. "You see how your Anglo friends treat us? We're through suffering, Ana! It's time to make them pay!"

He didn't see it. He didn't see that a club in a brown hand was no different from one in a white hand, that blood was blood. He *couldn't* see it.

"That's the difference between us, Rámon," she said. "Nobody owes me their blood. Not even you."

"*Jefe*," said a man from the door, urgently. "Time to go."

"Move, Ana," he said. "We have work to do."

She fought him silently until he hit her behind the ear with his fist. The world went bright red and cool black, and she felt herself being lifted and carried away.

She came to in a darkness that smelled like home. Not the clinic, with its astringent medicinal scents. Smells of cooking meat and cilantro, the bready smell of baking tortillas. *Mama*, she thought, but that was foolish, wasn't it? Even Rámon would not be bold enough to invade her mother's home, and even Mama would not be so hospitable as to cook for his private army.

No, the bed she was lying on had the harsh firmness of a folding cot. She tried to turn over and realized that she was tied to the frame, both wrists together. The ropes were tight enough that she could

feel her heartbeat pulsing in her fingertips—too tight
to squirm out of, certainly.

A door spilled sudden light on her, and she
squinted against it and the dull throb of a headache
and saw that Rámon was holding a flashlight, its
beam averted from her face to pool warm on the
concrete floor.

"You're awake," he said. "Good. I'll get you
some food."

She didn't bother to argue. He left for a moment,
taking the flashlight with him, but the door let in a
little gray illumination that defined the bare corners
of what must have been some sort of storeroom, raw
holes in the concrete walls where shelves had been
twisted free. The room was clean but very empty.
Her cot was the only furnishing.

Rámon came back as she sat up. The ropes
wouldn't let her straighten, and she glared at him
from her hunched position, refusing to lie down like
a good dog. He sat on the bed beside her, plate in
his hand, and rolled a steaming flour tortilla coated
with beans into a burrito.

"Open," he said. And waited. "Ana, you can
starve if you like, but it does me no harm and does
you no good. Eat. The food's hot."

It was clearly homemade, and she didn't think
they'd made it on their small field stoves. Someone
was bringing them meals—followers, most probably.
Wives. Girlfriends. Admirers.

She opened her mouth and took a bite of the tortilla. It tasted very good, the bread the perfect,
smooth texture, the beans spiced with onion and gar-

lic and hot peppers. She chewed and swallowed and took the next bite with more enthusiasm.

"See?" he said, still very gently. "There is no need to hate me, Ana, I don't want to see you harmed. You and I, we have history, yes? And we share ideals. We are not so different."

She stayed silent. He rolled another tortilla. She took a bite.

"You'll be pleased to know the rioting has stopped for the night. Maybe it will start tomorrow, maybe not. It's hard to tell."

She chewed and swallowed.

"I had to bring you, Ana. It's our last chance together, you understand? After this—" He hesitated, studying her. For a second he was the old Rámon, the boy she remembered, the one she'd made love to in the darkness. "After this the world changes, Ana. And I'm changing it. Rámon Cruz."

"Untie me," she said. He continued to study her, eyes quiet and soft. "Please."

"You know what I always loved about you, Ana? Your purity. You're like the heart of the sun. When you love, you love completely, and when you hate—" He shook his head and ate the last bit of the tortilla he was holding. "You've never been a good liar. Don't try to lie to me now. If I untie you, you'll do something that will make me hurt you."

"I'll kill you," she said. There was no boasting in it. She was stating a fact. Rámon nodded and stood up.

"Get some rest, Ana. You're going to need it." The smile this time was cold and distant. "You're going to be a hero for Aztlan yet."

"I spit on Aztlan, and I spit on you!"

She continued to curse him, in a low and shaking voice, long after his shadow had disappeared from the door, long after the darkness returned. Her muscles began to spasm again from the torturous angle of her wrists, and she finally, unwillingly, stretched out on her side on the cot, shivering.

Beyond the door someone was playing guitar, an old Mexican song she recognized but couldn't name. She didn't want to die here, in the dark, at the hands of Rámon Cruz.

But her only real choice was how she would die—like a child, crying, or like the woman she wanted to be. The one Gabriel would have respected.

She lay dry-eyed through the night, waiting. When the chance came, she was determined to take it, no matter what the cost.

The man who came to get her wasn't Rámon; she'd never seen him before. She wondered where Miguel was; she hadn't seen him at all, and that was odd. She tried to ask the man as he untied her hands, but he gave her a look that struck her silent more effectively than a slap. He left rope around one wrist and held the other end bunched in his fist; she was tethered like a dog, on a very short leash. He showed her to a narrow, windowless bathroom that was filthy beyond description, but her bladder had been aching for relief for hours and any was better than none. As soon as she was done, the man opened the door and pulled her out with a tug on the rope, towing her past a row of windows covered with ancient grime. The windows showed a gray glow—close to dawn? Or dusk? She had no idea of the time.

Rámon was waiting with his men; they sat at ease, most of them, with weapons close at hand. Guards were posted at the windows and doors. Even if she managed to get a weapon, she was dead before she took three steps, and so she stayed quiet, watching Rámon for some hint of what he wanted.

He looked bad in the early light, pale as a corpse. Sweat dotted his forehead. She got a vicious satisfaction at the thought that his wound might be turning septic, but it only lasted until he said, "Hold her," and she felt herself being grasped by two men, her arms spread wide. Rámon reached down into a box next to him and lifted out what looked like a vest, dark gray, covered with flat pockets. He limped to her and put the vest over one outstretched arm. She tried to kick him, but a fist slammed into her stomach and she lost the strength to do more than gasp for air. The vest slid along her left arm, then her right. By the time she'd recovered enough to fight again, it was done. They held her still as Rámon laced the front of it closed and knotted the cord. He stepped back to admire her.

"*Una soldada*," he said, and the others laughed. "Now you're one of us, Ana. Congratulations."

"What are you doing?"

He reached down into the box and held up what looked like a television remote control. It had only two buttons. He pressed the first one, and then a red light blinked on the second button.

"Now you're armed, Ana." He smiled that cold smile, the one she didn't know. "If I press the second

button, you become a pillar of fire, like in the Bible.
A martyr, isn't that what you always wanted? You're
going to die for Aztlan, Ana, whether you want to
or not. And we'll build a temple to you in the new
land, you and your brother.''

She realized what he had just done. He had made
her a bomb.

The vest was full of explosives, and he held the
detonator.

Chapter 28

She intended to keep her word to Pete, she truly did, but the silence of the house frightened her. She had a black-and-white television, its reception improved by a fantastic spike of tinfoil from its single antenna; with it she found one of the American television stations and watched part of a funny show she only vaguely understood. The English was too colloquial for her to grasp completely, though she knew the jokes were mostly sexual. Father Nani would be shocked, but then he'd be shocked when she confessed what she'd been doing with Pete, too. She'd find it hard to confess that with a true and contrite spirit.

As she rested her head on a pillow on the couch, she heard a knock. She switched off the television and opened the door without checking to see who it was. She had never feared for her safety as a *curandera*.

It was the young man who'd brought his daughter to her, the troubled one. She took in his flushed, anxious face at a glance, reached out for his hand, and drew him inside. "What is it?"

"My daughter," he said, and drew in a deep breath. "Can you come?"

"I—" She cast a helpless look at Jaime's picture, searching for some sign that he'd be with her. Nothing. "Of course. *Una momenta.*"

She gathered up cleansing herbs and a bottle of clean water, some cloths blessed by Father Nani. After a second's hesitation she put Jaime's picture in the bag with the herbs and gestured that she was ready to go.

The young man had a car waiting, a battered old American car with each piece a different color; the seats were more springs than cloth, and he apologized and put a piece of cardboard on the seat before letting her in. There were no seat belts. She held herself in place with both hands on the dashboard as he drove down the rutted dirt road, out past the markets and into the area across from the ASARCO smelter plant. Here there were no houses, only shacks built of discarded Sheetrock and rusting aluminum siding. Two rooms made a palace. There was no running water, no sewage, nothing but poverty and despair and, occasionally, a little love to sustain life and hope. The man pulled to a stop in front of one of the larger shacks and beckoned to her to hurry. She followed him up steps made of creaking slats to a floor that sagged beneath her weight, and a door that was little more than a sheet of plywood with a rusted latch.

Candles burned inside, and it was bitterly cold. The candles were almost all votives, and the largest, a blessed Virgin Mary, spread a jeweled glimmer of false beauty over the small room. It was neatly kept, but its emptiness cried out to her in waves of fear. This was what all of them dreaded. Most of Esmeralda's neighbors were one meager week from this house, this despair, this emptiness. A few pesos lost, and she might be here herself.

"This way," he said, and led her past the single table with its uneven chair. The chair did not match the table, and would have been scavenged from a dump site, probably on the American side. She glanced at the shelves that lined the walls and saw a few cans of tuna fish and spaghetti. At least they were still eating something more than the refuse from wealthier neighborhoods.

The little girl sat in the corner of the next room, a ghost in the darkness, her pale nightgown a memory of better days though it had become faded and patched and too short for her. She did not blink as Esmeralda approached. She was leaning against the door of a closed closet, an old, sturdy door with a crystal knob that must have been saved from their last home. The door was the nicest thing Esmeralda had seen in the house.

There was something about the girl, the way she sat, legs splayed in front of her, hands at her sides. She looked like a broken doll. Her head lolled forward at an uncomfortable angle.

Esmeralda's skin shivered on her bones as she remembered what the father had told her before. *She found her mother dead . . . suicide . . .*

Esmeralda said softly, "Her mother. Is this where she died?"

The father nodded convulsively. He was very pale. "She—she hanged herself—from the doorknob. With a piece of cord."

Esmeralda sank to her knees, watching the child; she pulled her bag close and opened it, searched through until she had found a sack of dried rosemary. She opened it and said, "Find me a broom. Whatever you have."

She did not touch the girl, except to be sure that there was no cord around her neck; there was nothing, but the child sat as one dead. Except for the rise and fall of her chest, she might have been her self-murdered mother. Esmeralda crushed a handful of herbs and whispered a prayer as she tossed them around the little girl. When the father brought the broom, she stood up and told him to leave the house.

"You won't hurt her?" he blurted, and immediately ducked his head in apology. "No. No, of course you will not. Forgive me."

"*De nada*," she said, and offered him a smile. "But you must trust me now. I will sweep out the spirits that surround her, and then we must talk, she and I. I must show her the way back."

She had known the child was *susto* since the last time she saw her—haunted by the horrors of her mother's death, severed from her good spirit and guardian. Now the child was *espanto*, and stood in the gravest danger of all. The devils had her, and it required skill and courage to save her. If it could be done at all.

Esmeralda took up the broom and, with careful concentration and the cheerful economy of a good housekeeper, began to perform a *barrida*, sweeping out the spirits as she prayed. At the door of the shack she swept out the rosemary and little swirls of dust, and in her mind she imagined the whirling, angry faces of devils cheated of their prize. She finished the prayer and set the broom on the porch, closed the plywood door, and turned back toward the bedroom.

The little girl was standing in the doorway, her eyes solemn and very dark. Her hands were clasped in front of her.

"Angela," she said. The name came to her suddenly, though she hadn't remembered it and the father hadn't reminded her. "How are you feeling?"

Angela came toward her, walking slowly, bare feet making little noise on the plywood floor. She might have been floating, so quietly did she move. When she was only a few steps away, she stopped and looked up into Esmeralda's eyes.

"He hates you," the girl said scornfully, and it was not a child's voice; it was a woman's, low and angry and very distant. "Why would he not? Your son has turned away from you. You're alone."

"I am never alone," Esmeralda said. "I am a child of God, like you, Angela."

The girl laughed. "You want to talk to your son again? Go to the devil. Go to the crossing. You'll meet your son there, in fire and death. It's possible you may even save a life if you go. But not your own."

"Who—" Even as she asked it, she knew. It was the voice of a woman lost between worlds, walking the shadows. Sometimes they saw deeply, those shadows.

It was the voice of Angela's mother.

"I'm tired," the voice whispered. Esmeralda hesitated, because there was no Jaime to help her, no power in her hands, but she couldn't turn away from the pain. She reached out and put her hands on Angela's head, traced the sign of the cross on her forehead, and sent all of the healing she could touch into the child's body.

Angela collapsed into her arms, her eyes fluttering closed. Esmeralda cradled her warm body close in the chill and watched a wisp of dust drift toward the door, hesitate, and then fade away into the wood.

Esmeralda held the girl for a long time, rocking her, before she opened the door and called to her father to come back inside.

"Then you've cured her!" he said excitedly when she told him what had happened. She handed over Angela with care and sadness, and shook her head.

"There is no cure for it, Victor. She is no longer *susto*, but she has learned to speak with spirits, and she will always have the ear for that. If we are lucky, she will learn the way of the *curandera espirita* and let her spirits teach her to heal herself and others."

Victor went very still, holding his daughter close. "*My* daughter? *Una curandera?*"

"*Es possible.*" She took a deep breath. "If her spirits are dark, then she will be *bruja*, Victor. You must take her to church and have Father Nani bless her, and you must pray very hard for her. She will not want to go to the church, but you must take her. And if you find her collecting bones and herbs, you must bring her to me or another *curandera espirita*, it's very important, yes? If you don't, she'll be lost."

Victor swallowed hard and nodded. Esmeralda

went past him to the other room, the one with the two narrow pallets of blankets and the chill and the closed closet door. She was careful not to touch the knob as she gathered her bag and herbs.

As she left the house to walk home again, she said, "One last thing. Take the door out and burn it."

It was already night outside, though the sunset lingered in an orange glaze over the mountains; to the east the sky was a rich velvet blue-black, glittered with flecks of ice that would become stars with true dark. On the American side of the border lights blazed, and cars moved in a continuous stream along the Border Highway. If she stood very still, she could hear the sounds of motors and music, the sound that she identified with El Paso and its busy, weary people.

She turned away from Victor's silent shack and began the long walk home. She would not, she was determined, listen to a dark spirit. She had been taught that there was always a price for it—but what Angela had said reminded her so strongly of Jaime's warning, fire and death, the devil and the crossing—

It's possible you may save a life, but not your own.

She would pray about it, she decided.

Chapter 29

November 27, 1996
Peter Ross

Agent Saletti flew back to her field office in Denver that night. The airport was under tight security, only passengers allowed inside, and though Pete and Agent Miller drove her to the terminal, she didn't say anything to them other than the automatic courtesies, the *pleases* and *thank-yous* of shock and grief. Pete got her suitcases out of the trunk for her—FBI agents packed light, but she was also bringing back Agent Garman's belongings, and that was a very heavy burden indeed. The porter he waved to hefted both bags easily. She might have walked away without another word if Pete hadn't said, awkwardly, "I didn't know him well, but I liked him. And he saved the life of a woman I love. I won't forget him."

She froze, her shoulders tight. Her head nodded stiffly, and her voice came late and tightly controlled as she said, "Well, that makes two of us. Did you know he was a ballroom dancer?"

"No."

"He could dance like Fred Astaire," she said softly.

"And he was married to a woman named Susan, and he has a baby named Jason. And I guess they'll get a phone call this morning."

She hesitated. From the car Agent Miller said, "Saletti."

"Sir." Her shoulders were like high-tension wire.

"It wasn't your fault. You did your best."

She turned to look at him, her eyes wide, her face expressionless. "Thank you, sir. But you weren't there, were you? So keep your opinions to yourself. And just so you know, I quit."

She walked away at a brisk pace, heels tapping, and the doors whisked open to swallow her up.

Agent Miller let out a long breath and traded a look with Pete.

"Is she really quitting?" Pete asked.

Miller leaned over and opened the passenger door for him. "I would. Hell, I still might."

They drove out through the heavy, slow airport traffic—people were leaving by whatever means they could, plane or car or bus. There was a car-to-car search at the entrance being run by the National Guard, and one at the exit, too, but Agent Miller was waved on after showing his credentials. On Montana Avenue, one of the main arteries of the town, cars moved in a continuous stream, heading east toward Carlsbad or west toward California; most of them carried Anglo passengers.

Agent Miller clicked on his radio and gave his call sign, then asked for a situation report.

"Sir, it looks basically quiet right now. We've got media everywhere, but they're out of the way at the

moment, and there haven't been any new clashes
since six o'clock. Looks like maybe a peaceful night."

"I'll believe that when the sun comes up," Miller
said, and signed off. He glanced over at Pete. "Bet
you wonder why you're driving around with me
today."

"Crossed my mind. I didn't think it was standard
Bureau policy to share."

"Agent Saletti wanted you here, and I wasn't prepared to say no to her, not today. I'm sorry about
your brother-in-law. Did you know him well?"

"Not well enough. I liked him. He had a lot of
class." That seemed a very poor epitaph. "How's
Ana taking it?"

"I suppose about as well as she can. I sent her
with an escort to pick up some things from the clinic;
they were supposed to go to her mother's house in
the Lower Valley when they were done. I haven't
heard back from them yet." Agent Miller checked his
watch and frowned, then reached for the radio. He
sent out a call sign Pete didn't recognize and waited
for a response.

Static. He repeated it three times, then switched to
the main headquarters call sign and asked an unfa-
miliar voice to locate Agent Ortega and have him
report in.

Instead of turning to head back to Fort Bliss, Miller
turned the car left, toward the border. Toward the
clinic. When Pete glanced at him, he shrugged.

"Might as well," he said.

"Two Anglo *federales* going into the *barrio*," Pete
said. "Sounds like a good plan to me."

Miller gave him a bleak grin and said, "If you're worried, lock your door."

The streets were deserted on the way to *La Clínica*, not a soul outside. Plenty of eyes, though. Pete could feel them and knew Agent Miller could, too. A black-and-white El Paso patrol car glided past them as they pulled in to the curb at the clinic; the cop nodded to Pete and pulled over on the other side of the street.

There was a rental car parked at the far corner, locked up tight. No sign of anyone else. Agent Miller peered in the windows and straightened up to look Pete in the eye.

"I don't suppose you like the looks of this," he said, "because I damn sure don't. Go get our friend over there."

Pete waved to the cop, who finished reporting his location and got out to join them at the protected brick wall next to the clinic door.

"I'll go first," Pete said, and found Agent Miller's hand holding him back. Miller, without a word, moved ahead of him and tried the clinic door. Nobody had locked it, and it opened with a whisper of weatherstripping. Pete drew his gun from his belt and saw Agent Miller do the same; the cop had already armed himself.

"Dr. Gutierrez," Miller called. "Agent Miller, FBI. Anybody here?"

He flipped on lights. The heating clicked on with a groan, and treatment curtains waved in the hot breeze, but there was no other sound.

"Check the beds," he told Pete, and Pete slid the first treatment curtain aside with a whisper of rings.

Clean sheets. He moved to the second one as the cop followed Miller to the door marked NO PASEN.

"Christ!" Pete said, and jumped back as he realized the second bed was full. It was a Hispanic man, well dressed in a dark suit. There was a neat hole in his temple and a spiderweb of blood across his face. Agent Miller spun and stared, his face going empty and tense. "One of yours?"

"Agent Ortega. I sent him with Ana." As Pete checked the FBI agent's pulse, Miller turned away and opened the door to the private stairs.

They all turned, weapons pointing the same direction, as a volley of knocks came from the locked unmarked door at the end of the treatment curtains. "Supply room," Pete said, and shoved beds aside in his rush to get there. The lock was a sturdy old combination model; he twisted it off with the help of a tire iron from the cop's patrol car.

Sister Teresa Gutierrez blinked at the light and the guns aimed in her direction. Her eyes focused on Pete and she said clearly, "They took Ana out of here. Hours ago. I don't know how long."

She looked pale and drawn, and for the first time in Pete's memory, she looked less than serene; she'd pulled away her coif and her black hair spilled over her shoulder in a thick, glossy braid threaded with silver. She looked strangely young without the wimple, oddly naked.

"You all right?" Agent Miller asked, taking her elbow. "No bumps and bruises?"

"No, I'm fine. They locked me in, but they didn't touch me." Her hands were shaking, Pete saw, and he reached out to take them. She met his eyes with a trace of embarrassment. "I—I don't do well in the dark. You understand."

He did. It was too much like the time she'd spent in a South American prison, waiting to die. He squeezed her cold fingers and said, "Of course. Rámon Cruz?"

"I didn't see them, but it seems to me that it must have been. I don't know what happened to the man with us—" Her eyes focused past Pete, at the body in the second treatment area. Her breath left in a rush, but she pulled it back in. "I hoped he'd gotten away."

"Anything you can tell me about these men? How many? What they were driving? Names?"

"If it was the same van I saw them put Gabriel into, it was a cream-colored cargo van with a sliding side door. No markings on it. Not a new van, old, boxy. I heard only one voice, but there must have been more."

"Why?"

She smiled. Pete answered for her. "Because Ana wouldn't have gone unless they overpowered her. Believe me."

Agent Miller said, without a pause, "We don't know she did go. She betrayed this guy, Pete. They're not afraid of leaving bodies. Let's check upstairs, okay?"

"I want to go," said Teresa, and she followed them up the stairs, a silent shadow in her long black dress.

There were no bodies upstairs, but Agent Miller's assessment was deadly accurate. Ana was missing, and these men were killers.

It was just a question of where she would die, and when, and how.

Things were getting complicated at the command center. Agent Miller arrived to discover that there were four agents from Washington, D.C., who outranked him, fresh off a military transport; he was thanked for his service and put on the bench, along with Pete. In fact, all of the local Border Patrol were benched or sent out on fence duty, even the special investigators. Pete figured the only reason he wasn't sent, too, was because they didn't know what to do with him. They didn't want him in reach of the media, but they didn't want to use him, either.

He had the feeling that they were going to assign him to coffee detail, and that wasn't going to do, not with Ana missing. She had very little time, and they were planning to waste it all.

He was debriefed by an agent named Nelson, near fifty and balding and so sharp that his glances gave paper cuts. Nelson told him everything was being done that could be done. He wasn't told the details.

"What do they think's going to happen?" Pete exploded after he and Agent Miller and a couple of other Border Patrol investigators were put in a room to write up reports. "Do they really think he's going to keep her alive? Or do they even care?"

"Of course they care. Look, Pete, I understand how you feel, but you've got to sit down and write this out. They need every bit of information you can think of. Anything about Ana, anything about Cruz. Most of the initial investigative reports were destroyed in the bombing, so they need you to reconstruct things

for them. Cruz's hangouts, his methods, his associ-
ates. You can do that. I know you can."

Pete put down his pen and stood up, grabbing his
jacket from the back of the chair. Miller leaned back
to look at him.

"You really think they're going to let you walk out
of here?"

"You really think they're going to want to try and
stop me?" Pete leaned over the table, picked up the
pen, and wrote five or six lines. He passed the paper
to Agent Miller. "This is every address we turned up
for anyone connected to Cruz, and believe me, it's
nothing. They won't go back that way; the drugs
were strictly fund-raisers. They're autonomous now,
and it's a military operation."

"So what's your plan?" Miller asked.

"How did they know Ana was at the clinic?"

Miller was silent. He knew exactly what Pete was
thinking.

"They're somewhere in sight of the building," Pete
finished. "And I'm going to find them."

As he started to go, one of the other Border Patrol
officers stood. "What're you carrying?"

"A nine."

The other man unsnapped a leather holder on his
belt, removed a magazine clip, and slid it to him.
"Don't go light."

The other investigator added a clip, too. Agent
Miller watched him pocket the extra ammunition
with a trace of a smile.

"No donations?" Pete asked.

"Look, I managed this thing right into a hole in
the ground. I've got a city in riot, scores dead, offi-

cers dead, agents dead—believe me, I'm not coming out of this alive, career-wise. I might as well go swinging." Agent Miller stood up and put on his own jacket.

"What about your report?"

"I can write my obituary later." He opened the door for Pete and looked outside, then gestured for him to follow. "I figure it'll sound better after I save your ass."

Chapter 30

The smell of the explosives made her throat dry, and eventually made her sick, but they didn't seem to care. *Of course they don't care,* she told herself in disgust. *You're the walking dead.* Her health was the least of their concerns.

Except for Rámon, of course, who seemed to care too much. She flinched away from him when he brought her food, but he wouldn't let her have her hands free to feed herself, and she knew she needed to eat to keep her strength. More tortillas and beans for lunch, now cold and not as appetizing. She asked to be taken to the toilet again, and Rámon allowed it, but she was given no chance to break free.

"Why did you blow up the Black Bridge?" she asked him, a blunt question after all the endless silence.

He gave her a hostile glare.

"I did not."

"Am I supposed to believe there are two maniacs bombing El Paso?" she snapped.

"We lost one of the packages that contained the explosive. It might have gone anywhere. We would never have destroyed the bridge, and we'd never have bombed *mojados.* They're the people we try to help."

"The way you used them to bring explosives in on their backs? That kind of help? Rámon, you're not only a *cabrón,* You're a hypocrite. How do you know the bridge didn't blow up because something went wrong with one of your 'shipments'?"

"Because," he said calmly, "we have no more shipments. We have everything we need. The package we lost was the last of them, and it was really just security; we had enough already. Whoever bombed the Black Bridge is our enemy, Ana, and maybe you even know who that could be. Somebody who was there when the backpack containing the explosives disappeared. Someone who hates Mexicans enough to persecute them as a profession. Someone for whom this is personal."

"What are you talking about?"

"Your ex-husband. Peter."

She laughed and was glad to hear the edge of contempt in it. "Peter Ross is many things, but he is not a *terrorista.*"

"I'm going to kill him," Rámon said as if he hadn't heard her. "Whatever happens today, I will make sure I send him to hell before I die."

"He didn't set the bomb!"

Rámon gave her an annoyed look. "Of course he did. Or someone just like him. It doesn't matter, I promise you. You don't have to worry. He *will* die."

There was a fever shine to his eyes, and for the

first time she realized that he might be sick enough to be unreliable. That was dangerous. He carried the remote control to her bomb vest clipped to his belt, and if she made him angry enough—

If she made him angry enough, maybe he would blow them all up. That was tempting but terrifying; she didn't know if she had it in her to be a martyr. She'd rather save her life, she decided, if she could. If Rámon gave her the chance.

She swallowed bile and said softly, "Good. I hope you do kill him."

"My little soldier. You know what today is?" he asked her. She shook her head. "Today is American Thanksgiving Day. Count your blessings, Ana. You've found your true calling."

At Mama's house, at any other time, she and Gabriel would be sitting through an interminable family dinner, all of the cousins and aunts and uncles, the children tearing through the house just ahead of punishment. Mama would make *menudo* and tamales. There would be bickering and laughter and warmth, and Ana's eyes filled with tears as she thought of Mama left alone, one child dead, the other missing.

"I hate you," she said to Rámon.

He looked up and smiled. "Hate is very close to love, *querida*, and you love me, too. You always did." He moved closer to her on the narrow bed; she tried to squirm away, but her hands had been bound again to the bed frame. "Don't worry. I won't force you. But this is the last day of your life, Ana. How do you want to end it? Most soldiers would want to make love before they die. Do you?"

She stifled the first torrent of abuse that came to

her lips, swallowed it, and said nothing. He touched
her gently on the cheek, warm, rough fingers gliding
down to her chin, down the column of her neck,
down.

"We were not so bad together, were we? Better
than you and your Anglo."

"Yes," she said through a very dry throat.
"Better."

His thumb stroked her pulse point below the ear,
and her breath caught. If she could make him come
closer, even with her hands tied, she might find a
way to kill him. Or detonate the bomb he'd dressed
her in.

"I don't think I can," he said. "It's my leg, you
see. It hurts. But the thought is very nice, Ana, and
I appreciate the offer. Some other time, if we both
live."

He pulled away. She twisted her body up and
kicked at him with all her strength. By luck she
caught him on the wounded thigh as he rose; he
collapsed against the bed with a choked scream,
knocking it aside, and she used the momentum to
flip the cot over. She could get to the knots now, but
she had only seconds to work them. Rámon was not
so badly wounded as all—

—that. Something cold touched her, just behind the
ear, like the pointing finger of Death. She froze, the
first knot half undone, and felt Rámon's fingers lock
around her neck. He moved the gun to where she
could see it and placed it between her eyes. His face
was red with fury.

"I try," he said, his jaw working unevenly; she
heard the grinding of his teeth under the words. "I

try to make you understand, but you won't. This is a sacred duty, Ana. And whether you like it or not, you are a messenger of the gods. We're going to do it together, and if you resist me again, *I will shoot you and drag you, do you understand me?*''

His voice rose to a rough, uncontrolled scream at the end. She held very still and felt the muzzle of the gun tremble on her skin.

"Yes," she whispered. Tears slipped free of her control. "I understand."

The gun went away. She felt him wrap his arms around her, and in that instant she could have found the remote trigger and set it off, killed him in the same blaze of fury that incinerated her, but for her soul she couldn't do it. She was too afraid to die.

And he wasn't afraid in the least.

After Rámon left, one of his silent *vatos* came in to untie her from the overturned bed. To her surprise, he stripped the rope off her wrists altogether and dropped it on the floor. She rubbed the chafed skin anxiously, truly afraid now because the only way he would let her go was in death.

The man said, "Turn around." She wouldn't have obeyed, but there was another man in the doorway, his gun held ready. She slowly turned to face the wall, already imagining the shot, wondering how it would feel in the seconds before it ended. She had no doubt it would be clean. They were soldiers.

God help her, she was terrified. If she hadn't already visited the bathroom, she would have lost control of her bladder. The man tapped her on one shoulder.

"On your knees," he said. "Hands behind."

She lowered herself awkwardly to the cold concrete floor and put her hands behind her back. An execution pose. She wouldn't know when it came, she hoped.

A cold click around her left wrist startled her, and she jerked, but not fast enough to avoid having the right wrist captured, too.

Handcuffs. She strained against them, unreasonably panicked, and froze as the man tapped her shoulder again.

"Up," he said. She couldn't. He tugged her arm until she managed it, moved her aside and set the cot back upright. He smoothed the blankets as if it mattered to her. "Sleep."

He left the room without a backward look. She sank down on the mattress as the door swung shut and the lock grated closed, and in the dark, all alone, she began to laugh.

"Pleasant dreams," she said, and laughed louder, laughed until she was weak and gasping, and then stretched out on the hard cot on her side and waited for dawn.

For the day of her death.

Chapter 31

November 27, 1996
Esmeralda Sanchez

Her television showed her hell. It seemed impossible that these things were happening just on the other side of the river, the invisible wall; it seemed impossible for these things to happen in America. But as she watched the confused, trembling pictures of mobs storming lines of police, of men and women being clubbed and punched and kicked, she found herself drawing her knees up to her chest and biting her lip and thinking how close she had come to being in that chaos. Of course, she knew it would not be the same everywhere—television lied that way, it showed only the worst of a bad situation. But still she had been there, not so far from where the helicopters circled and men fought for their lives, fought in anger for nothing but more anger.

She hoped Peter was safe, but there was no way to be sure of it. Jaime was as distant as ever, and she had no telephone to call America, and no car to drive over the border. *He is safe*, she told herself. *He will not leave me.*

But Jaime had left her.

She crossed the room and changed the television station to one that came in flurried with interference; the English was too rapid for her to understand, but she thought they were talking about the bombing of the Black Bridge. The ruin of it loomed on the small, grainy screen, the black trestles twisted and warped, the center of the bridge missing entirely. One side of it leaned at an alarming angle. *I was there. I stood on that bridge.* The thought seemed unreal. She had followed a child in a red coat, and maybe that had been God's will and maybe blind luck, but she had survived, and she had to believe that was God's hand at work. She turned away from the television to light a candle to the Blessed Virgin and went back to the couch to watch the news report.

A woman clutching a microphone ended the report from the bridge, and the station began a commercial that showed a happy Anglo family eating breakfast cereal. When it ended, the news showed more of the riot—or was it the same piece? She couldn't tell. What she could understand let her know that the pictures were old, and that there was no more fighting. Instead, the cameras showed a candlelit vigil, thousands strong, chanting in Spanish.

Was that better, she wondered, or worse?

Her attention was drawn by a knock at her door. She turned off the television and looked outside—not Victor tonight, or his daughter Angela, but a thin young boy of maybe fifteen who shuffled his feet and would not meet her eyes. He had a scar on his face, and a tattooed teardrop at the end of it.

"Yes?" she asked. The boy glanced up at her, then down again.

"I'm looking for Esmeralda Sanchez. *La curandera.*"

"Come in."

"It's you?" he asked.

"Yes."

He looked up now, dark eyes very bright and cold. "You know Peter Ross, *la migra?*"

Dread filled her stomach, weighed her down to a nightmarish slowness. The reporters, she remembered. Taking her picture, with Pete. *Our Lady of Miracles*, they'd called her; Peter had tried to make a joke out of it.

The boy looking at her smiled and said, "Rámon Cruz spits on you, *puta*," and took his hand out of his pocket. It held a gun.

She screamed and slammed the door; if she had not ducked away in the next second, the first bullet would have gone through her. She crouched and ran to the kitchen, unable to control her trembling or her hammering heartbeats. She heard the front door crash open and thought insanely, *Jaime! Help me!* But Jaime was far away, his spirit severed from her. She was alone now. No one to call on but God and her own strength.

I have no strength. But she did. She had lived through hell, she had buried her son, she had lived and loved, and she would not lie down for this angry, killing child.

Her flailing hand found a thin steel skewer that she had used to cook *barbacoa* for dinner. It was an ugly weapon, still crusted with blackened meat, but she gripped it hard and flinched back beside the wood-burning stove as the boy came into the kitchen, silent as a cat. Her arm touched the coarse black iron of the stove, and she almost cried out as it burned her. She bit her lip and blinked back tears of pain, her hands trembling almost uncontrollably, while the boy stepped closer, searching the dark room.

She saw him stiffen and knew he had seen her. In the second it took him to react, she lunged. She was aiming for his hand, but he moved too quickly, and the skewer's sharp point pierced his chest just below the armpit. She tried to stop it, but her fear drove it deep, and her flinch as the boy convulsively fired his gun at a wild angle buried the spike deeper in him. She grabbed for the gun. It was surprisingly easy to take it away from him; he reached out blindly for support and caught the edge of the cabinet by the sink. A dish rattled and fell. In the distance Esmeralda heard dogs barking.

"Bitch," he said in breathless amazement, and put his hand on the round top of the skewer that stuck from his side. His face turned the color of dirty linen. When he tried to breathe in, he coughed, and blood beaded on his lips. He pulled the skewer free with his left hand and dropped it to the floor, his eyes still on her but seeing someone else now, something distant. There was no blood, none that showed, at the wound. His heavy coat would have concealed it. She didn't dare come closer to him until his knees buckled and he slid down the cabinet to huddle like the child he was on the floor.

"I'm sorry," she said frantically, and knelt beside him, putting the gun aside. She reached under his coat to put pressure on the wound, her only thought

now that he was only a child, only a little older than
Jaime. She had killed a *child*. "Don't move. You'll be
all right. I'll get help."

His breath bubbled out red. She swallowed hard
and lunged for the front room, but his hand grabbed
her foot and toppled her and she fell stunningly
hard. She hardly felt him pull her slowly back
toward him. A boy's voice was talking in the distance—Jaime? Had he come back?

The boy said, "I'll take you with me, you *puta*,"
and she had only a second's flash to recognize the
skewer in his hand before he brought it down toward
her, had less than that to try to roll aside. Her greater
weight threw him off balance, and the skewer drove
painfully into the loose flesh at her side, stitching her
a wound of no more than an inch, back to front, and
this time as she rolled away he did not try to stop
her. She plucked the sharp metal free with shaking
fingers and screamed at him, "Why? Why did you
do this?" As if it mattered.

He answered her by laughing, showed his blood-
streaked teeth at her in a last gesture of defiance, and
collapsed to the floor. He looked surprised by that. It
hadn't been his plan. His rasping, wet breaths heaved
three or four times more, and then he was quiet.

As his blood crept slowly across the floor toward
her bare feet, she felt something cold pass through
the room, heard a mocking echo of laughter. She
knew she would never forget this moment, and the
smile on the boy's face.

Her neighbors came timidly, drawn by the noise
and her scream, and Señor Olivares looked the boy
over with the grave judgment of an old man, folded

his age-crippled hands, and said, *"Un delincuente.* The streets are full of them. God have mercy on his soul."

And he took Esmeralda across to his own house, where his wife fussed over her and tucked her into warm clothes and gave her sweet hot milk to drink while Señor Olivares and his oldest son went back. They returned a half hour later, and Señor Olivares told her it was done. He gave her a thick pad of folded American money that she knew had come from the boy's body.

She did not ask where the body had gone. She stayed another hour, while Señora Olivares and her granddaughter went across the street and cleaned the kitchen floor. When she was taken home and shown inside, there was no trace that anything had happened, except for the fading smell of gunpowder and the broken lock on the front door. Señor Olivares apologized and said his son would fix it in the morning, and in the meantime, would she like the loan of his dog?

"No, *gracias,"* she whispered. She hugged each of them in turn, her neighbors, her friends. "I can't thank you enough. I—"

"Esta bein," Señor Olivares said awkwardly, and shook his head. "We protect our own, you know that. He didn't belong."

And that was his epitaph, the boy whose name she never knew, with his scarred young face and cold young eyes. Perhaps he had never belonged anywhere.

She realized, with a sense of true horror, that if this Rámon Cruz was coming for her, he was surely coming for Peter Ross, too.

Chapter 32

They had a picture of Rámon Cruz, at least—it had the fake look of an age-enhanced photo, probably from his high school yearbook. The same yearbook that held Ana Gutierrez's picture, Pete realized with a deep stab of pain. He remembered looking through it with her, in those long-ago years when they'd still laughed together. She had been so pretty.

Was. Was still.

"Think anybody will recognize him from this?" Pete asked, and Agent Miller shrugged as he took his own copy of the picture from the folder.

"Probably not. Why don't we just ask if anybody's seen a small private army? That ought to do it." He paused in the act of getting out of the car. "Pete, we're on our own here. I left word at the command center, but you watch yourself. I can't swear to get to you."

"Just swear to get to Ana."

The day after Thanksgiving was cold and clear, the way most winter days were in El Paso, the sky a hard, clear blue with wisps of clouds that looked almost ghostly. The sun burned pure gold. Pete had changed his clothes to blue jeans and a red flannel shirt—something that wouldn't show blood, he'd thought crazily—and a thick, lined windbreaker to keep out the sharp, icy breeze. He wasn't wearing gloves; they slowed him down and he didn't want to take any chances on fumbling his gun.

The area around *La Clínica Libre* looked utterly deserted, like a movie set. As Pete passed a leaning chain-link fence, he studied the round sheet-metal shack behind it. Fluted edges creaked in the wind, and he noticed three of the grimy windows in front were broken. It was the shape of an aircraft hangar, but built on a budget; the old flaking sign said RAY'S BODY WORKS, but the place hadn't been open for years. Rotting tires made a looming pyramid in the back.

He decided it didn't feel right and kept walking, went to the corner, and looked across the street to see Agent Miller's trench coat disappearing in the opposite direction. They'd agreed to search in a one-block radius, rendezvous, and then go outward.

The next lot was empty except for tumbleweeds snarling the windward side of Ray's.

He saw a shadow in the window of the next building, and it moved quickly out of sight. His back tingled and he thought. *It's a big place*, but he kept walking. He didn't study the building directly, but his sideways impression was that it had once been a machine shop, with dirty, louvered windows set up high. The shadow he'd noticed had to have been at least six feet tall.

There was a gate in the chain-link fence, and as he

passed it he glanced at the lock. It had been rubbed with dirt, but it was new. He walked a half block farther and turned down an alley, pressed himself against the cold stone, and took out his radio.

"Miller."

"Here."

"I've got a possible over here, used to be a machine shop. New lock on the gate, shadow in the window. What do you think?"

"I think I shouldn't have had that last cup of coffee. Pete, stay where you are, I'll come to you."

"Go one street up. I don't want them to see another strange face around here. They might kill her if they've got her." *If she's still alive.*

"Got it." The radio clicked off in his hand, and he was fully prepared to wait for Miller to arrive except that he heard a soft scrape of metal from the street outside.

His angle was bad, but he thought he saw a man at the gate of the machine shop. The scrape was the gate shaking as he worked the lock.

"Miller?" he asked, keying the radio.

"On my way."

"Somebody's coming out."

Miller didn't answer. Pete kept the radio to his mouth and tried to maneuver minutely for a better angle, all too aware that they'd be looking for him, too.

The gate wheezed in the wind, rocking back and forth. He didn't see anybody near it.

"Maybe I jumped the gun," he said into the radio, and then he saw what was different.

The lock was gone.

"Maybe not," Miller said—not on the radio, behind him. The FBI agent joined him at the wall, breathing hard enough to plume white vapor into the air. "Man. Nice day for a run."

"Healthy mind, healthy body, isn't that the Bureau motto?"

"Something like that. I'm from L.A. originally, our motto there was 'don't get killed'. That seems pretty applicable here."

"I think somebody came out and took the lock off the gate."

"Maybe an invitation?"

"Maybe they're getting ready to leave."

Miller nodded. "You understand our situation, here, right? You're here to get your ex-wife out alive, I'm here to make sure I get Cruz. I need this, Pete. If I don't get him, I'm down in flames."

Well, at least he was honest. Pete looked over at him and nodded, too. "He's all yours."

"Then we should—"

Whatever Agent Miller was about to propose, it never arrived because they both heard the sound of a motor starting. Muffled but definite in the silence. Pete turned his attention back to the machine shop.

Two large doors were opening at the front of the building—they'd been oiled, or they wouldn't have been so quiet. A short Hispanic man came out and swung one side of the chain-link gate open, then the other. As he did so, a cream-colored cargo van crept out of the opening, its engine an uneven purr.

"Bingo," Agent Miller said. He sounded exultant as he switched channels on his radio to the frequency of the command center. He gave their position in terse, almost angry exchanges, ignoring the questions on the other end of what he was doing in the field, and clicked the radio off. "Back to the car. Maybe we can tail them, but it doesn't really matter. They're going to be followed from the air anyway. Our new system can paint the target with a targeting laser and follow it anywhere within five hundred miles. They're down."

"And Ana?" Some of the exultation faded out of Miller's face. "She's not a terrorist. I need to get her out of there."

The van turned onto the street with a quiet hiss of tires, and accelerated back in the direction of the clinic. Miller said briskly, "Time to debate it later," and took off at a jog after it. Pete cursed under his breath and followed.

They'd only gone three or four feet when the van suddenly skidded to a stop, the back door slammed open, and bullets raked the street. Pete threw himself flat and rolled for the scant cover of the curb; across from him, Agent Miller was following the same strategy. After what seemed like an eternity of whining bullets, Pete heard the van accelerate away and the mocking hooting of laughter.

Miller was back on his feet, unhurt, eyes blazing by the time Pete was sure all he'd collected were slider burns from the concrete. "Son of a *bitch!* Where are these guys from, L.A.? You okay?"

"I'm good. Come on."

He raced Miller back to the car, heart pumping adrenaline into his system faster than he could dump it. Cruz wasn't trying to be canny anymore; he wasn't being a good general.

He just wanted to go out in a blaze of glory.

* * *

"Wait," Rámon Cruz said softly, one hand on his driver's shoulder. He watched the two men, both Anglo, disappear around the corner back in the direction the van had taken. "Go. Quietly."

The driver inched the black late-model sedan out into the street and turned it in the opposite direction. Rámon turned toward his two men in the backseat, Ana Gutierrez held tight between them. The handcuffs must surely have been hurting her by now; he knew how agonizing they could be, and it gave him a certain cold satisfaction to see the pain on her face. He honestly believed, looking in her eyes, that she would blow herself up, so long as she could take him with her.

That would be a terrible waste. She didn't even know yet why she had been sentenced to die.

"A good general knows when to misdirect the enemy," he told her. "By the time the FBI takes that van, my men will have left a trail of blood from here to Sierra Blanca. Tell me, was that him? Your beloved Peter Ross?"

She said nothing, but he knew. He'd seen the photograph in the paper. Ross had traded one pretty Chicana for another, though his Mexican whore would be dead by now if Gato was half as reliable as Miguel had promised. He had thought about killing Ross first—had almost put a bullet in him as he lay in the street outside, pinned down by the van's fire—but he wanted Ross to appreciate the irony first.

"Cheer up, Ana," he told her, turning back face front. "We're going shopping. It's the holiday season. They say today's the busiest day of the year."

The sedan turned west, toward downtown.

*   *   *

The van wasn't trying to avoid pursuit; Agent Miller found it quickly once they'd regained the relative safety of the car and set out on the trail. In fact, it looked like the van was deliberately taking open roads, relying on increasing speed to get away, which was stupid. Surely they understood that with routine coordination the police would have them blocked off within minutes.

This wasn't the action of a man who'd kept his men moving undetected for days on end, who'd smoothly coordinated the bombing of an important government building. Rámon Cruz wasn't in the last-stand business, not yet.

"It's a decoy," Pete said aloud, and ducked as the van's back window exploded out in a shower of glass, and bullets raked the road ahead. "Slow down! It's a decoy, they want us to pursue!"

Agent Miller acted as if he hadn't heard—if anything, he sped up. "I'm not playing a hunch right now—it's too important. Keep your eye on the ball."

"I'm telling you—"

"And I'm telling you we're not giving them up!" Miller yelled the words like a challenge, and yanked the wheel to one side to avoid another random burst of gunfire from ahead. "You want out, jump. I'm not stopping."

His FBI coolness had entirely evaporated. Agent Miller was not reachable once he'd put himself in the chase, like a terrier on a rat. Pete clung to the dashboard, temporarily weightless, as Miller hit the brakes to avoid a thrown bottle of flaming gasoline; the fire bloomed behind them like a desert flower.

Ahead, just beyond the approaching bulk of a high school, a forest of flashing lights. The police had blocked the road. Agent Miller slowed the car and suddenly whipped the wheel, turning the car sideways to block the retreat; they were joined by two other police cars, sirens screaming. There were no roads for the van to turn off on; an open irrigation canal blocked them from the right, and on the left, one of El Paso's ubiquitous rock walls raised its thick, pointed head.

The van, instead of slowing, picked up speed. Miller leaned forward, peering over Pete's shoulder.

"They'll stop," he said. "They don't have a choice."

All Pete could think of was Ana, trapped in the van, fragile. He watched the van speed toward the crash, and every second seemed to go slower, each breath harder to swallow. He knew what would happen. He could see the way the van would bury itself in the steel frames of the police cars, shedding bodies and glass like a broken piñata.

Except that wasn't how it happened.

The van skidded to a stop less than a foot from the angled noses of the police cruisers. Pete couldn't hear the cops, but he knew they were shouting for raised hands, dropped weapons. They were telling them to get out of the van.

And they did. One after another, guns dropped out of the van's broken windows, and then five men came out, hands laced on their heads.

"I'll be damned," Agent Miller said. "Sometimes you just get lucky."

They walked to the van and the kneeling prisoners; the cops were busy handcuffing and reading the men their Miranda warnings, in English and Spanish. Agent Miller crouched down next to the first one and said, "Why'd you stop?"

The man turned to look at him, and for a second there was absolute amusement in his eyes. "Man, who you think we are? *Demente?* We don't die for nobody. Fuck that."

"Did he tell you to die?"

"He who?"

"Rámon Cruz." As Miller said it, Pete realized that Cruz wasn't among the men. Neither was Ana.

"Don't know him," the man said, and turned face forward again. He didn't resist handcuffs, but he didn't answer any more questions, either. None of them did.

"That's something," Agent Miller said. "At least they're not fanatics."

"If they're not fanatics, what are they?"

"Mercenaries. He's paying his men, but he's not paying them enough to die." Miller stared at the squad cars full of prisoners as they began to pull away. "Relax, Pete. I already sent units back to the machine shop. If he's there, they'll get him. If not, they'll find something to tell us where he went. We'll get him."

Maybe. Pete looked at the pile of guns next to the van as the El Paso police began bagging them for evidence.

"Did it occur to you that they may be smart fanatics?" he asked. "Maybe they're just living to fight another day."

"No such thing."

"Oh, I don't know," Pete said, and turned back toward the sedan. "I think *you're* pretty smart."

Chapter 33

November 28, 1996
The Bridge

They had not closed the border, of course. The rioting had been confined to a very small area, Esmeralda learned from a lady standing in line to cross from Mexico. The lady was a maid for a West Side family, and she said there really hadn't been all that much to it, the fighting. No one was alarmed. Besides, she told Esmeralda, why would they close the border? It was a day when most people crossed to buy things, both in El Paso and in Juárez. Merchants on both sides of the border would scream.

She'd forgotten how busy it could be on a bright, sunny day approaching Christmas. The line to cross from Mexico was very long, maybe a half hour or more to get to the turnstiles. She had her papers from Pete's apartment this time. Everything she needed. This time she would cross and take a taxi, using the money from her attacker's pocket, and she would find Ana Gutierrez and warn her not to cross the border today.

It was a simple warning. She did not think it would be difficult at all to convince her.

A man in line ahead of them with a portable radio turned it louder to let everyone hear the news report that the FBI had captured some of the men suspected in the bombing of the El Paso Border Patrol headquarters. They were not from Mexico, Esmeralda was relieved to hear. They were all American citizens, though Chicano.

There were a lot of Americans coming over the bridge from the other side today. She could tell by their conversations as they passed that they'd been waiting, too. They all had an indignant attitude about it, as if waiting were something that never happened for them. Maybe, she thought, it didn't. Maybe things were different in Texas that way.

But she didn't like the way they looked around at Juárez. They came to buy cheap liquor and souvenir serapes and gaudy sombreros, but they all thought that gave them the right to judge; she could see it in their stiff, hostile faces when they refused to look at her. There were times when she despised Americans. None of them would ever know or care about Victor and his daughter, who lived without heat or running water; if Victor and Angela made the harsh and dangerous journey to America, they'd be despised even more. If they built their own home, the Americans would whine about squatters. But they would use them to pick their fruit and dig their ditches and wash their cars. They would use them, like the woman in line ahead of her, to clean their homes and raise their children.

But they would always be intruders. Always Mexicans.

She knew this because she had heard two nurses

talking in the hospital about the cost of burying Jaime
in America. He hadn't been worth the price of a
grave to them.

She loved her country with a pure, burning passion that sometimes surprised her. She loved the people who lived here, in harsh and sometimes terrifying
conditions, who starved in famine and were cheated
in plenty. She knew that no matter what happened,
she would never live in America, not even as Pete's
wife.

And that made her very sad as she waited to cross
the border. Very sad indeed.

"Nothing," Agent Miller said. He sounded a good
deal more subdued than he had been at the victory
of the van; in fact, Pete thought, Miller sounded
downright depressed. The five men in the van
weren't enough. "Blood in the van, lots of it; we can
probably tie it to the murder of Gabriel Gutierrez,
at least."

Or Ana. Miller didn't mention that possibility, but
Pete knew it was there. As if Miller knew what he
was thinking, he said, "It's at least a couple of days
old. It's not hers."

But Ana wasn't in the machine shop, either. There
were signs of occupation, which told Pete that
Rámon Cruz no longer cared about staying hidden;
in fact, there were too many signs. Trash to sift, including leftover food. Newspapers. Candles and ker-
osene lamps. An empty green footlocker with
PROHIBIDO FUMAR stenciled on the side. Old bandages,
crusted with foul-smelling pus.

"Somebody's hurting," said one of the FBI forensic

team as he bagged the bandages. "We'll analyze it, but it looks like a pretty serious infection. Maybe life-threatening."

Bottles of aspirin, all empty, and some other prescription drugs that Pete supposed Ana had provided, or been forced to provide. He watched as they bagged the pills.

"Antibiotics and pain relievers," Miller said as he read the labels. "Empty. Either they didn't trust Ana to refill them or they didn't have time—I guess that's why the aspirin."

"This is getting us nowhere," Pete said, and walked out of the cavernous room to a smaller one that was probably used as a cell. He looked at the folding cot, the ropes still lying on the floor. Ana had been kept here. He closed his eyes and tried not to think about what had happened here, but it was hard to turn it off at will. He'd always had an active imagination, but he'd never expected it to hurt so much.

A stir of activity at the door brought him out of hell; he turned back to the main room and saw that they had someone against the wall, hands outstretched. A woman. Hope flared but was quickly doused when Agent Miller saw him coming and shook his head. Even without the warning, he would have known it wasn't Ana as he approached. Too short, too round, the hair too long. She was dressed in a faded print dress too tight in the hips and cheap scuffed shoes rounded at the sides by her weight.

There was no fear in her face as she was allowed to turn around.

"Margarita Barrachia," she said. There was bleak pride in her eyes. "You're looking for Rámon Cruz."

She spoke Spanish. Pete stepped forward and said, in the same language, "Yes. Do you know where he is?"

She studied him without surprise or interest. "You are with the government?"

"Yes, señora. My name is Peter Ross." He could see the name didn't mean anything to her, and was glad; they didn't need any side issues just now. "You know Cruz?"

She nodded. "He slept at my house, ate my food— I brought them food here, only two days ago. And that was when he told me."

"Told you what?"

It was hate looking out of her eyes, a shine like silver, almost blinding. He repeated his question when she didn't answer.

"He told me my husband, Miguel, died for his *compadres*. Died like a soldier." The glitter in her eyes grew harsher. "I didn't care about that. But I wanted him back, so I could have a mass said for him. So his family could grieve."

Pete saw that the FBI agents were restless, so he translated in a low voice. She waited for him to finish, a patience all out of tune with the look in her eyes.

"He told me he'd buried Miguel himself. He lied to me. The *policía* showed me Miguel's body, dumped in an alley like a dead dog. Rámon lied to Miguel, and then he lied to me."

Agent Miller tried to break in, but Pete said again, "Do you know where he is? How to find him?"

She blinked, and for a second the hate focused

squarely on his face, hot as a searchlight; he had to focus not to flinch.

"You will kill him?"

Pete thought of a few dozen answers, ranging from *of course* to a flat, inflexible *no*, and chose, "If he tries to kill us or anyone else, yes, we will."

"I heard him talking when I was bringing the food," she said. "They were looking at a map. It was of the border crossing. The one downtown."

Pete's heart tripped. It was the bridge he took every week, the one so close to Esmeralda's house in Juárez. It was the primary bridge for Americans going to the Juárez shopping areas. It was the main bridge for Mexicans crossing to shop in the U.S.

Margarita straightened her shoulders and smiled and said, "Now you kill him. For me."

The car parked in an area Ana was only vaguely familiar with; she didn't know downtown streets at all, and the buildings were not memorable. She knew where to find the winglike sweep of the Civic Center Auditorium, and the courthouse where she'd gone for jury duty, but that hardly qualified her as tour guide. She thought that the Border Highway was to the left, beyond it the green sweep of Chamizal National Park, shared with Mexico.

"You might as well tell me where we're going," she said to Rámon, too tired now to be afraid. Her throat was dry, her head pounding; she didn't think she'd had anything to drink for nearly a day. Rámon shook a handful of aspirin from a small bottle, swallowed them with a mouthful of bottled water, and looked at her in the rearview mirror.

"We're here," he said. "Just a little walk, Ana. Not far at all. Of course, you may have to go slowly for me."

He grinned humorlessly. Fever had flushed his skin but left his skin dry; he looked gaunt and very ill.

"Rámon, you can still give up. They'll take you to the hospital, save your life—" She did not say they'd save his leg. She knew the smell of rot. "It's stupid to throw yourself away like this. What are you proving?"

"I'm proving that there are still patriots," he said. "We're going to walk to the Border Patrol station at the middle of the bridge, and I'm going to shoot the guard in the head. My men will shoot anyone who tries to run from the bridge on the American side. I will read a small message, and then I will let everyone leave except for you. It could not be simpler."

"You'll all die." She said it for the benefit of Rámon's men, but she got no reaction. "Don't you understand? He's committing suicide! You can't let this happen!"

"You think my men will listen to you? You're corrupt, Ana. You turned your back on your own people. Oh, you pretend you are one of La Raza, but that's bullshit. You went to American schools and American college, and you married your nice little Anglo boy."

"You don't know anything about me!" she shouted at him. He turned and leveled a finger at her.

"I know *everything*, Ana. You think I picked you by *accident*? You're full of cheap sentimentality, but you're coconut, brown outside, white inside. You murdered the children of immigrant women. You think I don't know about the abortions you did?"

The words punched into her like wounds, left her weak and disoriented. She searched for words, but nothing came. Rámon's eyes were full of feverish contempt.

"I picked you because you were a traitor and a *puta*, and before I'm finished with you, the world will witness how Aztlan punishes its enemies."

She couldn't answer. Tears tore at her throat, but she refused to let them out. Years of bitterness between her and Pete, years of guilt, too, made worse because he'd forgiven her but she'd never fully forgiven herself. But *damned* if she would show Rámon Cruz how badly he had hurt her.

Blood splashed on the door of their home in Dallas. She'd thought at the time that it couldn't get any worse, the hatred; she'd sickened of the strain, and she'd run away from it. But the blood followed.

She wondered if Rámon really understood that.

He checked his watch. "I'll give you a little time to think about it," he said. "It's early yet. If you pray, you'd better do it now, because in a half hour you'll be dead."

"You're crazy," Agent Miller said flatly, but he hung onto the passenger strap as Pete floored the sedan and raced through another intersection. He took the on-ramp to Interstate 10, heading west at nearly sixty miles an hour, far too fast for traffic and the angle of the merge, but he didn't care. There was a chance.

"We're never going to make it in time," Miller

said, trying again. "Even if we do, we can't just go charging in."

"I'm not planning to."

"You've got a plan?" Miller was clearly skeptical. Pete grinned, but there wasn't any humor in it.

"What's the matter, Miller, you never heard that improvisation is the mother of all screw-ups? Come on, you're the one who wants Cruz bad enough to put your ass on the line. Don't tell me you're going to back out now. *We know where he is.*"

Miller leaned his head back against the upholstery, closed his eyes, and said, "Whatever you're going to do, I don't want to know about it. As far as I'm concerned, I already lost track of you. You're on your own, understand?"

Miller was a smart man. He knew that whatever it was Pete was planning to do, it wasn't anything that would look good on an FBI field report, or in a congressional subcommittee, come to that. Pete, on the other hand, no longer cared.

"Don't worry," he said. "I already lost myself."

He stopped the sedan three blocks from the international bridge, bailed out with the engine still running, and walked, not ran, up the hill, strolling past the line of people waiting to cross and ignoring how they glared at him. He didn't see Ana, though he had a bad moment at the sight of two Hispanic men in heavy coats who might have been part of Cruz's crew. He kept walking.

He walked to the Border Patrol booth, knocked on the door, and held his identification up to the window. When the guard answered the knock, he motioned for him to open up.

As he closed the door behind them, sealing them both in the observation room, he looked the guard over. He didn't know him, but he recognized him from other trips to the other side of the border. The guard blinked in surprise as Pete drew his service weapon and pointed it at him.

"Let's understand each other," Pete said very evenly. "I don't have time to explain things to you. This is the short version. Nod if you understand me."

The guard nodded.

"Let me have your shirt, your shades, and your hat."

In the distance Ana heard sirens.

"*Jefe*," the man sitting to her right said. "They're coming."

"Get her out of the car," he said. She tried to fight them, but there was no way for her to manage it with her hands still manacled behind her, numb and aching with strain. Her shoulders ached so badly she almost screamed when one of the men shoved her next to Rámon. They closed and locked the car doors, and she stood shivering in the wind, the vest heavy as lead against her chest. She felt sick and dizzy and wondered how it would look for him if the martyr to the cause threw up all over his explosives.

Rámon threaded his arm through her pinned right one and said, "If you don't walk with me, Ana, I will put a bullet through the first person I see, and it will be your fault. Do you believe me?"

"Yes." She did. There was a gun in Rámon's right hand, half hidden in the folds of his brown overcoat. His driver and the other two men fell in behind

them, and as Rámon limped forward she heard them
follow at the same pace. It was absurdly like a funeral procession. She knew she was crying again,
tears whipped away from her cheeks by the cold, dry
wind, but that didn't matter.

She wished she could tell Pete that she was sorry,
that the destruction of their lives together hadn't
been his fault. He was the kind of man who blamed
himself, and who constantly searched for answers to
questions that had none.

She wished him peace.

The sirens were still coming, but the wind shifted
and she thought that now they were heading away
from her, down into the Lower Valley. No one knew
where they were. No one was coming to help her.

Then you have to help yourself. The thought surprised
her out of the black, clinging despair of the past few
minutes. *Do what you have to do. Die if you have to,
but don't let them use you like this!*

Before the thought was complete, she shoved hard
against Rámon, sending him off balance; his grip
pulled her with him. She pivoted on one foot as he
reeled, and slammed a knee not into his crotch, but
into the pulpy softness of his wounded thigh.

He screamed, a high, thin scream like a little girl,
and she was a little sickened at the intense agony on
his face. The gun came at her and she thought with
a sense of black relief, *It's done,* but instead of shooting her he hit her with the butt, a blow that shattered
all thought out of her head and sent her stumbling
back into the two men behind her. She tasted blood,
and when she tried to focus her eyes the world
seemed weirdly bright and floating. There was very

little pain, but she had that liquid sensation she knew was shock. He had hurt her. Maybe very badly.

She couldn't stand on her own. One of the men held her upright with a grip on her shoulder, a pain that cut dimly through the fog and made her take some of her weight on shaky knees. Her head felt cold, her neck hot.

"Bring her," Rámon ground out through clenched teeth. He clung to the arm of his driver, limping worse than ever, and she saw that blood and serum were spreading through the fabric of his khaki pants.

She hadn't been able to get to the detonator, or she would have blown them all to hell, no matter what the consequences to her soul. She'd do it now if she saw a chance.

She would not let Rámon Cruz use her.

She was half dragged the rest of the way up the hill; it seemed dreamlike to her, and she saw people looking uncomprehendingly in her direction, faces clenched in disapproving frowns. They thought she was drunk. She almost giggled, but her mouth felt loose and strange. She tasted blood again and wondered where it was coming from. *Concussion.* The word drifted up, severed from some deep anchorage in her brain. *Depressed skull fracture.* What did that matter? The only thing that mattered now, the only thing in the world, was to stop Cruz from killing someone else.

She lifted her head as the thought drilled home and saw that they were stepping onto the international bridge, the concrete and steel symbol of peaceful trade. There were so many people, many of them Tejano like her, prosperous, well-dressed Hispanics with no loyalty to or interest in Mexico except as a place to buy bargains. So many people.

So many children.

When she opened her mouth to scream, she saw Rámon staring at her and remembered what he'd said. He'd shoot someone if she resisted. He'd promised to let everyone off the bridge once he'd read his statement.

She didn't think he'd keep his word, but her courage failed her. She couldn't take the risk. He looked from her to a young Anglo boy, no more than twelve years old.

She swallowed the cry.

It was too late, in any case.

Rámon's driver let go of him, and Rámon rocked slightly for balance, found it, and lifted his gun in his right hand. With a surprisingly strong voice he shouted, "Nobody moves!"

Nobody did. They stared at him, stunned into silence, more than fifty people waiting in the line that snaked from the Border Patrol booth back toward the safety of the American street. Rámon's men spread out like hunting tigers, herding the people into a tightly packed circle while Rámon limped up to the light green-painted Border Patrol guard shack.

Ana watched as the Border Patrol guard opened the door and stepped outside, the shadow of his hat and glint of sunglasses making him strangely familiar to her.

"Officer," Rámon said, and pulled his lips back in a snarl. "The border is closed."

He shot the Border Patrol guard three times in the chest.

The guard collapsed backward, arms flinging wide. He had never drawn his gun.

She dimly heard the people screaming, some of them throwing themselves flat on the pavement; she swayed and fell to her knees. The bridge seemed to be slowly tilting away from her.

Rámon limped back into the soft focus that was her field of vision, and took a grip of her hair. The agony that flared from that was as bright as the sun, and it blotted out everything, even the terrible confusion of what to do now.

"Listen!" Rámon screamed in English. "I want the Chicanos to step out. Only the Chicanos!"

His men broke the paralysis by pulling people out of the group; after four or five were forced out, more followed, or were dragged out by their families. The Hispanics separated from the Anglos. Rámon looked at them, maybe forty people, and said softly, "You are the children of dogs and whores, but it is not your fault. You have the power to take back your land and make it new again. Remember this day, because it is the beginning of your lives. Run!"

He fired his gun into the air, and some of them screamed. All of them ran, stumbling over each other, their retreat a vibration against Ana's knees through the bridge. She saw that the police had arrived just beyond, a Christmas parade of lights.

Rámon put away the gun. He took the detonator from his belt and held it in one hand.

"The rest of you," he said, and looked at the twenty or so Anglo men, women, and children huddled together by the fenced wall, "I want to tell you a story before you die."

* * *

Esmeralda heard the shots and saw people running, not to the other side, the American side, but across toward her. The Mexicans waiting in line scattered. She did not know what was happening, but fear made her run up the hill instead of down, to batter on the window of the Mexican border guard's booth. He stared at her, whey-faced, and shook his head. He was crouched down on the floor.

"*Teroristas!*" he shouted at her.

"Let me through!" she screamed back. She pushed the unyielding turnstile—locked in place. "For the love of God, let me through! I can stop him! I know how to stop him!"

It was more than that. She *had* to go, knew it as surely as she felt the ache in her hand that told her where sickness was. Her whole body ached with this sickness, and the need, the imperative, to be the cure. Jaime had told her. Angela's dark spirit had told her, too.

She held all their lives.

Unexpectedly, the turnstile clicked. She shoved through and ran through the empty chain-link passage, breath burning on her lips, fear tearing at her like a tiger. *You'll die.* Angela's dark spirits bared their teeth at her and drew claws down her back. *Let them all die in fire. What matter? Save yourself.*

She was *curandera*.

She would not turn away from death, even her own.

"There was a young Tejano girl," Rámon said, and shook Ana for emphasis. She cried out, the pain crescendoing to a white fury at her temple. More blood in her mouth. The kind cushion of shock was almost gone now, and she knew she was losing herself to the injury, her balance gone, her strength fading. She couldn't remember what it was she was supposed to do, only that it was very important. "This girl, she abandoned her family and her faith. She became a doctor, a respected person, and she married an Anglo and she moved to a big Anglo city. You know what she did there? She performed abortions. She murdered Chicano children for *money*. I don't care that she aborted her own baby. It was the child of a whore and an Anglo *cabrón* who hated the sight of a Mexican's face, and it deserved no chance to live. But I *do* care that she killed *my* baby."

"Your—" Ana couldn't think, couldn't imagine what he meant. "Your baby?"

"One of your patients, *Doctora*. A woman you don't even remember. She was my wife and she came to you with money and you killed my child. You thought you wouldn't pay for that?" He pulled up on her hair, and she felt something tear at the top of her head, tasted more blood and knew it was sheeting down her neck. "I am the first priest of Aztlan, Ana, and I sentence you to death for the murder of my son."

He let go of her. The relief was so intense that she doubled over, sobbing, but he wasn't done. He dragged her by the arm to the chain link that covered the concrete wall of the bridge and unlocked her handcuffs.

The chance to resist was meaningless. Her hands fell to her sides like dead clubs, numbed and blue from the hours he'd kept them pinned. He grabbed her left wrist that still wore one cuff closed and fastened her to the fence.

"I never knew," she whispered. He held her face in his hand for a few seconds, thumb digging into her cheek. His eyes were as black as midnight.

"I know," he said. "And that's why I can't forgive you."

He moved away from her, never taking his eyes from the tourists herded so effectively as a shield between him and the police at the far end of the bridge, and for a few seconds she did not realize where he was going.

He was going to the turnstile. His men held their ground, keeping the knot of Anglo prisoners herded together.

He was running. He'd never intended to die with her. He was going to escape to Mexico and come back again, another army, another bombing, another row of body bags.

She laughed. He stopped at the sound, staring back at her, his face flushed and pinched with the fever.

"Coward," she said. The word carried clearly to him, and he never knew what it cost her to say it. "You don't believe in Aztlan. You don't believe in anything except your own hate."

He had the detonator in his hand, a slender black shape.

"Time to go, Ana," he said, and pushed against the turnstile.

It didn't move. He pushed again, harder, frowning.

The dead Border Patrol guard, half in and half out of the guard shack, rolled over on his side and started to draw his gun. Rámon saw him at the same instant Ana did, and froze, a strange smile on his face. *He's going to press it*, she thought, but the thought failed to seem important. She was too tired to care anymore.

The world came suddenly into focus for her. The Border Patrol agent.

It was Pete.

He didn't know about the explosives, or about the remote detonator. If he fired, Rámon would have time to press the button.

"Pete, no!" she screamed, and saw him hesitate.

She saw a shadow on the other side of the man-high turnstile. A slender hand reached through the bars toward Rámon, whose eyes were still on the Border patrolman.

The hand took the remote detonator from his fingers.

Esmeralda did not know what it was, but she knew it was important, because her fingers ached so when she touched the black, smooth plastic box. She took it with one quick, convulsive move and breathed out a quick gasp of triumph, because a cool child's hand stroked her cheek and she heard Jaime say, very clearly, *I love you, Mama. You are very brave.*

Even if she had thought to do it, she couldn't have gotten out of the way before the man with the devil's eyes turned, a gun in his hand, and shot her. She had never been shot, and did not know there would be so much pain to it, so much heat. Her legs folded underneath her and the world spun white and gold and blue and she saw Jaime smiling at her, but there

were tears in his eyes and she wished she could cry,
too, for pain and for joy.

I don't want to go, Jaime. Please!

He kept one hand on her face, where he always
touched her. He was wearing the same shirt she remembered, the checked one he'd liked so much, and
the new shorts and the small red canvas shoes. He
looked so clean, so peaceful. Wind ruffled his hair,
and stars sparked and died in his eyes.

Am I dying, Jaime?

*You died in the desert, Mama. Remember? With me.
Your spirit went with me in the dark to keep me safe.*

She didn't remember, but she supposed it was
true. How remarkable, to be a *curandera espirita* and
not even know that her soul was gone with her heart
into the ground.

How very strange.

The second's distraction gave Rámon time to fire
at the woman on the other side of the turnstile before
he swung around to shoot the Border patrolman. He
would aim for the face this time. No mistakes.

His leg gave out as he turned. It collapsed in a
hail of pain, and he smelled death and rot and
thought not of Aztlan, but of Ana, who would live
after all.

What a bitter thing to know. He almost laughed
as he raised his gun, knowing he was too late.

He met Peter Ross' eyes over the barrels of their
guns.

He never felt the shot that blew open the back of
his head.

*   *   *

The shot fired by Rámon's driver missed Pete's head by a fraction of an inch. As the driver aimed again, sure he would hit *la migra* this time, he felt the muzzle of a gun at his head and a voice said in English, "FBI. Drop it."

It took him a second, but he did. Unlike Rámon, he wasn't enough of a martyr to die today.

Agent Evan Miller took him and the other two men into custody.

Pete got to his feet shakily. It hurt to draw breath, and he knew he'd be black and blue under the bullet-proof vest from the impact of Rámon's bullets, but that was a small thing. He started toward Ana, who crouched against the wall, her head lolling drunkenly. Agent Miller got there first, and Pete stopped in his tracks as he heard a woman's voice whisper, "Pedro?"

He turned back to Rámon Cruz. Beyond him, the shooting victim lay on the far side of the turnstile.

Esmeralda Sanchez lay on Mexican soil, her hair spread out around her like a soft velvet fan. Her eyes were wide and fixed at the sky. He couldn't move because it couldn't be true. Surely a merciful God wouldn't let it be true.

Her chest rose and fell, slowly and unevenly. The paralysis left him at the sight of that tiny, significant motion, and he dragged Cruz aside and pushed the turnstile. It didn't move.

She took another breath, slower, more shallow.

He looked toward the window where the other Border patrolman, bare-chested because Pete was wearing his shirt, stared over the counter at him.

"Unlock it!" Pete screamed. "Now!"

The metal turned with a click. He fell out into the bright sun and threw himself down next to Esmeralda. Blood on her clean yellow shirt. The blackened neat circles of two shots to the chest.

She breathed in again. Out. Her eyes were so wide, her face so pale. There wasn't much blood under her.

"I'm here," he said, and took her hand. "Don't go, Es. Please don't go."

"Is—okay—" she whispered in her fragile English. "I need—go. *Por Jaime.*"

"Jaime's dead!" He squeezed her hand tightly, watching her lips turn slowly blue as she breathed so very shallowly. "Please. Please stay. He doesn't need you. *I* need you. I need you, Esmeralda, please, God, I love you."

He heard the click of the turnstile behind him. Somebody gave orders for paramedics into the radio, but that didn't matter. Nothing mattered except the next faint breath she drew.

Her eyes moved away from the empty sky to slowly focus on him. He felt her hand tremble and let her pull it free. She touched those long healing fingers to his face, slid them back to his temple to that spot she'd touched so many times before. He felt it this time, a tingle like a touch on his brain. Power beyond love. Love beyond pain.

"There," she said. "Gone. Now—you—live."

Something warm fluttered up from her lips, maybe his name. He felt it go into him and through him and past him into the quiet desert sky.

"Esmeralda," he said. There was no strength in the hand that fell away from his head. No resistance when he took it in his own. Nothing left in the eyes but a strange, familiar glitter that he didn't recognize until a tear slid silver from her eye and he realized that Esmeralda had cried, at last.

She was gone.

Chapter 34

December 25, 1996
Peter Ross

He brought her roses, bright red ones tied with bright blue ribbon. She would have smiled, he knew; she would have lifted them to her nose and smelled them, glanced at him in shy delight, and he closed his eyes and remembered the hollowed dimple in her cheek that the smile would have revealed.

The simple stone marker read, ESMERALDA ELENA SANCHEZ, the dates of her birth and death, and the phrase he had paid to have added.

SHE WAS LOVED.

He couldn't sit for long, even though the day was clear, the wind cool. He felt too close to her, and far too distant. *You told me I was lost,* he said to her as he stood. *But you never showed me the way back. I'm still lost, Es. Maybe more than ever.*

There was no trace of cancer in his head. The tumor was completely gone. The black irony of that hurt him like a new wound.

Merry Christmas, Es.

He turned at the sound of footsteps on the white

gravel path; a woman was approaching from the dusty shadows of the parish church, her head covered by a mantilla. As he watched, he recognized the walk, the tilt of the head, and the single white rose in her hand.

Ana.

She stood a little way from him, her dark eyes unreadable. The mantilla covered the close-shaved hair where doctors had treated her skull fracture, and he thought she looked elfin like that, strangely innocent.

"I thought you might be here," she said, and the voice was different, too, softer, more forgiving. "I can go if you want. I don't want to disturb you."

She placed her single rose on the grave beside his bouquet, touched the stone of the marker, and murmured something under her breath that sounded like a prayer. When, he wondered, had Ana learned to pray?

"How are you?" he asked. The lace mantilla fluttered around her face, and she reached up to tame it with those slender surgeon's fingers. She raised her head and looked straight at him, *into* him, with a candor that he'd thought they'd left behind years ago.

"Hurt," she said. "Like you. And alone."

Without warning her eyes went liquid with tears, Ana, his concrete-and-stone wife, who never wept. He took her in his arms and held her, and felt for the moment, at least, that there was some hope in the world.

Some beauty.

Something warm touched his face, the remembered

brush of fingers, and he felt laughter shiver through him like warm sun.

Es, he thought, and opened his eyes to the day. He couldn't see her standing there, but he felt it again, that gentle touch of peace.

Pedro, he heard, or thought he did, in the wind's murmur. *We are never alone.*

Author's Note

Some of the geography of El Paso in this book is fictional, and some is not; the tension in El Paso between the Anglo and Hispanic/Chicano/Tejano community(ies) is real. The Aztlan movement is also real, though certainly not a violent insurgence, and at no time have the people in this movement advocated violence. The existence of neo-Nazi hate groups is, as I'm sure you know, not fictional at all, and neither is the fact that they have successfully infiltrated government agencies and police departments.

Many thanks to my "beta testers"—Carolyn Bullard, Rachel Scarbrough, Dianne Ray, Joanne Madge, and Jayne Largent. Without them . . . you know the drill.

We can find a thousand reasons to hate each other. Look for the reason to love.

No Gray In Between?

i'll tell you what blackandwhite is

black is racism
white is racism
black is right
white is right
black is wrong
white is wrong
white is today
black is tonight

black is white is/black is white is/black is white is/
white is black/is nigga is/spade is spic is/moulie is
coon is/honkie is poor white trash/is wop is dago/
is kyke is chink/is nip is cracka/is kraut is gook. . . .

is you all out of your blackandwhite minds?

—Kathleen Sager

Reprinted by permission from
A Little Piece of My Heart:
The Collected Works of Kathleen Sager
Aegina Press, 1998